Death in Pont-Aven

Published by Hesperus Nova
28 Mortimer Street, London W1W 7RD
www.hesperuspress.com

First published in the German language as
Bretonische Verhältnisse. Ein Fall für Kommissar Dupin
by Jean-Luc Bannalec © 2012,
Verlag Kiepenheuer & Witsch GmbH & Co. KG,
Cologne/ Germany© 2012, Jean-Luc Bannalec

English translation © Sorcha McDonagh, 2014

This edition first published by Hesperus Press Limited, 2014

Typeset by Madeline Meckiffe
Printed in Great Britain by CPI Group (UK) Ltd

ISBN: 978-1-84391-498-3

Jean-Luc Bannalec

Death in Pont-Aven

Translated by
Sorcha McDonagh

nova

Une mer calme n'a jamais fait un bon marin.
A smooth sea never made a skilled sailor.
– Breton proverb

For L.

The First Day

The seventh of July was a magnificent summer's day, one of those majestic Atlantic days that always lifted Commissaire Dupin's spirits. There was blue everywhere. By Breton standards, the air was already very warm for so early in the morning but it was a perfectly clear day. There was a distinct sharpness to everything. Just last night it had looked like the end of the world was nigh; heavy, low-lying clouds, ominously black and monstrous, had raced across the sky as the rain came down in torrents of biblical proportions.

Concarneau – or the gorgeous 'Blue City' as it is called to this day because of the gleaming blue fishing nets that lined the waterfront in the last century – was glittering in the sun. Commissaire Georges Dupin was sitting in the *Amiral*, at the very end of the bar, the newspaper spread out in front him as usual. Above the beautiful old covered market building where you could buy fish fresh from the sea every day (whatever happened to find its way into the local fishermen's nets early that morning) the round clock read half past seven. The very traditional café and restaurant where he was sitting, a former hotel, was right on the waterfront opposite the famous old town. The *ville close* had been built on a small, flat island that lay like a picture postcard in the large harbour surrounded by strong walls and towers. This was where the languid River Moros flowed into the harbour.

Dupin had spent his whole life amidst the glamour of Paris, but two years and seven months ago he had been 'relocated' to this remote backwater due to 'certain disputes' (as the internal memos had put it) and ever since then had drunk his *petit café* in the *Amiral*; it was a ritual as delightful as it was inflexible.

The rooms at the *Amiral* still had that wonderful atmosphere reminiscent of the nineteenth century when world-renowned artists, and then later Maigret, had stayed there. Gauguin once got himself into a brawl right outside after some sailors insulted his extremely young Javanese girlfriend. The *Amiral* had gone downhill over time, but then twelve years ago Lily and Philippe Basset – both from Concarneau but whose paths happened to cross in Paris – decided they had other plans and took it over. And they had made something of it again. It was indisputably the secret hub of the village. As atmospheric as it was, it was still authentic – no fussy decor or folk music here. Most of the tourists preferred the 'prettier' cafés further down by the large square, so one usually had the place to oneself.

'Another coffee. And a croissant.'

Lily could tell from the Commissaire's expression and abrupt gestures just what her customer wanted, despite the fact that he had muttered his order to himself rather than saying it out loud. This was Dupin's third coffee.

'Thirty-seven million – did you see, Monsieur le Commissaire? It's up to thirty-seven million now.' Lily was already standing at the espresso machine, which was one of those ones that made proper noises. It still impressed Dupin every time he saw it.

Lily Basset was perhaps in her early forties, a very pretty woman with curly, dark blonde hair and boundless energy and enthusiasm. Those green eyes of hers were always watching. Nothing escaped her – it was truly remarkable. Dupin liked her very much, and Philippe too, who was the restaurant's absolutely superb, yet utterly unpretentious chef, even though neither of them spoke very much. In fact, perhaps that's why he liked them. Lily had accepted the Commissaire from the outset – which was a big thing here anyway, but even more so because Parisians are the only people whom Bretons consider to be true outsiders.

'Damn it.'

Dupin realised he definitely wanted to have a bit of a flutter. The enormous lotto jackpot that had the whole country on tenterhooks still hadn't been won last week. Dupin had confidently filled in twelve rows and managed to get one number right in two – different – boxes.

'It's Friday already, Monsieur le Commissaire.'

'I know. I know.'

He would go to the *Tabac-Presse* in a minute.

'Last week all the lottery tickets were sold out by Friday morning.'

'I know.'

Dupin had slept dreadfully, in fact he hadn't slept properly in weeks. He tried to concentrate on his newspaper. In June, the northern part of Finistère had had a measly sixty-two per cent of the sunshine of an average June – a hundred and forty-five hours. Southern Finistère had managed seventy per cent, neighbouring Morbihan, just a few kilometres away, had notched up at least eight-two per cent. The article was the lead story in *Ouest France*. Astonishing weather statistics were one of the paper's specialities – indeed they were a speciality of all Breton newspapers and all Bretons in general. 'For centuries', this was the key, very dramatic point, 'no other June has provided us with so devastatingly few hours of sunshine and warmth.' The same old story. And the article ended with the inevitable, 'That's just how it is, the weather is beautiful in Brittany… five times a day.' It was like a patriotic mantra. But only Bretons themselves could complain or laugh about Breton weather; when other people did it, it was considered extremely rude. In the nearly three years Dupin had spent here, he had learnt that this was true of all things 'Breton'.

The piercing sound of his mobile made the Commissaire jump. It got him every time. Labat's number flashed up on the screen. Labat was one of his two inspectors. Dupin's mood darkened, and he let it ring. He would see him at the station in half an hour anyway. Dupin thought Labat small-minded, unbearably keen and sycophantic, yet also driven by hideous ambition. Labat was in his mid-thirties, rather stocky, with a round baby face, slightly protruding ears, a bald patch that he couldn't quite pull off – and he considered himself irresistible. He had been assigned to Dupin right at the beginning and the Commissaire had made numerous attempts to get rid of him. He had been pretty thorough in his efforts, but so far without success.

The phone rang a second time. Labat was always so full of his own importance. The phone rang a third time. Dupin realised he was feeling a little uneasy.

'Yes?'

'Monsieur le Commissaire? Is that you?'

'Who else were you expecting on my phone?' barked Dupin.

'Prefect Guenneugues just called. You've got to stand in for him. Tonight, the Friendship Committee from Staten Stoud in Canada.'

Labat's dulcet tones were obnoxious.

'As you know, Prefect Guenneugues is the honorary chairman of the committee. The official delegation is staying in France for a week and tonight they are the guests of honour at the Bretonnade in Trégunc Plage. Due to unforeseen circumstances, the Prefect has a few things to take care of in Brest, and is requesting that you welcome the delegation and their chairman, Docteur de la Croix, on his behalf. Trégunc is in our jurisdiction after all.'

'What?'

Dupin had no idea what Labat was talking about.

'Staten Stoud is twinned with Concarneau, it's near Montreal, the Prefect has some distant relatives there who...'

'It's quarter to eight, Labat. I'm having breakfast.'

'It's very important to the Prefect, it was the only reason he called. He asked me to inform you immediately.'

'Inform me?'

Dupin hung up. He had no desire to devote even a moment's thought to this. Thank God he was too tired to get properly worked up about it. Dupin couldn't stand Guenneugues. What's more, he still had no idea how to pronounce his name, which admittedly was not an infrequent occurrence for him where Bretons were concerned. This often landed him in embarrassing situations since he had to deal with people all day.

Dupin turned back to his paper. The *Ouest France* and the *Télégramme*, those were the two big local papers and they were devoted to Brittany in a way that was both affectionate and proud; after a page of very concise international and national news dealing swiftly with world events, there followed thirty pages of regional and local, mostly very local, reports. Commissaire Dupin loved both papers. After his 'relocation' he had, at first unwillingly but then with growing interest, begun his study of the Breton soul. Next to meeting the people, it was these small, seemingly insignificant stories which had taught him the most. Stories about life at the 'End of World', the 'finis terra' as the Romans – those invaders! – had called the most remote tip of this wild, craggy peninsula that stretched out into the raging Atlantic. It was a name the *département* retained to this day. Amongst the locals – the Celts! – the land of course wasn't known as the 'End of the World', but in fact its exact opposite: 'Penn ar Bed', literally the 'Head of the World', or 'The Beginning of Everything'.

The phone rang again, and yet again it was Labat. Dupin could feel the anger rising up inside him despite his fatigue.

'I won't be able to make it tonight, I have things to do, official duties, tell that to Geungeu... tell that to the Prefect.'

'A murder. There's been a murder.'

Labat's voice was quiet and flat.

'What?'

'In Pont-Aven, Monsieur le Commissaire. The owner of the *Central Hotel*, Pierre-Louis Pennec, was found dead in his restaurant a few minutes ago. The police in Pont-Aven were called.'

'Is this a joke, Labat?'

'Two of our colleagues from Pont-Aven should be there by now.'

'In Pont-Aven? Pierre-Louis Pennec?'

'Excuse me, Monsieur le Commissaire?'

'What else do you know?'

'Only what I've just told you.'

'And it's definitely murder?'

'It certainly looks that way.'

'How so?'

Dupin was annoyed by his own question almost before it had passed his lips.

'I can only tell you what the caller, the hotel chef, told the officer on duty, which he then –'

'Fine. But what's it got to do with us? Pont-Aven is in the Quimperlé jurisdiction – this is Derrien's case.'

'Commissaire Derrien has been on holiday since Monday. We're in charge when it comes to serious matters. That's why the station in Pont-Aven –'

'Okay, okay... I'll head there now. You should too. And call Le Ber, I want him to come straight away.'

'Le Ber is already on his way.'

'Good... Unbelievable. Fucking hell.'

'Monsieur le Commissaire?'

Dupin hung up.

'I've got to go,' he called in Lily's direction, but she was engrossed in a telephone call. Dupin placed a few coins on the bar and left the *Amiral*. His car was parked in the big car park on the waterfront just a short walk away.

'Absurd,' thought Dupin as he sat in his car, 'this is absolutely absurd.' A murder in Pont-Aven, at the height of summer, just as the tourist season was about to turn the village into a big open-air museum, as they said so scornfully in Concarneau. Pont-Aven was an idyllic place. It must be years since the last murder in this picturesque – to Dupin's taste much *too* picturesque – village. At the end of the nineteenth century it became known around the world for its artists' colony, largely because of Paul Gauguin who was of course its most prominent member. Now Pont-Aven turned up in every French guidebook and every history of modern art. And on top of this, the elderly Pierre-Louis Pennec was a legendary hotelier, an institution, just like his father before him, and indeed his grandmother, the famous founder of the *Central*, Marie-Jeanne Pennec before that.

Dupin fumbled about with the ludicrously small buttons on his car phone. He hated it.

'Where are you, Nolwenn?'

'On my way to the station. Labat called just now so I'm up to speed. I suppose you'll want Doctor Lafond.'

'As quickly as possible.'

There had been a different forensic pathologist in Quimper for the last year and Dupin couldn't stand him. Ewen Savoir was a bumbling young snot-nosed fool. Impressive instruments and gadgets but he was stupid, and terribly long-winded. Admittedly Dupin couldn't exactly claim that he liked grumpy old Dr Lafond; he and Lafond clashed too if things weren't going quickly enough for Dupin, and then Lafond would fly off the handle, but his work was simply excellent.

'Savoir drives me absolutely insane.'

'I'll take care of everything.'

Dupin loved hearing this sentence from Nolwenn's mouth. She had been the secretary to his predecessor and his predecessor's predecessor. She was wonderful. Marvellous, absolutely marvellous.

'Good, I'm at the last roundabout in Concarneau. I'll be there in ten minutes.'

'This sounds like a nasty business, Monsieur le Commissaire. It's unbelievable. I knew old Pennec. My husband did a few jobs for him a few years ago.'

For a moment Dupin was about to ask what 'a few jobs' meant, but he let it go. He had more important things to worry about. To this day he didn't quite understand what Nolwenn's husband actually did for a living, he somehow just seemed to pop up everywhere, always doing 'a few jobs' for all sorts of people.

'There's going to be such a fuss. An icon of Finistère. Of Brittany. Of France. *Mon Dieu*... I'll be in touch.'

'All right. I'm already at the station.'

'Speak to you soon.'

Dupin drove fast; far too fast for these narrow streets. It was hard to believe that old Derrien had chosen this time to go on holiday for the first time in years. He would be away for ten days. His daughter was getting married; the wedding was in Réunion which even Derrien thought was an utterly preposterous idea.

The groom came from the same sleepy backwater she did, three kilometres from Pont-Aven.

Dupin fiddled with the car phone again.

'Le Ber?'

'Monsieur le Commissaire?'

'Are you there yet?'

'Yes, I just got here.'

'Where's the body?'

'Downstairs in the restaurant.'

'Have you been in yet?'

'No.'

'Don't let anyone in. Nobody goes in before I get there, including you. Who found Pennec?'

'Francine Lajoux. An employee.'

'What's she saying?'

'I haven't spoken to her yet. I've honestly only just got here.'

'Right. Okay. I'll be there right away.'

The pool of blood looked grotesquely large to Dupin. It had spread out in a shapeless mass across the uneven stone floor. Pierre-Louis Pennec was a tall man, thin, wiry, with short grey hair. An imposing figure, even at ninety-one years old. Pennec was lying on his back, his corpse strangely contorted, his left hand touching the hollow of his knee, one hip badly dislocated, right hand on his heart, face horrifyingly distorted. His eyes wide and fixed on the ceiling. He had a number of obvious wounds to his upper body and throat.

'Somebody really battered Pierre-Louis Pennec. An old man. Who would do something like this?'

Le Ber was standing two metres behind Dupin, they

were the only people in the room. There was disgust in his voice. Dupin was silent. Le Ber was right, though: this really was a brutal murder.

'Fucking hell!' Dupin ran his hand fiercely through his hair.

'Presumably those are knife wounds, but there's no sign of the murder weapon.'

'Let's not panic, Le Ber.'

'Two officers from Pont-Aven are securing the hotel, Monsieur le Commissaire. I know one of them, Albin Monfort. He's been a policeman for a good while. A very good policeman. The other one is called Pennarguear. I didn't catch his first name. Still very young.'

Dupin laughed in spite of himself. Le Ber was still young himself. He was in his early thirties and this was only his second year as an inspector. He was precise, quick, intelligent. But he was always very serious and spoke in a solemn manner. Sometimes he had a mischievous glint in his eye which Dupin liked to see. And he never made any fuss.

'Nobody's been into the room yet, have they?'

Dupin had already asked this question three times, but it didn't irritate Le Ber in the slightest.

'Not a soul. But the pathologist and the scene of crime team should be here soon.'

Dupin understood. Le Ber knew that the Commissaire liked to have a quiet look around by himself before the rabble descended.

Pennec was lying in the furthest corner of the room, right in front of the bar. It was an L-shaped room, with the restaurant in the long front section and the bar in the small bay that branched off it. From the restaurant there was a little corridor to the kitchen which was in an annexe behind the main building. The door was locked.

The stools stood in a neat row at the bar, apart from one which was pushed back a little. There was a single glass on the bar, and a bottle of lambig, the apple brandy Bretons were so proud of – as they were of anything genuinely Breton or anything they considered to be so. Dupin liked it too. The glass was almost empty. There was no sign of a struggle; in fact, there was nothing unusual in this part of the room at all. It had clearly been carefully tidied and cleaned by the hotel staff the evening before, as had the rest of the room. The tables and chairs were arranged with scrupulous precision, the tables already laid, the tablecloths rustic and colourful, the floor spotless. The restaurant and the bar must have been renovated not too long ago; everything looked so new. And it was well insulated, too, nothing could be heard from outside, nothing at all. Nor from the street, even though there were three windows, or from the foyer, where the main entrance was. The windows were shut tight – Dupin inspected them carefully.

There was an eeriness about the contrast between the careful order and cleanliness – the sheer banality of the room – and the gruesome sight of the corpse. The obligatory prints of paintings from the time of the great artists' colony hung on the whitewashed walls. You could admire these prints even in the smallest cafés and shops in the village. Pont-Aven seemed to be wallpapered with them.

Dupin went over the whole room very slowly a few times without looking for anything in particular, but found nothing. He clumsily took his little red notebook out of his trouser pocket and scribbled a few things on the page, practically at random.

Somebody tried to force open the door but Dupin had locked it from inside, so they knocked loudly. Dupin was tempted to ignore it, but didn't protest when Le Ber looked enquiringly at him and then went towards the door. It crashed open. All of a sudden, Salou had burst into the room and Labat's eager voice was announcing, 'Doctor Lafond is here. And the forensic experts, René Salou and his team.'

Dupin heaved a deep sigh. He always forgot about Salou and his 'scene of crime work'. René Salou was the greatest forensic expert in the world. He had turned up today with three people in tow who were now skulking behind him in silence. Dr Lafond was the last to come in, heading straight for the body. He murmured a barely audible '*Bonjour*, M'sieur' in Dupin's direction. It didn't sound unfriendly.

Salou turned briskly to Labat and Le Ber.

'Gentlemen, if I could ask you to leave the room until our work is finished here. Only the Commissaire, Doctor Lafond and I should be here while my team is working. If you could have someone stand guard? *Bonjour*, Monsieur le Commissaire. *Bonjour*, Monsieur le Docteur.'

Dupin was finding it difficult to keep his anger in check. He didn't say a word. The two men had never had much time for one another.

'Docteur Lafond, if you would be so good as to make sure you don't leave any new evidence behind you? Thank you.'

Salou had produced his bulky camera.

'My team will get started on the fingerprint work straight away. Lagrange, I want potential fingerprints first, from the bar, the glass, the bottle, from everything near the body. I want you to be systematic about it.'

Lafond placed his bag on one of the tables near the bar, utterly calm and showing no sign of having heard Salou's words at all.

Dupin went to the door. He had to get out of there. He left the room without another word.

By this time, there was considerably more noise coming from the little reception desk in the foyer. The news had definitely started to spread through the hotel and from there through the whole village. Some guests were standing at reception, all of them talking at once. Behind the crowded desk stood a short-haired, somewhat gaunt little woman with a large, pointy nose who was speaking in a firm voice. She was trying hard to seem calm.

'No, no, don't worry. We'll sort it all out.'

A murder in the hotel where you wanted to spend the most glorious weeks of the year; Dupin understood why the guests were upset, but he also felt sorry for the woman. It was just before the tourist season and Le Ber had said half of the hotel was booked up. Twenty-six guests were already there, four of them children, most of them from abroad; the majority of French people weren't on holiday yet. The influx wouldn't start properly for another week. Still, even if the hotel wasn't booked out, the guests who *were* there were coming in and out, in the evenings and at night. Anyone who committed a murder somewhere like this would have to reckon with the possibility that somebody would notice something – that he would be seen, for instance, when he left the hotel through the foyer, or that someone would hear the struggle, a cry for help, Pennec's scream as he fought for his life. Surely there were staff staying in the hotel at night too. It was a risky place to commit a murder.

Le Ber came down the stairs. He gave the Commissaire a questioning look.

'That's the way it is, Le Ber. The crime scene belongs to the professionals for now.'

Le Ber started to say something but stopped. He had learnt it was best not to ask Dupin about his methods or strategy. That was the only thing that used to annoy him about Le Ber when he first arrived, and sometimes it still happened – Le Ber always wanted to understand Dupin's approach.

'Where are the local police officers? Reception will have to be moved. I want to have this area free.'

'Labat took them upstairs. He wanted to start questioning the guests about last night.'

'I want only guests and staff coming in and out of this hotel from now on. Someone should be on duty in the foyer. Not you, someone from the local police force. You said an employee had found Pennec?'

'Yes, Francine Lajoux. She's worked here for more than forty years. She's upstairs in the breakfast room now with a chambermaid. She's in shock but we've called a doctor.'

'I'd like to speak to her.' Dupin hesitated a moment, undecided. Then he took out his notebook. 'It's five past nine now. Labat called at 7.47. He had just been informed by the police in Pont-Aven. They had taken a call from the hotel here. Madame Lajoux must have found Pierre-Louis Pennec around half past seven. That's not even two hours ago. We don't know anything yet.'

Le Ber couldn't believe that the Commissaire had actually made notes like this, even though it was generally known that Dupin had a note-taking method that was, to put it mildly, very unique.

'Pierre-Louis Pennec has a son, Loic. There's also a brother, a half-brother. He lives in Toulon. The family should be informed soon, Monsieur le Commissaire.'

'A son? Where does he live?'

'Here in Pont-Aven with his wife Catherine, down by the harbour. No children.'

'I'll go and see him straight away. But I'll speak to Madame Lajoux first.'

Le Ber knew it would be useless to argue, knew what the Commissaire was like when he was on a 'proper case'. And this was a proper case.

'I'll get you Loic Pennec's exact address and the phone number for the half-brother. André Pennec is a well-known conservative politician in the south, he's been a member of parliament for twenty years.'

'Is he here now? In the area, I mean?

'No, not as far as we know.'

'Okay. I'll call him later. No other family?'

'No.'

'Get Salou to tell you everything when he's finished. And Lafond is to call me, even if he says that he won't comment until his report is complete.'

'Okay.'

'And I want to speak to Derrien. Somebody needs to

try and get hold of him immediately.'

Derrien would be sure to know Pont-Aven like the back of his hand. His knowledge would be helpful. And it was really his case after all.

'I think Monfort is already doing that.'

'What does the son do? Does he work in the hotel too?'

'No, probably not. All Labat knew was that he had a small company.'

'What kind of company?'

'Honey.'

'Honey?'

'Yes, *miel de mer*. The beehives have to be twenty-five metres or less from the sea. The best honey in the world, according –'

'All right. Our priorities, Le Ber: I want to know what Monsieur Pennec did in the last few days and weeks, in as much detail as possible. Day by day. I want everything written up as accurately as possible. Everything, even the everyday stuff. His rituals, his habits.'

One of the guests at reception suddenly raised his voice.

'We are going to get all of our money back. We're not going to accept this.' An unpleasant little creep, heavy-set and greasy. His wife looked on obediently.

'We are going to leave this minute – that is exactly what we are going to do.'

'I don't think you will be leaving now, Monsieur. Nobody is leaving.'

The man turned to Dupin, bristling with anger. He was going to lose his temper any moment now.

'Commissaire Dupin. Commissariat de Police, Concarneau. First you are going to be questioned by the police, along with every other guest.'

Dupin had spoken so quietly he had practically hissed. Combined with his impressive build, his words had the desired effect. The little man took a few swift steps backwards.

'Inspector Le Ber,' Dupin, speaking loudly and formally now, 'the police officers will question Monsieur,' he stopped and prompted the man with a look, so that he meekly stammered 'Galvani', 'the police will question Monsieur Galvani and his wife about last night. Thoroughly. Take personal particulars, check their identification.'

Dupin was tall, strong and well-built, with shoulders that cast quite a shadow. According to the local gossip, he was carrying some extra weight; so nobody was ever expecting the skilful speed and fine precision of which he was so effortlessly capable. He certainly didn't look like a commissaire, even less so in the jeans and polo shirts which he almost always wore – and Dupin liked to exploit this fact.

Monsieur Galvani spluttered something incomprehensible, and looked to his wife for protection, as she was a good head taller than he was. Dupin turned aside, and saw the hotel employee smiling furtively at him. He smiled back. Then he turned to Le Ber who was frowning and looked quite embarrassed.

'The most important thing is that you and Labat reconstruct yesterday and last night in as much detail as possible. What did Pennec do? Where was he and when? Who saw him last?'

'We're working on it. The chef was probably the last person to see him.'

'Good. Which staff members are at the hotel this morning?'

Le Ber took out a very small black notebook. 'Mademoiselle Galez and Mademoiselle Jolivet, both very young, chamber-maids, and Madame Mendu, who, if I understand correctly, is going to be something of a successor to Madame Lajoux. And she's also responsible for the breakfast. Madame Mendu is standing over there.'

Le Ber motioned discreetly towards reception with his head.

'Then there's Madame Lajoux and the chef, Edouard Lenaff. And an assistant of his.'

Dupin made a note of everything.

'The chef? At this hour?'

'They get all their supplies from the big supermarket in Quimper very early in the morning.'

'What's the kitchen boy called?'

Le Ber rifled through his notebook.

'Ronan Breton.'

'Breton? His name is Breton?'

'Breton.'

Dupin wanted to say something but didn't.

'And the chef was the last person to see Pennec alive?'

'So it would seem at this point.'

'I want to speak to him as soon as I'm finished with Madame Lajoux. Just briefly.' Dupin turned away and climbed the stairs. Without turning around he called, 'Where on the first floor is it?'

'It's on your right, the first door.'

Dupin knocked gently on the door to the breakfast room and went inside. Francine Lajoux was older than Dupin had expected – definitely over sixty, pure white hair, an angular face with deep wrinkles. She was sitting in the far corner of the room and beside her was a buxom little red-haired chambermaid with a somewhat chubby but pretty face – a Mademoiselle Galez, who gave the Commissaire a friendly and relieved smile. At first Madame Lajoux hardly seemed to notice that the Commissaire had come in, continuing to stare motionlessly at the floor.

Dupin cleared his throat.

'Hello Madame, my name is Dupin, I am the Commissaire in charge. I'm told it was you who found Pierre-Louis Pennec's body this morning.'

Madame Lajoux's eyes were red from crying and her mascara had run. For a moment nothing happened but then she turned her gaze to the Commissaire.

'An abhorrent murder, isn't it, Monsieur le Commissaire? This is an abhorrent murder. Cold-blooded murder. I have been a loyal employee of Monsieur Pennec for thirty-seven years. I was never even off sick once… Well, maybe twice at most! It looked like he had been beaten up, didn't it? The murderer must have made those stab wounds with a huge knife. I hope you catch him quickly.'

She didn't speak in a hurried way, but she did speak with impressive speed, without pauses and with a lilting intonation.

'Poor Monsieur Pennec. Such a wonderful man. Who could have done such a horrible thing? Everyone liked him, Monsieur le Commissaire. Everyone.

Everyone respected him, respected and admired him. And in our beautiful little Pont-Aven! Horrible. Such a peaceful place. The pool of blood was so big. Is that normal, Monsieur le Commissaire?'

Dupin didn't know how to respond. Or what he should respond to for that matter. Feeling rather worn out, he placed his pad in front of him and made a note. There was an odd pause. Madame Galez took a surreptitious peek at his notebook.

'I'm sorry, I know it must be awful for you to have to think about this again, but can you tell me about how you found the body? Was the door open? Were you alone?'

He was well aware that this was not a particularly sympathetic response.

'I was completely alone. Is that important then? The door was closed, but not locked like it usually is. Yes. Monsieur Pennec locks it when he leaves at night. Even at that stage I thought something wasn't right. I think it was quarter past seven or thereabouts. I make the breakfast every morning you know. I've been here at six o'clock every morning for the last thirty-seven years. Thirty-seven years! Six o'clock on the dot. The teaspoons were missing. The breakfast ones. You know when there aren't that many guests, we just do breakfast up here but in the tourist season we do it in the restaurant too. I wanted to get some teaspoons from the restaurant. They're often missing, we need to fix that. I'm always saying it! I must speak to Madame Mendu again. I didn't see anything out of the ordinary in the restaurant, just the body. Poor Monsieur Pennec. Do you know why nobody

27

heard anything last night? Because of the big festival. It was so loud everywhere, all over the village, it's always like that when there's a festival on. It gets so rowdy. I didn't get a wink of sleep before three o'clock. And yes, I was on my own. I screamed. And then Mademoiselle Galez came. She brought me here. She's such a dear, Monsieur le Commissaire. This is so awful.'

'So you didn't notice anything unusual last night or in the last few days? Anything about Monsieur Pennec, here in the hotel? Think back. The smallest detail could be important. Something that may seem insignificant to you.'

'Everything was as it always is. In perfect order. That was very important to Monsieur Pennec.'

'Nothing at all then.'

Madame Lajoux made a gesture of resignation.

'No, nothing at all. We've all spoken to each other as well. All the hotel staff who are on duty today, I mean. Nobody noticed anything unusual.'

'In general terms – do you have any idea what might have happened here?'

'Monsieur le Commissaire!' She looked absolutely indignant. 'You're asking as though something criminal has happened here.'

It was on the tip of Dupin's tongue to observe that murder was generally considered a crime. 'Out of all of Monsieur Pennec's employees, you had worked for him the longest, is that correct?'

'Oh yes.'

'So of all the people here in the hotel, you knew Monsieur Pennec best.'

'Of course. An establishment like this one, Monsieur

le Commissaire, is a lifetime's work. A true calling, as Pierre-Louis Pennec always used to say.'

'Did anything catch your eye in the restaurant or the bar? Apart from the body, that is.'

'No. The tourist season is just starting, you know. It's always really hectic around now. There's so much to do.'

The expression on her face changed dramatically. Now she spoke very slowly, in a laboured, strained voice. 'There are terrible rumours going around, you know. People say we were having... we were having an affair, Monsieur Pennec and I. In the years after his wife so tragically died. A boating accident. I hope you won't take any notice of those brazen liars, Monsieur le Commissaire. A grotesque lie. Monsieur Pennec would never have done anything like that. He continued to love his wife even after she died and he remained faithful to her always. In any case... Just because we were so close and so friendly. People have active imaginations sometimes.'

Dupin was somewhat baffled.

'Yes of course, Madame Lajoux. Of course.'

There was a small pause.

'What else can you tell me about the accident?' Dupin hadn't asked this question with any particular purpose in mind.

'It happened out of the blue one day. It was dusk and Darice Pennec went overboard in a storm. Nobody wears lifejackets here, you know. They were coming back from the Glénan Islands. Do you know the archipelago? Probably not, apparently you're new round here. It's absolutely beautiful. Just like in the

Mediterranean. Some people even think it's like the Caribbean. Dazzling white sand.'

Dupin would have liked to say that he obviously knew the Glénan Islands, that he had in fact been living here for almost three years. In Breton eyes, if your family hadn't lived in Brittany for generations, you were 'new' here. But at some point he had come to terms with this and given up arguing.

'Storms blow up so quickly here, you know. She disappeared immediately. The sea does that sometimes. He was out until the following morning looking for her. That was a long time ago now, twenty years or so. She was fifty-eight years old. Poor Pennec, he was almost fainting with exhaustion when he came back in to land.'

Dupin decided not to delve any further.

'And what about you?' Dupin turned smoothly to Mademoiselle Galez, receiving an indignant look from Madame Lajoux in the process. 'Did you notice anything in particular yesterday, today or in the last few days? It could be a small detail.'

The chambermaid was surprised by how abruptly he had switched his attention to her. She looked a bit frightened.

'Me? No. I had so much to do.'

'Do you know if anyone went into the restaurant this morning after you and Madame Lajoux?'

'No. I locked the door.'

Dupin made a note.

'Very good. When did each of you see Monsieur Pennec for the last time?' Dupin stopped short. 'Alive, I mean?'

'I left at half eight yesterday. I always leave at half eight. For the last ten years I mean. Before that I was here every evening too, but I'm not up to it any more. Not like I used to be. Before I left, Monsieur Pennec and I did speak briefly about things to do with the hotel. It was just like it always is.'

'And you, Mademoiselle Galez?'

'I'm not quite sure. Maybe around three o'clock yesterday afternoon. I saw him before that, as he was coming out of his room that morning, around seven o'clock. He asked me to do his room straight away.'

'He has a room here? Monsieur Pennec lived in the hotel?'

Mademoiselle Galez gave Madame Lajoux a look that was difficult to interpret, and Madame Lajoux took over.

'He has a house on rue des Meunières, not far from the hotel, and he has a room here, on the second floor. He's been sleeping here more and more in the last few years. It was just too much hassle to go home at night. He was there till closing every evening you see, he never left before midnight, never. He kept an eye on everything. He was an excellent hotelier you know. Like his father and grandmother. A great family tradition.'

'Why did his room need to be done immediately?'

Mademoiselle Galez seemed to consider this for a moment. 'I don't know.'

'Was that unusual?'

Again she seemed to be trying to think carefully. 'He didn't say it often.'

'What did Pierre-Louis Pennec still do at the hotel? Is there a business manager or someone like that?'

'Monsieur le Commissaire!' There was outrage in Madame Lajoux's tone and expression. 'Monsieur Pennec did everything himself. Everything. He has managed the hotel since 1947. I don't know if you know the story of the *Central*. You're so new here after all. You should know it! This is where modern art was invented. Gauguin had his famous school here, the Pont-Aven School.'

'Madame Lajoux, I –'

'Pierre-Louis Pennec's grandmother founded all of this, she was the one behind it all. She was a close friend of the artists and encouraged them as much as she could. She even built them studios. You ought to know all of this, Monsieur le Commissaire, Marie-Jeanne is in all the history books and art books. Without Marie-Jeanne Pennec's guesthouse and Julia Guillou's hotel right next door, none of it would have existed. Sometimes the artists lived and ate here free of charge, most of them hadn't a penny to their names anyway. And...' She had to pause to draw breath, she looked absolutely outraged now. 'And it's a huge injustice that continues to this day that they make more of a fuss about Mademoiselle Julia than they do about Marie-Jeanne Pennec. Are you aware of all this, Monsieur le Commissaire?'

'I – no. I had no idea.'

'You're going to have to buy a book about it. No buts. The bookshop is just by the bridge. And read up on everything. It's all common knowledge here.'

'Madame Lajoux, I –'

'I understand, the main thing is the police investigation now, of course it is. You had asked whether Pierre-

32

Louis Pennec managed the hotel by himself? That was the question. Oh yes! He ran it for sixty-three years, can you imagine? He was twenty-eight when his father, the wonderful Charles Pennec, died. He died quite young. He had inherited the hotel from his mother. She –'

Madame Lajoux broke off and looked like she was reminding herself to concentrate.

'When the time came he was twenty-eight and Pierre-Louis had no fear of the burden of tradition. He took over the hotel and has run it by himself ever since.'

Francine Lajoux sighed loudly.

'And as for me, I'm responsible for breakfast, the bedrooms and the chambermaids, as well as reception, reservations and all those things. I mean, Madame Mendu really does it these days, has for a few years now. She does it well.' Madame Lajoux paused for a moment, took a breath and then spoke so quietly it was almost inaudible, as though she were exhausted, 'But I'm still here.'

Mademoiselle Galez came to her aid.

'Madame Mendu took over the job of housekeeper from Madame Lajoux. You must have seen her out there at reception. She has an assistant, Mademoiselle Jolivet, who works at reception in the afternoons and as a waitress in the restaurant in the evenings. Then Madame Mendu works the reception in the evening and of course every morning too.'

When the chambermaid had finished speaking, she looked uncertainly at Madame Lajoux. Quite rightly, as it turned out a moment later.

'But those are all menial tasks. The management

was done entirely by Monsieur Pennec. I –' Her tone had been scornful. She broke off abruptly, evidently shocked at herself.

'Is everything all right, Madame Lajoux?' Dupin knew he had almost enough information.

'Yes, yes. My nerves are somewhat on edge.'

'Just a few more things, Madame Lajoux. What did Monsieur Pennec typically do at the end of the day?'

'If the restaurant was still busy, he made sure everything was running smoothly, discussed the important things with Madame Leray and the chef. Corinne Leray doesn't come in until late afternoon. She runs the restaurant but otherwise she has nothing to do with the hotel. Is that what you wanted to know, Monsieur le Commissaire?'

Dupin noticed that his little diagram of the names of the hotel staff, their responsibilities, hierarchies and working hours had become extremely confusing. 'And then? Later, I mean. At the end of the day?'

'At the end of the day, once he was finished with everything and the tables in the restaurant had been set for the next day, he would still always be standing at the bar. Fragan Delon would be there sometimes. Or one of the regulars. Or a local. But usually he was by himself.'

Mademoiselle Galez apparently felt the need to clarify this.

'Monsieur Delon was Monsieur Pennec's best friend. He often came to the hotel, sometimes for lunch, and sometimes in the afternoon or evening time.'

'Mademoiselle Galez! It is impossible for outsiders to judge whether people are best friends. It's a very private matter.' Francine Lajoux gave the chambermaid a reproachful look, as a teacher would an impertinent student who had been showing off inappropriately. 'They were friends. More than that, we can't say. And they didn't always see eye to eye.'

'Was Monsieur Delon here yesterday?'

'I don't think so. But you'll have to ask Madame Mendu. Mademoiselle Galez and I aren't here in the evenings.'

'What time did Monsieur Pennec usually finish up at the bar? Did he always drink a lambig then?'

'So somebody's already let that one slip. Yes, a lambig. It's our apple brandy! As good as a calvados, believe me, they just do more advertising! Pierre-Louis Pennec only ever drank lambig from Menez Brug. He went to the bar around eleven every evening and he always stayed half an hour, never longer. Does that help?'

There was a knock at the door and a moment later Le Ber was standing in the doorway, speaking frantically.

'Monsieur le Commissaire, Loic Pennec is on the phone. He and his wife already know.'

At first Dupin wanted to ask how the news had reached them, but he knew this would be a ridiculous question to ask. The wholevillage would obviously know by this point. He should have thought of that.

'Tell him I'm coming straight away. I'll be right there.'

Le Ber disappeared into the corridor again.

'Thank you very much, both of you. You've given us some important information. You've been really helpful. I would like to ask that you let us know immediately if you think of anything else. I'm sorry to have taken up so much of your time.'

'I want you to find the murderer, Monsieur le Commissaire.' Madame Lajoux was stony-faced.

'You can get in touch at any time, Madame Lajoux, Mademoiselle Galez. I will definitely be in touch. Probably very soon.'

'Whenever you need, Monsieur le Commissaire,' they said, almost in unison.

Le Ber was standing right next to the door when the Commissaire came out.

'Monsieur and Madame Pennec are expecting you in –'

'Le Ber, when the forensics team is finished, go into the restaurant with Madame Lajoux. I want her to double check whether anything is missing or altered – best do the whole hotel. And ask Madame Mendu whether Pennec's friend Fragan Delon or anyone else was here late last night. Whether someone was at the bar with Pennec yesterday, however briefly. Oh yes, and speak to Madame Leray!'

'Okay. I have a complete list of all the hotel staff.'

'Are there any other entrances to the hotel?'

'Yes, you can get in through the kitchen. The entrance is in the courtyard, you just need to go down the little alleyway behind the hotel to get to it. There's a big, cast-iron door there, but it's practically never used and they keep it locked. The key is hanging up in reception.'

'What kind of festival was on in Pont-Aven last night?'

'Oh, just the local *Fest-Noz*, you know? It's when –'

'I know what it is.'

They were held throughout the summer, the 'traditional Breton dance festivals' with their traditional folk music. They weren't exactly Dupin's cup of tea. They were held in a different village every evening, no matter how small a village might be, and there was endless folk dancing.

'Monsieur le Commissaire, you should really be –'

'The chef, just briefly.'

Le Ber had obviously already thought of this. With a gesture that had only a touch of resignation about it, he pointed along the corridor.

'We've taken one of the free rooms.'

He made another attempt, 'If you want, I'll speak to the chef.'

'We'll do it very quickly.'

'Apparently Edouard Lenaff doesn't like talking very much anyway, Monsieur le Commissaire.'

Dupin looked at Le Ber, a little irritated.

'What?'

The room was amazingly spacious and bright for such an old building and it was furnished with simple but pretty white wooden furniture, old oak parquet and pale upholstery. There was a lanky youth at a small table near the door, somehow managing to look utterly indifferent. He took almost no notice of them when they came in.

'Hello, Monsieur. Commissaire Dupin, Commissariat de Police, Concarneau. I understand you saw Pierre-Louis Pennec yesterday evening.'

Lenaff gave a brief, friendly nod.

'When was that?'

'Quarter to eleven.'

'Are you sure of the time?'

Lenaff nodded again.

'How are you so sure?'

'I was done for the day, the kitchen just needed tidying. It's always about quarter to eleven then.'

'Where exactly did you see him?'

'Downstairs.'

'More specifically?'

'On the stairs.'

'Where did he go?'

'Down the stairs.'

'And you?'

'Outside. I wanted a smoke.'

'And what direction was he headed?'

'No idea. Towards the bar, I think. He always went to the bar later on.'

'And did you speak to each other?'

'Yes.'

The conversation wasn't exactly flowing. Dupin had no idea where this chap got the passion that he evidently put into his cooking. He wasn't a top chef, but Dupin knew the restaurant was well respected. Even Nolwenn had recommended it, which meant he must be good.

'What did you talk about?'

'Nothing major.'

Dupin's astonishment prompted Lenaff to add a little more. 'Plans for today.'

'What do you mean?'

'What we would cook today, the dish of the day and stuff. We always have a special dish of the day. That was important to Monsieur Pennec.'

An astonishingly detailed outburst, thought Dupin. 'And that's all you talked about, nothing else?'

'No.'

'And you didn't notice anything about Monsieur Pennec? Was he acting out of character at all?'

'No,' answered Lenaff, as expected. 'Not at all.'

Dupin sighed. 'So he seemed normal to you?'

'Yes.'

'Was he alone? Did anyone join him?'

'I didn't see anyone.'

'And apart from that, did you notice anything unusual? In the hotel or about anyone else?' Dupin knew the question was pointless. Before Lenaff could answer he added: 'I would ask that you come to us immediately if anything of interest does occur to you. You're an important person for us. Presumably Pierre-Louis Pennec went to the bar after your conversation and he was probably murdered there just a short time later. Do you understand why your testimony could be of great significance?'

Even at this, Lenaff's gaze and facial expression did not change. Dupin hadn't really expected them to.

'I've got to go. I'm sure we'll see each other again in the next few days.'

Lenaff stood up, silently shook the Commissaire's hand and left. Le Ber and Dupin were left alone in the room.

'Huh.' Dupin stood up too and turned to go. He couldn't suppress a grin. In some ways it had been a very Breton conversation. He secretly quite liked the chef. And had decided to come and eat here sometime. He had learnt a lot.

'What do you think, Monsieur le Commissaire? It would be incredibly unlucky if nobody saw or heard anything at all last night.'

Dupin was tempted to say that this wouldn't be the first time he had been incredibly unlucky but he restrained himself. 'We'll see. Nobody is to go into the rooms downstairs, Le Ber. When our colleagues are finished, we'll lock everything up. I'll see the Pennecs now.'

Dupin left.

Le Ber was used to this by now. The Commissaire was obsessed with having the crime scene locked up indefinitely, even if it was a public place, for far longer than the forensic team needed. He wanted it kept locked until he was sure there was nothing more to be gleaned from it. It always caused a huge amount of trouble. This habit of his didn't have anything to do with any police guidelines – it was just that the Commissaire had his own ideas, and Le Ber knew it would be pointless to discuss it. He had also learnt that these unorthodox methods could have astounding results. During Dupin's first investigations in Brittany he had had serious arguments with any number of people, not just with Guenneugues, and Dupin hadn't always won. But ever since his first successes as a Commissaire, especially after solving the sensational murders of two tuna fishermen in his second year, a case which was etched into Bretons' memories and made Dupin very well known in the region, there had been far fewer arguments.

The *Central* was on Place Paul Gauguin, the village's pretty little main square. It was a beautiful, dazzlingly white building from the end of the nineteenth century and it had obviously been lovingly and carefully looked after over the decades. It was right next to the much larger *Julia Hotel*, the famous hotel that had once belonged to Julia Guillou. The *Julia* had later become the town hall and had housed part of Pont-Aven's art museum for a number of years. The sycamores that Julia Guillou had had planted in the face of bitter resistance from the local authorities still stood in front of the hotel. They had been planted to provide her guests, the artists, with some cool shade on the terrace in summer.

Loic Pennec and his wife lived on rue Auguste Brizeux, not far from the *Central*, but then nothing was far from the *Central* in Pont-Aven. Commissaire Dupin was glad of the walk, not least because he really needed another coffee. He always needed coffee, lots of coffee, and he felt he needed it more than ever today. Without a sufficient amount of caffeine, his brain didn't work properly; he was absolutely convinced of it.

Dupin crossed the famous stone bridge over the Aven and took a sharp left onto rue du Port, which led straight down to the waterfront where it met rue Auguste Brizeux. Down here by the harbour, imposing hills rose on either side of the legendary Aven. Dupin had to admit they had chosen an excellent area to settle way back when, this place where the Aven flowed into the sea – more specifically, the place where the river, which initially wove through the winding valley like a little mountain stream, became a kind of inlet, which then meandered picturesquely for more than seven kilometres to the open sea, branched off into countless tributaries and occasionally formed beautiful lakes. The river and sea were inextricably bound by the tides.

Dupin was so overwhelmed by the number of bars and cafés in Pont-Aven every summer that they all blurred into one uninviting mass. Having almost made it to the harbour, he picked one of the cafés that did without those huge enlarged photos of crêpes and cakes. The coffee came quickly, but it was incredibly bitter. It did help a little, but Dupin didn't order a second one. He was thinking. He couldn't form a proper opinion of Madame Lajoux, he didn't know what to make of her. One thing was for sure – she wasn't as naive as she let on. He got out his notebook and made a few notes. There was quite a lot in his notebook already – never a good sign. The less he knew about which way the wind was blowing in a case, the more 'very important' notes he made. There was still an air of the surreal about the whole case, but that was a familiar feeling for him too. If he were honest, he knew he had felt that way quite often. He had to pull himself together now. There had been a murder. This was his area of expertise.

The Pennecs lived in one of the dozen or so imposing villas made from dark, almost black, stone along the waterfront. Dupin thought they looked dreary and impersonal, and were too big to blend into their surroundings. An enamelled plaque at the entrance read 'Villa St Gwénolé'.

'Do come in, Monsieur, please.'

Dupin had only needed to hold the doorbell down

for a second. The door had been opened almost immediately. Catherine Pennec was standing in front of him in a black, high-necked dress. Her voice was quiet and subdued but sharp too, it suited her wiry frame.

'My husband will be down soon. We'll sit in the drawing room. Would you like a coffee?'

'Yes. Yes please.' Dupin wanted to get rid of the disgusting taste of the last one.

'It's just along here.'

Madame Pennec led the way into the large drawing room.

'My husband is just coming.'

She left the room through a narrow door. The house was furnished in a very middle class way. Dupin had no idea if they really were antique pieces. Everything was in perfect order, it was almost painfully neat.

Dupin could hear someone coming down the stairs into the hall, and a moment later Loic Pennec was standing in the doorway. He really did look astonishingly like Pennec senior. Dupin had seen photos of Pierre-Louis Pennec in his younger years in the lobby of the hotel, photos of him with famous guests in the sixties and seventies. Loic Pennec was as tall as his father, but a good bit heavier. He had the same short, very thick grey hair, the same distinctive nose, the mouth was just a bit bigger and narrower. Like his wife, Loic Pennec was dressed very formally, in a dark grey suit. He looked drawn and pale.

'I'm terribly sorry to –' began Dupin.

'No, no. Really. You have a job to do. We want you to make progress as quickly as possible. This is all so awful.'

Loic Pennec also spoke in a subdued voice, stuttering a little. His wife had come back with the coffee and was sitting beside her husband on the sofa. Dupin had taken a seat in an armchair which was part of a set, dark wood, pale upholstery, lots of trimmings.

This wasn't an easy situation. Dupin hadn't responded to what Pennec had said, busying himself with taking out his notebook instead.

'So do you have any leads yet, anything from the initial forensic work? Anything that you're following up?'

Catherine Pennec seemed relieved that her husband had taken up the thread of the conversation again. She tried to look composed.

'No, nothing. Not yet. It's not easy to imagine what motives there could be for murdering a ninety-one-year-old man, apparently so loved and respected by everyone. A horrific crime. I'm terribly sorry. You have my sincerest sympathies.'

'I can't take it in.' Loic Pennec's voice was losing its clipped composure, becoming totally flat. 'I don't understand it.' He buried his face in his hands.

'He was a wonderful man. A great man.' Catherine Pennec put her arm around her husband.

'I wanted to tell you the news myself, and I'm really sorry that you found out some other way. In such a small town, I should have known.'

Loic Pennec still had his face buried in his hands.

'It's not your fault, you have a lot to do.' Madame Pennec held her husband even tighter as she spoke. It looked more like protection than comfort.

'Indeed. Especially at the beginning of an investigation.'

'You've got to catch the murderer quickly, he must be brought to justice for this barbaric act.'

'We are doing everything in our power, Madame. And I'll certainly drop in again soon. Or one of my inspectors will. There's obviously a lot of information you could help us with, but for the moment I don't want to impose on you.' Dupin checked himself – he couldn't end the conversation so abruptly. 'Unless of course there's anything you'd like to let us know at this stage, anything that you think might help in solving your father's murder.'

Only now did Loic Pennec raise his head again. 'No, no, you shouldn't have to wait, Monsieur le Commissaire. I want to help, if I can. Let's talk now.'

'I thought –'

'I insist.'

'It would be good if you could go over the hotel with one of my inspectors as soon as possible to see if anything strikes you. Whatever it might be. The smallest detail could be significant.'

'My husband is going to take over the hotel. He knows every inch of that building, every nook and cranny. He practically grew up there.'

'Yes. Of course, Monsieur le Commissaire. Just tell me when.' Loic Pennec seemed to have composed himself somewhat.

'But you should know that my father-in-law didn't keep any valuables in the hotel. Or large sums of cash. There's nothing actually worth stealing in the whole place.'

'My father didn't much care for expensive things. He never did. He was only ever interested in the hotel. It was his calling in life. He had a savings account at the *Crédit Agricole* for sixty years, that's where the money was and whenever he'd amassed a certain amount, he bought another property. That's how it was for the last few decades. He invested all his money in real estate. He wasn't big on saving or anything like that.'

Pennec almost seemed relieved to be able to talk now. Madame Pennec was looking intently at her husband. Dupin wasn't sure what that look meant.

Loic Pennec continued, 'Otherwise he never bought anything big. Apart from his boat – he never stinted on boat maintenance. There may have been a certain amount of money in the restaurant till in the evenings, I don't know. I'm sure that's something you could check.'

'My colleagues have looked at everything, the hotel till, the restaurant till. Nothing unusual so far.'

'Anything is possible these days!' Madame Pennec said indignantly. 'He owns four houses in Pont-Aven. And the hotel of course.'

'He was obviously a good businessman, your father. He's made a considerable fortune.'

'Some of the houses need basic work done. A lot ought to have been renovated years ago, certainly the roofs on two of them. And you've got to bear in mind that the tourists want houses by the sea. The prices are far lower here, but he only ever wanted to buy in the village. The rents are lower, too.'

'He didn't put up the room prices for twelve years – or the rent on his houses.' Madame Pennec sounded scornful. A moment later she looked embarrassed and promptly fell silent again.

'What my wife is trying to say is that my father could definitely have made more profitable business decisions. He was a very generous man. Like his father – and my great-grandmother. A patron of the arts, not some greedy businessman.'

'And more generally, has anything occurred to you that you think might be significant? People whom your father might have had a dispute with, who had annoyed him or were annoyed by him? Anything your father told you in the last few weeks or months, anything that was playing on his mind.'

'No. He had no enemies,' Pennec broke off, 'as far as I know. Why would he? He rarely had disagreements with people. I mean serious disagreements. Apart – apart from with his half-brother – they'd had a falling out. André Pennec. A successful politician, he built his career in the south. I hardly know my half-uncle.' He broke off again for a moment. 'He didn't talk much about his emotions. My father, I mean. Our relationship was very good. But he never said very much. I don't know the story of what happened with his brother.'

'Does anyone else know it?'

'I don't know if my father ever really told anyone. Maybe Delon. Maybe his half-brother's wife knows the story. His third wife. Much younger than him. My father and his brother haven't spoken much for the last twenty or thirty years. André is twenty-two years younger than my father.'

'So your grandfather had an extra-marital affair?'

'Yes, that's exactly what happened. With a woman from the south of France, still young, in her early thirties. It didn't last long.'

'It lasted long enough though. It went on for over two years,' Catherine Pennec added.

Pennec gave his wife a withering look. 'Anyway, the woman got pregnant and moved back to the south, to be near her family. My grandfather didn't see his son very often. And then he died. André couldn't have been more than twenty at the time. I really wouldn't know who even knows this story still, except for André.'

Dupin made copious notes. 'And Fragan Delon was your father's closest friend?'

'They were old friends, yes, since childhood. Old Delon is a private man. He's been on his own for a long time too, I don't think life has been too kind to him.'

He had to speak to Delon, that's something he'd already resolved to do during his interview with Madame Lajoux.

'Do you know Fragan Delon well?'

'Not particularly well, no.'

'And are you familiar with your father's will?'

The question came without warning. There was a look of mild indignation on Pennec's face. 'You mean the document itself? No.'

'Didn't you ever speak about it?'

'Well of course we did. But I never saw the will. He wanted me to take over the hotel. We've spoken about that a lot over the years. Time and time again.'

'I'm very glad to hear that. Such a famous establishment.'

'It's a… it's a huge task. My father took it on sixty-three years ago when he was twenty-eight years old. My great-grandmother, Marie-Jeanne, founded it in 1879. I'm sure you already know that.'

'A *real* Pennec, she could see what the future would hold: tourism. And the artists of course. She knew them all. All the artists. She was buried in the same grave as Robert Wylie – an American painter. That's the status she had.' Madame Pennec's voice was solemn with pride.

Dupin had the feeling that he would be hearing the story of the *Central* and the Pont-Aven School again during this case. Every Breton schoolchild could recite the story about the hotel and the artists in their sleep. Marie-Jeanne really had recognised the signs of a new time: the invention of 'summer retreats', an emerging preference for the coast and the sea, the beach and the sun, and she'd opened a simple hotel on the Place Municipale. Robert Wylie had been the first artist to come here, arriving in Pont-Aven as early as 1864 and bringing his friends with him soon after. Everyone was mesmerised by the 'perfect idyll'. The Irish, the Dutch, the Scandinavians and then the Swiss followed – and more than a decade later, French painters came for the first time; the locals just called them all 'the Americans'. Gauguin came in 1886; the artists' colony turned into the Pont-Aven School, and it invented radical new art.

There were of course many things that drew the artists to Brittany and Pont-Aven, to the ancient Celtic land, Armorica or the 'Land in the Sea' as the Gauls called it. There was the ever enchanting landscape with its traces of the mysterious eras of menhirs and dolmens, hints of the land of the druids, great legends and epics. They certainly also came because Monet had been working on Belle Ile for a number of years and you could just about see Belle Ile from the mouth of the Aven. Or maybe it was because they were looking for the untouched, the simple, the unspoiled, and here they found the agricultural and rural, the old customs and festivals, and because they had an unbretonic tendency to be drawn towards anything wonderful or mystical. These were all reasons but in fact the two manageresses, Julia Guillou and Marie-Jeanne Pennec, and their incredibly generous hospitality had played an important role. They had seen it as their mission to make the 'biggest open-air studio' as comfortable as possible.

'Yes, Monsieur Pennec, you really do have to have a calling for it. It's so much more than a business.' Dupin surprised himself with how dramatic he sounded. Recalling such greatness was visibly doing both of the Pennecs good. 'When will you see the will?'

Loic Pennec cast an irritated look towards Dupin. 'I don't know yet. We will have to make an appointment with the notary.'

'Apart from you, was anyone else mentioned in your father's will?'

'No. Why do you ask?' Pennec hesitated. 'I obviously don't really know.'

'Will you change a lot?'

'Change? Change what?'

'At the hotel. In the restaurant.'

Commissaire Dupin realised his question had sounded a little crass, even to him. He had no idea how he had hit upon it just then. This conversation had gone on for too long, and it was time he wound it up.

'I mean, it's perfectly correct – and also necessary, for every generation to innovate. It's the only way to preserve the old, the only way to keep tradition alive.'

'Yes. Yes. You're right. But we haven't thought about that yet.'

'Of course. I understand. It wasn't an appropriate question to ask anyway.'

The Pennecs looked expectantly at him.

'Do you think your father would have told you about serious disputes or conflicts he might have had?'

'Yes, of course… At least I think so. He was a very stubborn man. He always had his own ideas about everything.'

'I have taken up enough of your time. Please excuse me. I really will go now. You are grieving. This is a terrible crime.'

Madame Pennec nodded firmly. 'Thank you, Monsieur le Commissaire. You are doing your best.'

'If anything else occurs to you, please get in touch. I'll leave you my number. Don't hesitate, no matter what it might be.' Dupin placed his card on the coffee table and put away his notebook.

'We will.'

Loic Pennec stood up. His wife and Dupin rose to their feet too.

'We hope you make progress quickly, Monsieur le Commissaire. I would be more than a little relieved if you were to catch my father's killer very soon.'

'I'll let you know as soon as there is any news.'

Loic and Catherine Pennec went with him to the door. They were emphatically polite in their farewells.

It had turned into a truly beautiful summer's day. By Breton standards it was positively hot, just nudging over the thirty degree mark. It had been stuffy in the Pennecs' villa and Dupin was glad to be outdoors again. He loved the constant, gentle, almost imperceptible breeze from the Atlantic. It was already much later than he had thought it was, the morning was long since over. In this weather people went to the beach so that Pont-Aven itself was quite peaceful down here by the harbour.

It was low tide now and the boats lay on their beam ends on the muddy ground as if at rest. It was like a still life. Dupin kept forgetting. Little Pont-Aven was made up of two unlikely halves: the upper part and the lower part by the harbour. Or to be more exact: the river and the sea. And although they were so close together there was a different feel to each one and they had completely different landscapes and atmospheres. He was sure that this had fascinated the artists too. He could clearly recall coming here from Concarneau for the first time and parking on Place Gauguin. It had been such a change. Even the air was different. Inhale in Concarneau and you tasted salt, iodine, seaweed, mussels in every breath, like a distillation of the entire endless expanse of the Atlantic, brightness and light. In Pont-Aven it was the river, moist rich earth, hay, trees, woods, the valley and shadows, melancholy fog – the countryside. It was the contrast of 'Armorica' and 'Argoat', or as they were called in Celtic, the 'Land of the Sea' and the 'Land of Forests'. Dupin had learnt that the world of the Bretons essentially consisted of these extremes, as it had done throughout Brittany's lengthy history. Before he moved to Brittany, he wouldn't have been able to understand how these two worlds could be so close together and yet so far removed from one another, so very different from one another. Pont-Aven was mainly Argoat, it was countryside, farmsteads, agriculture; but it was Armorica too, down here at the port that is, where the high tide brought everything with it, the sea, everything it contained, its whole atmosphere. Sometimes you could see magnificent sailing boats along the – as a proud sign declared – 320-metre-long quay, leaving you in no doubt you were by the sea.

Dupin was ravenous. He realised he hadn't eaten anything since the croissant that morning. He often forgot to eat when he was caught up in a case, but only noticed when he started to feel dizzy. He decided, albeit reluctantly, to nip up to Place Gauguin and try one of the cafés there. They had looked a bit more like proper restaurants. And what's more he could keep an eye on the hotel from there.

At the top of the hill he chose the café on the other side of the little square, opposite the *Central*. There wasn't much going on. Dupin sat down at a table on the very edge of the square. A handful of people were still standing in front of the *Central*, deep in conversation. The sun was beating down on Place Gauguin now, so that Julia Guillou's sycamore trees really came into their own. Dupin ordered himself a *grand crème*, a *jambon-fromage* sandwich and a large bottle of Badoit. A very friendly waiter confirmed his order with a nod. Dupin had actually fancied a *crêpe complète*; he loved them, especially the runny egg on top of the ham and cheese in the middle, but he was strict with himself about following Nolwenn's rule: only have crêpes in good crêperies.

Dupin sank deeper into his surprisingly comfortable chair. He watched the comings and goings in the square. Suddenly a huge black limousine caught his attention. It inched across the square, almost mocking in its slowness.

His phone rang. Dupin looked at the number: it was Nolwenn. But he answered a little gruffly anyway.

'There have been lots of calls for you, Monsieur le Commissaire.'

'I thought there might be.'

Whenever he turned off his mobile – as he had just now at the Pennecs – all calls were forwarded to the office.

'I'm just eating something. Trying to, anyway.'

'*Bon appétit.* Prefect Guenneugues, Le Ber, three times, Doctor Lafond, Doctor Pelliet, Fabien Goyard, the mayor of Pont-Aven. And – your Laure. The Prefect is very concerned –'

'Mon Dieu. He can take his stupid committee and go… And it's not "my Laure".'

His relationship with Laure was over, as far as he was concerned. Probably. At least he was almost sure it was. Like all those other flings he'd had since he 'fled' Paris, at some point they just fizzled out for whatever reason. He was still persuading himself it was over, what he'd had back then with Claire, those seven years in Paris. He was still trying to convince himself of that. But this wasn't the moment.

'What committee? The Prefect wanted to say how concerned he is about this terrible murder because there's going to be such an outcry.'

'Really? Oh.'

'Doctor Pelliet said it was important. But he didn't want to tell me anything else.'

'I'm eating right now.'

'Feel free.'

Doctor Pelliet was Dupin's grumpy GP in Concarneau. Dupin couldn't imagine what he wanted. His last visit was months ago and they had discussed everything there was to discuss. There was something about his doctor wanting to speak to him urgently that he didn't like.

The sandwich was dreadful, it was dry and the baguette was overbaked, but he ate it anyway, even considered ordering a second as he really was awfully hungry. The coffee wasn't any better than the last one either. Dupin's mood was black. Even in the car this morning he hadn't been under any illusions. The pressure to solve the case, or at the least to have something substantial to show for his work *very soon* would be huge. And the pressure would be coming from all sides. The murder of someone like Pierre-Louis Pennec would affect Bretons deeply, and on top of that the tourist season was almost here. Nobody wanted a murderer free to walk the streets right now. The most unpleasant thing would be the many 'influential' people, politicians, all the higher ups, who would think they could just share 'suggestions' with him in any number of ways. He was aware of all of this and he hated it. There would also be, he was well aware, daily calls from the Prefecture in Quimper.

The phone rang again. Le Ber. Dupin knew he should answer it but he let it ring. It died away and started again a moment later. Nolwenn again.

'Yes?'

'Doctor Pelliet just called again. He called personally, not his receptionist.'

'Did he say what it was about this time?'

'No, just that you should get in touch. He didn't even ask you to call soon. But you know what he's like.'

'Fine, I'll call him.'

Dupin got out his wallet, gloomily placed the money on the little plastic saucer and set off. It had been a stupid idea to come here. As if this would have been a proper restaurant! And what could he possibly have seen on the square in front of the hotel? What had he been thinking?

Next on his agenda was the visit to Fragan Delon. He looked up the address and phone number in his notebook.

Fragon Delon answered immediately; the phone had rung twice at most.

'Yes?'

He sounded perfectly calm.

'*Bonjour*, Monsieur. Commissaire Dupin here. I'm investigating the murder of Pierre-Louis Pennec.'

Dupin waited but Delon didn't respond.

'I would like to meet you. I'm sure you could help us. We have to build up a picture of Pierre-Louis Pennec, his personality, his life. As I understand it, you were his closest and oldest friend.'

Delon didn't react at all. Even after a long pause.

'Are you still there, Monsieur Delon?'

'When do you want to come over?'

His voice didn't sound at all unfriendly, not in the slightest. It was very quiet, very clear.

'I could be there in a quarter of an hour. In twenty minutes.'

He still had to call Le Ber back. Le Ber would definitely have a lot of things to discuss.

'All right.'

'See you soon then, Monsieur Delon.'

Delon hung up even more quickly than Dupin did.

Dupin had taken a little map of the city from reception. Delon lived on the western edge of Pont-Aven, a quarter of an hour's walk according to Dupin's best guess.

Le Ber had a lot to report. And at the same time not very much at all. There had been five of them, Le Ber, Labat, the two police officers from Pont-Aven whom they'd already met (Monfort and Pennarguear) and one more police officer. They had questioned all the guests and employees for the first time, made lists, searched the hotel again. The usual routine. The scene of crime team and Lafond had finished their examinations, but their reports weren't complete yet. On first inspection they hadn't found anything remarkable.

If he were honest, nothing relevant, not one thing of any relevance, had been discovered so far. Most significantly it seemed nobody had seen or heard anything last night. Nobody had seen anyone in the hotel who wasn't meant to be there, nobody had seen anyone entering or leaving the restaurant after it closed. In all probability, the chef really had been the last person to see Pennec alive. Pennec had stayed in the restaurant and kitchen the whole evening, had had conversations here and there, had been at different tables, had spoken to the staff. Nobody had noticed anything unusual about him.

Dupin was familiar with this kind of case. Everything had been 'as per' – right up until the murder had happened, of course. Nothing was out of the ordinary, apart from Pierre-Louis Pennec having a conversation with a stranger outside on the square in front of the hotel and that he maybe seemed a little worked up – 'maybe'. That was the only remarkable thing, and it had been reported by three members of staff, although only Madame Lajoux had spoken of the conversation looking somewhat heated. But nobody could say who the stranger had been. Labat had taken on the task of tracing him. It was all they had at the moment.

Dupin was almost at Delon's house already. He reached for his phone again. He couldn't stop thinking about the Dr Pelliet thing. What was so urgent that his GP would call out of the blue twice in quick succession?

'Doctor Pelliet's office, Mademoiselle Dantec speaking.'

'*Bonjour*, Mademoiselle Dantec. It's me, Georges Dupin. Doctor Pelliet –'

'Yes, the doctor is trying to get hold of you. I'll put you through.'

Mademoiselle Dantec suited Dr Pelliet perfectly, they were an ideal match. No mincing of words, no shilly-shallying.

'Monsieur Dupin?'

'Yes, speaking.'

'I've got to speak to you. In person.'

'In person? You mean you want to meet up?'
'Yes.'
'Do you think we could leave it until I... in the next few days I think I could –'
'I think we should speak very soon.'
'Do you mean today?'
'Yes.'
'I'm on a case you know and –'
'So today then?'

How was he going to manage this? But he knew he would say yes. Had to say yes. He never stood a chance where Dr Pelliet was concerned. He would manage it somehow, just before the surgery closed. Pelliet hadn't been waiting for a response.

'I'll be expecting you.'
'What do you mean? Now?'
'Surely you're still in Pont-Aven. It'll take you half an hour.'

Dupin tried again: 'I'm really sorry, it's just not possible. I'm on my way to an important meeting right now.'

'It's about the case.'

Dupin fell silent.

'The case? I mean... you mean the murder of Pierre-Louis Pennec?'

'Yes.'

Dupin knew it didn't make sense to ask anything more on the phone. He sighed gently.

'I'm on my way, Docteur.'

Dupin drove an old dark blue Citroën XM. It was big and difficult to manoeuvre. Dupin loved his car, although he didn't nurse any great passion for cars generally. He was constantly making it clear that he had liked Citroëns before Nolwenn enlightened him that they were – indeed how could it be otherwise with items of such quality – Breton cars. They came from Rennes, as did Charles Vanel; Charles Vanel and of course lots more.

It took him an awfully long time to get to Concarneau. In summer the tourists crawled along in their cars through the narrow streets between Concarneau and Pont-Aven, and they always cut through the pretty little village of Névez that he was so fond of. And since most foreigners either didn't know the traffic rules for *rond-points* or didn't know how to handle them in a confident French manner, there was often some rather impressive gridlock on the road into Névez (as indeed there was at all the *rond-points* along on the way).

As he drove along, Dupin puzzled over how Pelliet could be involved in the case. Nolwenn had recommended Dr Pelliet to him back when he had first arrived in Concarneau. Nolwenn's children were already Pelliet's patients. Since then Dupin had gone to him with everything, no matter what it was, and Pelliet always knew what to do.

As he drove over a large bridge that looked like it was propped up on stilts, Dupin realised how happy he was to be back in Concarneau. The bridge ran between two hills high above the Moros, and ended on the outskirts of town. He took the first right onto rue Dumont d'Urville, drove past the market hall and turned right onto rue des Écoles.

Dr Pelliet had his surgery in an old fisherman's cottage, one of the many traditional, narrow houses that stood in two neat rows along the waterfront. He parked at the stunningly ugly new church, one of the few ugly buildings in Concarneau, and walked the last few metres.

'How's the stomach?'

Dupin was confused for a moment. Pelliet's receptionist had sent him straight into the examination room and Pelliet was sitting opposite him now in a big old armchair behind his desk. Dr Pelliet was perhaps in his early sixties, a native of Concarneau. Downstairs on the surgery sign it said 'Dr Bernez Pelliet', not Bernard. He was tall and thin, with a long face and a high forehead. The most striking thing about the impression he made was the utter calm that he radiated, he seemed like nothing could ever faze him.

Dupin had been having recurrent stomach problems for years and they had been very bad several times a few months ago. Pelliet had listened for a few minutes and then said, 'Nervous stomach. And too much caffeine. If you want I can examine you anyway.'

'It's fine, thank you.' He found the stomach thing a bit embarrassing in this professional situation. 'I mean, good. Better. Yes, quite a bit better.' He knew he was not coming across as professionally as he might have hoped.

Pelliet looked up from his papers and gazed at him somewhat sceptically. He spoke firmly: 'Now then.'

Dupin was relieved, Pelliet's tone of voice having

made it clear that the stomach topic had been dealt with. Pelliet still held his gaze. Dupin had fumbled for his pen as discreetly as possible. In vain. The notebook was already in his lap but the pen was missing.

'He wouldn't have had much longer to live.'

These words came as a complete shock. Dupin thought he would continue, but Pelliet considered this enough to be going on with. Pelliet always spoke with the same clear, unemotional, yet not exactly cold voice, which perfectly suited his personality. It was clear who Pelliet meant, but Dupin's question still slipped out:

'Pennec?'

Pelliet didn't take any notice of it.

'The heart. He would have needed multiple bypasses soon. Significant narrowing of the arteries. It's a miracle he survived the last years, months and weeks at all. The chances were slim. Very slim indeed.'

'You know about his heart? I mean, you're *his* doctor too?'

'I can barely call myself his doctor. He never let himself be examined, not even once in the last three decades. Nothing at all, not even the simplest check-up. He only came because he's had back problems for many years; he used to get injections for it now and then. On Monday morning he came in with chest pain. The pain must have been bad, but he only agreed to an ECG under protest.'

Pelliet paused.

'And?'

'He should have had an operation. On the spot. He didn't want it.'

'He didn't want anything done to him?'

'He said, "At my age, you're done for once you start having operations."'

Pelliet's face was inscrutable.

'How much longer would he have had to live?'

'As I said, medically speaking,' Pelliet overpronounced every word, 'he in fact should have died long ago.'

'And what about medication? Was he given any tablets?'

'He categorically refused them.'

'And? What did you say?'

'Nothing.'

'But he knew that it was going to kill him?'

'Yes.'

Pelliet paused and then said in a tone of voice that put a definitive end to this line of questioning:

'A mentally sound man. And ninety-one years of age.'

Dupin fell silent for a moment.

'Did anyone know about his illness – about his situation? How serious it was?'

'I don't think so. I don't think he would have been comfortable with that. He never made much of a fuss. He even asked if my receptionist knew about it and was relieved to hear that she doesn't really understand medical terminology.'

Noticing Dupin's astonishment, Pelliet added: 'A very strong-willed man.'

'So he wasn't weak then? Wouldn't someone have noticed his condition? In the last weeks at least?'

Nobody had mentioned noticing any change or even frailty in Pennec.

'That's just the way it is, you know. A strong will.

A proud man. And in any case he hadn't been all that sprightly for a long time. Ninety-one.'

Pelliet said this last word very slowly and looked Dupin calmly in the eye as he did so. He wouldn't get anything more out of Dr Pelliet. Everything had already been said.

'Thank you. This information is extremely important.'

Dupin knew that the word 'important' was pushing it a bit here. And he wasn't basing it on any solid fact. Right now he had no idea if it would be at all significant for the case. The only thing he knew for sure was that this information had made the case more complex.

'Do you have any leads yet, a hypothesis?'

Dupin was relieved by this unexpected question, it lessened the feeling he had had throughout the conversation, the feeling that he was sitting here as a patient. He made an effort to answer confidently, but he didn't quite manage it.

'We are investigating various leads.'

'So nothing at all yet. Yes. It's an awful case. A really awful case.'

The doctor's voice had changed for the first time; there was some true emotion in it now. He stood up and held out his hand to Dupin.

'Thanks again, doctor.' Dupin leapt up far too quickly, shook Dr Pelliet's hand, turned around and left at a smart pace.

Back out on the street again, Dupin tried to marshal his thoughts. He really had no idea where to begin with this bit of news, but it was serious. The victim of a brutal murder, a very old man, had had a life-threatening heart condition, and would in all likelihood have died a natural death any moment – literally any second. He had been well aware of this fact, but nobody else had even hinted that they had known about Pennec's condition or noticed anything unusual about him. Could he possibly have kept his condition to himself, as Pelliet supposed? In that case they were random, coincidental facts, Pennec's murder and Pennec's terminal illness. But then again maybe that's not how it was at all. But Pennec was certainly aware that his illness could catch up with him at any time – and that changed everything *for him*, it must have. Everything. Even for a ninety-one-year-old.

Dupin could feel himself becoming anxious. He didn't like this one bit. He dialled Labat's number.

'Labat – I want to know what Pierre-Louis Pennec did this week, every day since Monday. Everything we can find out. What did he do, who did he see, speak to, call? Question everyone one more time about those four days, and let Le Ber know. We're concentrating on those four days. From Monday morning till last night.'

'Just those four days? Why?'

'Yes. Well, no. Not just those four days of course. But mainly that period. To begin with.'

'And how come? Why mainly those four days, Monsieur le Commissaire?'

'A feeling, Labat. A feeling.'

'We're concentrating all of our police resources on a feeling? I still have a few urgent things to do, Monsieur le Commissaire.'

'Later, Labat. I'm going to see Fragan Delon now.'
Dupin hung up.

Nolwenn had called Fragan Delon and postponed Dupin's visit until five o'clock. It was now half past four. He would quickly buy a few pens at the *Tabac-Presse* around the corner that he always went to. He usually bought the same cheap black bic biros because he was forever losing them faster than he could buy them again. He needed a few notebooks too – Dupin had used the same notebooks since his training days, Clairefontaine ones, a bit narrower than A5, unlined, bright red; he spotted them amongst everything else at a glance. He had had hopelessly bad handwriting ever since his schooldays. He also wrote words in completely different sizes – the used pages looked chaotic to the uninitiated. He went over his notes again and again during a case. If he were honest, he couldn't explain the strict criteria he had for what he wrote down and what he didn't. Simply put, the principle was this: whatever he thought was important at a given moment, no matter what the reason, he wrote it down. There were keywords, sketches, charts and sometimes they ran riot across the page. He needed to do it because his memory worked, to his great annoyance, only haphazardly. It retained things he didn't need or want to know any more, the smallest, most obscure details; other things however, that he absolutely wanted and needed to remember, vanished.

It was busy in the *Tabac-Presse* on Pénéroff Quay, the biggest square in the town. In fact the whole village had been busy over the last few days. Concarneau was getting ready for the highlight of the year, the festival to end all festivals, the *Festival des Filets Bleus*.

Dupin loved this shop; like all good *Tabac-Presse* shops, it was full to bursting; every corner, every centimetre, was taken up with newspapers, magazines, books, notebooks, stationery, sweets, plastic nick-nacks and all sorts of junk.

Dupin's phone rang. Private number. He had just paid and was almost back out on the street again. He answered without giving his name.

'Monsieur le Commissaire?'

'Speaking.'

'It's Fabien Goyard here. I'm the mayor of Pont-Aven.'

Dupin had heard of Goyard, but couldn't remember the context. He hated politicians with very, very few exceptions. They always gave away the most important lines of inquiry. And they considered people like Dupin sadly naive.

'I'm calling because I'm very interested in finding out whether you've made any progress with your investigation. What a horrible thing to happen in our little Pont-Aven – dreadful, absolutely dreadful, and this close to the tourist season. You've got to think about –'

A sudden feeling of the worst contrariness came over Dupin. It is an inalienable truth that for the 'important' people of the world it's always about two things: money and personal reputation. Not that Dupin would have cared, but it was annoy-ing and what's worse, it wasted time. And his boss Guenneugues was no help – on the contrary in fact. The mayor was still talking, that typical mix of submissiveness and command in his voice. Dupin interrupted him:

'We are doing our best, Monsieur le Maire. Believe me.'

'Are you aware that not only have some guests from the *Central* left the village, but some tourists from other hotels too? Do you know what this means? And during this financial crisis too! We have fewer guests this year anyway. And now this.'

Dupin didn't say a word. There was a long pause.

'So do you have a hunch, Monsieur le Commissaire? If I may say so: in a small village like this one, this kind of thing can't happen without leaving significant clues.'

'Monsieur le Maire, it's not my job to have hunches.'

'But who do you think murdered Pennec? A local or an outsider? That's what you should be concentrating on.'

Dupin sighed openly.

'Do you think the murderer is still in the village? Could he kill again? It would cause such panic.'

'Monsieur le Maire. I've just seen that an important call is coming in on my other phone. As soon as there are relevant developments I'll be in touch. I promise.'

'You've got to understand my position, I –'

Dupin hung up. He was very proud of himself. He could rein in his emotions far more easily now than he could before. He did not want another relocation. Sometimes he had to keep his mouth shut, no matter how hard it was. In Paris he had found it extremely hard on a number of occasions. In the end, according to his file, his downfall had been the time he had chosen a very big public event to 'seriously insult' the mayor of Paris – who interestingly later became the president of France. And of course insulting his superiors, or as it was put in writing, his 'sustained, malicious verbal abuse' hadn't exactly helped.

By now he was quite good at holding his tongue, he thought, as he had just proven to himself. But he wasn't pleased about it. He really resented having to keep his anger in check in these kinds of situations. And that's also why he found it a bit sad, because he lacked some of the 'hidden depths', which now seemed a quasi-requirement for his profession: drug addiction, or at least alcoholism, neuroses or depression to a clinical degree, a colourful criminal past, corruption on an interesting scale or several dramatically failed marriages. He didn't have any of those things to show off about.

By now Dupin had reached his car. He would be at Fragan Delon's more or less on time.

Dupin had had high hopes for his conversation with Fragan Delon. But if he were to be honest, it hadn't revealed anything particularly significant.

It seemed to Dupin that Francine Lajoux and Fragan Delon were the people to whom Pennec had really been closest. If he had trusted anyone with his worries or anxieties then they would have been the most likely candidates. But Delon had not known anything about his serious health problems, and consequently nothing about whether Pennec had trusted anyone else with the knowledge. He knew nothing about any argument or disagreement that Pennec might have been having with anyone in the last few months or weeks, or even whether there'd ever been one, apart from with his half-brother.

On this topic, Delon suddenly became animated, almost talkative. He had strong opinions on the cause of the rift in the Pennec family and he had an opinion on the relationship between Madame Lajoux and Pennec. He was sure that there had never been an affair – not that Pennec had ever said so in as many words, Delon was just sure of it. And he had expressed this – as he did everything in this conversation – in a few, sparing words, albeit in a friendly way. Delon didn't think the relationship between Pennec and his son had been a close one. As with all private matters though, Pierre-Louis Pennec apparently hadn't told him much about it. 'We spoke about other things, not about ourselves.' That was certainly not unusual for two Bretons, especially of their generation. And even though Delon hadn't said a word about it, his profound sense of grief was apparent.

Dupin had already learned from Le Ber that Delon had not seen Pennec in the three days before his death. Delon had been staying with his daughter in Brest, so he wasn't any help in reconstructing how Pennec had spent the days since Monday and his visit to Dr Pelliet.

What Dupin had established was this: the hotel had been the centre of Pierre-Louis Pennec's life. This legacy and all of the duties that went with it. Pennec had been involved in many committees and clubs in the community that tried to 'preserve tradition' and was equally involved in encouraging young artists in Pont-Aven.

Crucially, Dupin had also learnt a bit more about Pennec's life and personality. He'd learnt about his tastes and habits, things he was passionate about and discussed with Delon. They had played chess for over fifty years, ever since they had been young men, mostly in the evenings. Sometimes *pétanque* too of course, down by the harbour with the other local men. He and Delon took Pennec's boat out together once a week to go fishing, whatever the weather. Spring and autumn were best, when the big shoals of mackerel were passing by the coast. They had drunk a lambig together one or two evenings a week at the hotel bar.

All in all Dupin left feeling a little disappointed. But he liked old Delon.

Now that the streets around Place Gauguin in the old town centre were filling up with people again, it was pandemonium. Most of the holiday-makers were back from the beach and they wanted to wander through the shops and galleries a little longer before looking for a restaurant. There was an incredible number of art galleries here. It was only now, during the tourist season, that it really became apparent. They seemed to have shot up out of the ground like mushrooms. Although most of the galleries were near the museums, Dupin had counted twelve on the rue de Port alone, a quiet little road that wound down to the harbour. Reproductions of all the paintings from the Pont-Aven School were on sale of course, ranging from cheap to extremely valuable, but also for sale were numerous originals by contemporary painters who sought their fortune here in this epoch-defining place. Dupin found all paintings quite repulsive.

He couldn't see any sign of the holiday-makers deserting Pont-Aven in large numbers or deciding to avoid it. At the *Central* itself, a few little groups were standing around, speaking in a somewhat subdued manner and pointing here and there. Only in the morning had there been signs of something approaching irritation for a few hours; by the evening the place seemed to have returned to the old familiar tourist routines.

It was seven o'clock now and Dupin was feeling slightly dizzy again. He hadn't eaten anything since that sandwich in the afternoon. There were still things he needed to do today. He took out his phone.

'Nolwenn?'

Dupin had called her on the office number, he knew she would still be there.

'Yes, Monsieur le Commissaire?'

'I'd like to speak to the notary who looked after Pierre-Louis Pennec's will tomorrow morning. And please could you get us access to Pennec's bank accounts? I want a clear picture. Of his properties too.'

When he followed 'official procedure' with these kinds of things, it always got more complicated and technically they'd need a warrant. Given a few hours, Nolwenn could have it sorted without a fuss.

'Duly noted. Le Ber tried to reach you a few times and wants you to call him back. He's got some news.'

'Is he still in Pont-Aven?'

'He was still there half an hour ago.'

'Tell him I'll be at the hotel soon and we'll speak then.' He hesitated. 'Labat and the two police officers from Pont-Aven should also be on standby.'

He hadn't intended that at all, but it was good to stay in the loop. Maybe they had made some progress, especially on the issue of what Pennec's last days looked like.

'André Pennec called. He heard what happened from Loic Pennec. He arrived here in Pont-Aven in the early afternoon.'

'He came straight away? He dropped everything and came?'

'He'd like to see you tomorrow morning. He suggested eight o'clock.'

'Excellent. I'd like to see him too.'

'I'll set it up. Will you meet him at the hotel?'

Dupin thought about it for moment. 'No. Tell him the police station. My office. Eight is fine.'

'Are you coming back here, Monsieur le Commissaire? I'm actually just about to head home.'

'Go ahead. I won't be coming in again today.'

'It's going to be busy in Concarneau tonight; the first festival pre-events are on. Bear that in mind when you're coming back... The Prefect has asked that you call him back and so has the mayor of Pont-Aven. I told them both you were in wall-to-wall meetings until late tonight.'

'Wonderful.'

Dupin admired Nolwenn. She was unshakably pragmatic and determined. Nothing was too much for her; it always just seemed to be a question of the – correct or incorrect – approach to something. What had won him over immediately on first being introduced were her alert eyes, sparkling with strong-willed intelligence. She was a good-looking woman, late fifties, rather short with cropped blonde hair. Nolwenn was indispensable to him in general, but particularly because of her practically limitless local and regional knowledge. She was born and brought up in Concarneau – in Konk-Kerne, as the Bretons called the town – and never left. She was a Breton woman through and through, still fundamentally suspicious of France. After all, Brittany had only been a part of France since 1532, 'for a piffling five hundred years' – an annexation! Nolwenn helped him to understand the soul of Brittany and its people. In the beginning he'd had no idea how essential this would be for his work. Since his first day she had been giving him lessons in Breton history, language, culture and Breton cuisine (*no* olive oil – butter!). She had put up two phrases in little blue frames above his desk for him. First, the famous quote from Marie de France in the twelfth century: 'Brittany is poetry'; second, an entry from an encyclopedia in tacky decorative lettering: 'The Breton may have the same appearance as his storm-tossed, rugged land, a melancholy disposition and a cautious nature, but he also has a lively, poetic imagination, inner sensitivity and often great passion, hidden behind external roughness and calm.' Dupin thought the phrase itself was evidence of their lively, poetic way with words. Yet it had become clear to him over time that there was a ring of truth to those words.

One of their private jokes was that Nolwenn made up for the – somewhat difficult – traits of the Bretons: their infamous stubbornness, their pig-headedness, their cunning, their taciturnity on the one hand and garrulousness on the other, and that distinctive preference for Breton comparatives and superlatives. The biggest producer of artichoke in the world, the second greatest tidal range in the world (up to fourteen metres!), the region with the most traditional costumes in the world (1,266 sub-varieties), the biggest tuna harbour in Europe (Concarneau), the world's biggest accumulation of seaweed and algae, the most read daily paper in France (*Ouest France*), the highest concentration of historical monuments, the most canned fish producers in the world, the most seabird varieties in all of Europe. Not forgetting of course the 7,770 saints invoked (with varying degrees of devotion) to cure all aches and pains (saints that neither the world nor God has ever heard of). Some of the statistics weren't very impressive in themselves, but did sound very impressive when delivered in emphatic Breton tones; for example that there were four million Bretons or that Brittany made up a sixth of the landmass of France – Dupin didn't actually think it was very much, but maybe it wasn't such a bad thing.

Even if Dupin had found the move from Paris to the end of the world very difficult at first, he had long been 'a bit of a Breton' at heart. Nolwenn complimented him on it whenever he made progress under her beady eye (even if he wouldn't admit it to himself or to anyone else because he was seen as a dyed-in-the-wool Parisian here in the back of beyond). And Nolwenn was doubly strict when judging a 'Parisian', which she was convinced was for Dupin's own good. Of course this praise remained very superficial; Dupin mustn't go getting any ideas. Because in fact even if he married a Breton woman, had Breton children and spent his twilight years here, he would always remain an 'outsider'. Even after two or three generations, his great-grandchildren would be sure to hear murmurs of 'Parisian'.

As evening came on, the light became more and more bewitching. The colours of witchcraft: everything shone brightly, warm, soft and golden. It always seemed to Dupin as though the sun mysteriously made everything glow for a few hours before it set. Things weren't simply lit up: they radiated light from within themselves. Dupin had never seen this kind of light anywhere else in the world, only in Brittany. He was sure this must have been one of the main reasons the painters came here. He still found it a bit embarrassing when he caught himself – the city slicker par excellence – in sentimental raptures over nature like this. And he had to admit that it was happening to him more and more.

Dupin was approaching the *Central*. Someone had erected a large, handwritten cardboard sign at the entrance to the restaurant: 'The restaurant is temporarily closed. The hotel is open.' There was a note of despair to it. He turned into the little alleyway to the right of the hotel and walked up to the cast-iron door at the entrance to the courtyard of the hotel. Suddenly he was completely alone. Nobody strayed here from the main square, and no noise reached this far. The door was closed and locked, in accordance with regulation; the scene of crime team had done their job. It didn't look like the door was used much anyway.

'Monsieur le Commissaire. Here – I'm over here.'

Dupin raised his head glumly. Labat was standing just a few feet away in the courtyard of the hotel.

'Ah. Let's go inside.'

It was eerily quiet inside the hotel. One of the chambermaids was hanging around the reception desk looking lost. Dupin hadn't even tried to remember her unpronounceable Breton name. She was in her own little world, twisting a strand of hair round and round her finger, only briefly looking up as they walked past her.

Dupin turned to Labat. 'Where are the officers from Pont-Aven – the ones that were here before, I mean? And did you get hold of Derrien?'

'They still haven't got through to Derrien, unfortunately. They are trying to get in touch with him via the first hotel he stayed in. Pennarguear has just left. He had been on duty since midday yesterday. Monfort is still here, he's still doing interviews. They've both got a lot done today. The cooperation is fantastic.'

'Very good. Very good!' Dupin practically sounded triumphant. At least Derrien had left good people here.

'We've built up a provisional picture of Pierre-Louis Pennec's last days, and a bit more besides. Shall we start there?'

'Absolutely.'

The door to the room they had chosen as their headquarters was open. For some reason it looked quite pathetic now in the evening light. Le Ber was sitting at a small desk, the only one there was in the room. He looked pretty shattered – Labat did too if truth be told. They went in. Dupin sat down on one of the many chairs.

Labat took up the thread of their conversation again. 'Maybe we should in fact begin –'

'The daily routine, Pierre-Louis Pennec's last four days!'

'I just wanted –' Labat composed himself and reported: 'Usually his days went like this: Pennec got up early, at six every morning. In recent years he has mostly slept here at the hotel. He'd come downstairs at half past six.'

Labat was now completely and utterly in his element. Dupin couldn't stand Labat's pride in his own meticulous legwork. He spoke in an artificially concise way, ridiculously solemn over the most banal details. But Dupin paid close attention.

'He used to have his breakfast in the small breakfast room, usually alone, sometimes with staff or with Madame Lajoux in order to discuss hotel and restaurant matters. He would stay there when the first guests arrived. There is a large group of regular guests who happily come every year for years on end, decades in some cases.'

'Do you have all their names?'

'Yes. Pierre-Louis Pennec would be there or somewhere around the hotel until nine or half past nine, pottering around doing this and that. Then he used to go for a walk. He only started doing that a few years ago.'

'On his own?'

'Yes, usually alone.'

'Where did he go?' Dupin wasn't particularly interested in the answer, but Labat's being such an unbearable know-it-all always made Dupin want to test him. But Dupin always seemed to draw the short straw.

'Pierre-Louis Pennec's walk took him up the main street, then right, back down to the river and along the right hand bank. At the outskirts of the village –'

When Dupin's mobile rang, even Labat and Le Ber jumped. Dupin picked up automatically.

'Yes?'

'It's me.'

It took Dupin a moment to recognise the voice. And then he stammered anyway.

'Yes?'

'It's Laure. I could drop by tonight after work. Or oysters, we'll go out for oysters. I –'

He still missed that.

'I'm in the middle of a case. I… I'll be in touch.'

Dupin hung up. Le Ber and Labat looked annoyed.

He would really need to think about how he was going to sort out the Laure thing. It had been going on for three months and he still didn't know what he wanted. It couldn't go on like this.

'I'll continue then.' Labat sounded noticeably put out.

'So, Pennec would then go on a bit further, through the wood. Always the same route, but probably different distances along it. The whole walk lasted between one and two hours, depending. In the last few months he most likely didn't go all that far any more. Afterwards Pennec spent time at the hotel again. They would be getting lunch ready. It wasn't unusual for him to arrange to meet someone for lunch. He always stayed down here, as he did at dinnertime too. Kept an eye on things. For many years he then used to go up to his room at around half past two to relax. Finally he ran errands and did his shopping at around four or half past. By six o'clock he was back in the hotel. Preparations for the evening, dinner, conversations with staff, the chef, the guests. An early dinner in the breakfast room with the staff around half past six, before the influx of guests. They always ate the dish of the day, that was very important to Pennec – everyone should always have a good meal. Pennec would dart here and there during dinner, keeping an eye on everything, greeting people, seeing them to the door, going from table to table every so often and spending a lot of time in the kitchen. Sometimes at the bar.'

Le Ber chipped in for the first time. 'Pennec always stood at the bar for half an hour before the restaurant opened at half seven. Acquaintances or friends would come past. Special guests. Pennec himself rarely went out. He met people here. Never for very long. According to all of the staff, he was rarely on his own around this time. These last few days were no different. And we have the names of all the people he saw recently.'

Dupin made a few cryptic notes for himself; the rituals that people created for themselves in their daily lives, their free time, interested him. Nothing showed the essence of individuals more clearly, he was convinced of it; it was here you began to understand them.

Labat continued in his stern, systematic way.

'Then at the end of the day there was the lambig at the bar, often alone. Once or twice a week with Fragan Delon, or even with another very trusted person. It was probably a great distinction to be invited to have a drink with Pennec.

'And recently? Since Monday?'

'Well,' Le Ber took over, 'it's hard to tell. What we've got between Monday and today is still tentative. On Monday morning Pennec was out for two hours after breakfast. We don't know where yet. He didn't say anything to anyone at the hotel, but that's not unusual. He rarely said where he was going when he went out and he didn't have a mobile. He went to the barber on Monday afternoon at four o'clock, the one down by the harbour, and he stayed for around an hour. He's been going there for decades. He had called the previous Thursday and booked an appointment.'

Pennec was in fact quite a peculiar chap. Dupin would have expected someone to cancel their barber's appointment after being given the kind of news that Dr Pelliet had given Pennec.

'We'll be speaking to the barber.'

'Yes, you definitely should. People tell their hair-dressers so much. Even the most private people.'

Yet somehow, after everything he had learnt about Pennec, Dupin wasn't counting on it in this case. Not if he had judged Pennec's personality correctly.

'He was with Madame Lajoux at the bar before dinner on Monday evening, talking about business, nothing unusual according to Madame Lajoux's statement. After the restaurant closed he was by himself at the bar, Fragan Delon usually liked to come for a drink on Mondays but he was away. Frédéric Beauvois came on Tuesday morning around nine o'clock and stayed for about an hour. He's a retired art teacher and chairman of the local art society amongst other things. He also runs the art museum, just around the corner from here. Pennec donated money to the museum now and again although we still don't know the extent of these donations. From time to time Beauvois does tours of Pont-Aven for special guests at the request of the mayor and Pennec; so the *Central* is of course a must-see on the tour. The next one would have been tomorrow morning. Beauvois put together a little leaflet for Pennec a few years ago which is available all over the hotel, *The Artists' Colony of Pont-Aven and the Central Hotel.* Pennec paid for everything, including the printing. He was absolutely determined to get it revised and expanded. That's what they had wanted to talk about.'

'How do you know?'

'Madame Lajoux. And Delon knew a bit about it too, although none of the details.'

Delon hadn't mentioned anything about someone called Beauvois to Dupin.

'Madame Lajoux knew that Pennec wanted to see Beauvois about the brochure.'

'What does amongst other things mean?'

'Amongst other things?'

'What is Beauvois "amongst other things"?'

'Oh – he's the chairman of lots of clubs and associations.'

Le Ber looked at his notes.

'There's the Friends of Paul Gauguin Association, the Friends of Pont-Aven Association, the Organisation for the Remembrance of the Pont-Aven School, the Art Patrons' Club and –'

'That's okay, Le Ber.' Dupin was familiar with this kind of thing. Every town in Brittany had more clubs than residents.

'When was the meeting arranged?'

'Probably only Monday. They met regularly. Pennec ate dinner with the staff as usual this week.'

'What else?'

Le Ber glanced at his notes. 'Monsieur Pennec's son

was there on Wednesday evening. But of course you must know that from Loic Pennec himself.'

It occurred to Dupin that he hadn't specifically asked about these things when he was at the Pennecs'. But it hadn't been that kind of visit.

'The son usually came once a week. Mostly just for half an hour before dinner, he used to stand at the bar. He never stayed long. On Thursday the head of Pont-Aven's small harbour came, Monsieur Gueguen. He has an unbelievable number of job titles too; he is, amongst other things, chairman of several friendship committees that Pennec was on. The conversation took a little longer than the usual half hour. It went on until around quarter to eight. It was mainly about Pennec's mooring for his boat at the harbour. He wanted to keep it as it's such an excellent spot. We spoke to Gueguen briefly. He didn't have anything of interest to report. Pennec seemed normal to him.'

'Pennec's boat is in the harbour here?'

'He's got two boats. They're both here in Pont-Aven.'

'Two boats?' Up to this point only one boat had ever been mentioned.

'Two motorboats. One is bigger and newer. Jeanneau Merry Fisher, 7.15 metres.'

Le Ber's eyes gleamed.

'And a very old one, probably much smaller. The old one is in the harbour too but further down. Apparently he uses the new one almost all the time now, including on his fishing trips with Delon.'

'And the other boat, what did he use it for?'

'Apparently he barely used it. For going down the Aven, into the Belon sometimes, getting oysters.'

'Anything else? Labat, what have you got?'

'The hotel staff haven't noticed anything in the last few days. We've spoken to them all in detail. They say he behaved completely normally.'

'I've heard that one before.'

Labat didn't let this get to him. 'We've asked them to get in touch straight away if anything occurs to them.'

'Keep going.'

'And then there were three people with whom Pennec had more in-depth conversations recently, two of them regular guests. One conversation on Tuesday evening for half an hour before dinner, and one on Wednesday, that was late in the evening at the bar, also around half an hour. We have their details. Le Ber has already spoken to both of them. They were conversations about the weather, food, Brittany. About the tourist season. The third conversation was the one we've already told you about, the conversation he had with that stranger.'

'When was that?'

'Wednesday afternoon. In front of the hotel.'

'Ah yes.'

Dupin leafed through his notebook somewhat at random.

'We absolutely have to know who that was.'

'We're on it. Pennec spoke to the chef every night. You know that already. You've spoken to him at length of course.'

Now Le Ber took over again. 'We've also started checking the telephone calls. He had a private line in his room, but he usually made calls on one of the three cordless phones from reception. He almost always had one of them on him, even when he was upstairs in his room. All the calls from these handsets end up on the general list of calls for the main line, which handles all the hotel and restaurant phone calls. So you can't tell who placed a given call.'

'I want to know everything.'

Labat wanted to say something but stopped himself. Le Ber continued.

'In the last four days before his death he talked to his half-brother on the phone once, we know that at least. He called André Pennec from his landline and they spoke for ten minutes on Tuesday afternoon. You of course wanted to speak to André Pennec yourself. We've got short calls to Delon from his handset in the last three weeks, one to a notary here in Pont-Aven, one each to the art teacher and the mayor.'

'Which calls were this week? The one to the notary?'

'Yes, Monday afternoon.'

'Have you spoken to her?'

'No, not yet.'

'Is she Pennec's notary? I mean is she the notary who looked after Pennec's professional affairs? His will?'

'We don't know yet.'

'We need the will. Speak to Nolwenn tomorrow morning. She wanted to make an appointment for me with the notary who executed Pennec's will. What was the name of the notary he called?'

'Danielle Denis. I'm told all the "best people" in Pont-Aven have her look after their affairs.'

'Madame Denis?'

'Yes.'

'Okay.'

Dupin knew her vaguely. She was, he knew, a very highly regarded person in the area and in Concarneau too. Undoubtedly an attractive woman, probably early forties, a little bit younger than him, who was admired and respected for her elegance, unerring style and fierce intelligence. 'A real Parisian' one might have said, although Madame Denis had spent her entire life in Pont-Aven. She had only lived in Paris during her student years and hadn't been particularly impressed by it.

'Tell Nolwenn to find out if Madame Denis is Pennec's notary. First thing tomorrow morning. And make an appointment for me to see her. How many calls on the general landline list are from this week? I'm talking outgoing calls.'

'At least four hundred, maybe five hundred numbers.'

'Call all of them, find out who Pennec called and what it was about. I want to hear about every phone call Pennec made in the last few weeks. Find out all you can. Concentrate on this week.'

Le Ber's face showed he hadn't expected anything less. Labat's face reddened slightly.

Dupin knew that anything they could establish from investigations of this – extremely laborious – kind would only be useful if the murder had *not* been a 'coincidence'. If something happened 'spontaneously' that evening, as an escalation of something that was hidden before, then none of it would be of any use at all.

'We need a bit of luck now.'

Labat looked at the Commissaire somewhat scornfully. 'It could also be someone who's not in the picture at all.'

'I'll speak to the half-brother first thing tomorrow morning. Did Lafond call again? Or Salou?'

'We've spoken to both of them again. Salou doesn't want to say anything yet, we don't think he's got anything for now. You know he would have shown off about it straight away. Doctor Lafond believes it was definitely a knife rather than a sharp, pointed object. Four entry wounds. Time of death was somewhere between eleven o'clock and one o'clock, according to his initial, provisional estimates.'

Dupin was surprised that Lafond had said anything before his report was complete – that wasn't usually his style.

'But he doesn't know anything else,' said Le Ber before Dupin could ask his follow-up questions, 'not how long the blade was, how big the knife was, what kind of knife it was.'

'None of that gets us any further.'

Dupin took a look at his watch. Half past eight. Labat and Le Ber had got a lot done, there was no doubt about it.

'That was some good work, Inspector Labat, Inspector Le Ber. Very good work. You should be off home now.' Dupin meant it.

Labat was visibly annoyed by the elaborate praise and the Commissaire's concern. Neither inspector seemed to know what to say. Dupin rescued them. 'See you tomorrow then.'

The two inspectors stood up, still a little unsure, as if they still weren't certain whether they could trust the Commissaire's words.

'Really. I'm only staying a little while longer myself. Go to bed early. Get some rest. Tomorrow is going to be another tough day. *Bonne nuit*.'

Labat and Le Ber paused again in the doorway.

'*Bonne nuit*, Monsieur le Commissaire.'

Then they hurried away.

Dupin wanted to go back to the restaurant and bar, seeing as he'd had to leave so abruptly that morning. He wanted to take another look at everything. He took down the crime scene cordon, opened the door, and locked it again from the inside. Everything looked exactly as it had when Pennec's body was found, and crucially it looked exactly the same as it had looked two nights ago when the murderer left the hotel after the crime. Dupin went up to the bar, to the place where Pennec had been lying. He knelt down and looked around from this lower angle. It was truly unsettling to see how utterly peaceful and pleasant the room was.

The walls were whitewashed, rough plaster. Prints, paintings and copies in narrow frames jostled for space on the wall, close together or on top of one another, practically covering up the walls in the restaurant and bar. Landscapes for the most part, the Pont-Aven landscape and coast, the mills. Breton farm-girls. Dupin hadn't noticed quite how many paintings there were that morning.

The dining room of the *Central* was not beautiful, but if you wanted you could imagine yourself back to its great, glamorous days – there were still enough traces of those times. You could sense the erstwhile charm and elegance. Pont-Aven had a unique blend of the provincial, born of the poverty of its origins as a fishing and farming village, combined with a sophistication thrust upon it in more modern times by the arrival of artists from Paris and the wider world. Dupin recalled a photograph he'd seen in a book about Pont-Aven in Nolwenn's office. It was of a group of artists sitting on a wall on a moss-covered stone bridge, all of them looking into the camera. Most were well dressed in big hats and fine, if threadbare, suits. Three or four houses in the background showed the harsh realities of the area, farmers and fishermen struggling to survive. To the left of the bridge was the *Central*. They were all there, the whole Pont-Aven School, Gauguin, his close young friend Emile Bernard, Charles Filiger and Henry Moret. If Nolwenn started listing them off, the list became endless; Dupin only knew a few himself. The artists had obviously made a joke of it, the famous 'Bretons', putting on the wooden shoes that tapered at the toe, stretching their legs out in front of them so that the shoes were as prominent as possible in the photo.

Suddenly there was a knock at the door that made Dupin jump. Another knock. Scowling, he went to the door and opened it. Madame Lajoux stood in front of him.

'Could I come in for a minute, Monsieur le Commissaire?'

Dupin composed himself. 'Of course. Please come in, Madame Lajoux.'

Francine Lajoux moved tentatively, stopping after a few steps.

'I'm finding it difficult, Monsieur le Commissaire.'

She looked like she'd aged years since that morning. It was terrible to see; her face was haggard, her eyes red. Dupin noticed for the first time how snow-white her hair was.

'This must be absolutely awful for you, Madame Lajoux. You and Monsieur Pennec were very close.'

'This is where he was murdered.' She struggled to remain calm, seeming to summon all her strength.

'Would you prefer to go outside?'

'No, no. Yes, we were very close, you know, Monsieur le Commissaire, but...' she looked uncertainly at Dupin, 'but never too close, if you know what I mean.'

'Absolutely, I know what you mean. I didn't mean to imply anything.'

'Everyone always talked. And the way everyone has been looking at me since this morning. Such nasty gossip. He loved his wife. I don't care about myself you know, Monsieur le Commissaire, I care about him. His reputation.'

'Don't take any notice of them, Madame Lajoux. Ignore it.'

Madame Lajoux kept her eyes lowered. 'Do you know anything more yet, Monsieur le Commissaire?'

'We know some things, but not enough.'

'Can I help? I'd like to. The murderer has to be caught and punished. Who could possibly have committed a crime like this?'

'You can never tell.'

'You think so? Really? That's a horrible thought.'

'Have you seen André Pennec yet?'

The change of topic was abrupt, but Madame Lajoux answered immediately and in a clear voice.

'Oh yes. He had the audacity to take a room here in the hotel. Madame Mendu let him have one. He came in this big fancy limousine straight from the airport. What a ridiculous man! And it's a bold move to stay here. Such hypocrisy, Monsieur Pennec wouldn't have been happy about that. He left the hotel straight after he'd brought his things to his room. He drove off in his big car.'

'Do you know where he went?'

'He didn't tell anyone anything.'

Dupin took out his notebook and made a note. 'Madame Lajoux, I would actually like to ask you to do one thing: think about Pierre Louis Pennec's last four days very, very carefully one more time. We've got to know what he did in those last four days. It would be extremely helpful.'

'Monsieur Le Ber has already asked me about that. I've told him everything I know, Monsieur le Commissaire.' She hesitated for a moment. 'Monsieur le Commissaire, is it true that the murderer always returns to the scene of the crime at least once?'

'It's complicated. There are no rules when it comes to murder cases. None at all, believe me.'

'I see. I read it in a book once. A commissaire said it.'

'Madame Lajoux, you shouldn't take anything you read in a crime novel too seriously… I have another question for you: do you know the art teacher who runs the little museum?'

Dupin had plucked up the courage to ask a few more questions after all. Francine Lajoux seemed to have become stronger during the course of the conversation – talking obviously helped her.

'Of course, I know him well. A truly wonderful man. Pont-Aven has a lot to thank Monsieur Beauvois for. Monsieur Pennec had a lot of respect for him. This new brochure was very important to Monsieur Pennec.'

'How far did they get with it?'

'I'm not sure, I think there was a first draft. With a photo of the restaurant, maybe two, one from back then and one from today. This was Pierre-Louis Pennec's favourite room in the hotel. At the beginning of last year we renovated everything on the ground floor, the walls, the floor. We even got a brand new air-conditioning system. He never spared any expense where the hotel was concerned.'

Dupin noticed now for the first time that the air in the restaurant was not in the least bit stuffy, despite the warmth of the day and the fact that the room had been locked up. The air-conditioning was clearly doing a very good job.

Sighing, she continued, 'Monsieur Pennec was always happy here. He was here every evening. Until closing time.'

'What did you talk about this week over dinner? Did he say anything about his half-brother? Either this week or recently?'

'No, nothing at all.'

'Did he talk to you about his son from time to time?'

'No. He almost never spoke about him. Just about the son's wife sometimes, Catherine Pennec. He got worked up about her every now and again, I don't think he liked her. But I shouldn't be saying this.'

It was clear Madame Lajoux was holding back.

'What did he get worked up about?' Dupin blinked.

'I'm not sure. She wanted new furniture for the house, something along those lines. He always thought she was living beyond her means and trying to play the *grande dame*. But I really shouldn't be saying things like this,' she hesitated, 'she's certainly not a murderess, even if she's not a nice person.'

'Feel free to speak your mind.'

She sighed again deeply. 'Why did the murderer kill Monsieur Pennec here? Do you think he knew him and knew that he was here every evening? Was he watching him that evening and saw that he was alone?'

Madame Lajoux seemed utterly exhausted again and a little shaky.

'We don't know yet. Madame Lajoux, it would be best if you went home now. It's late. You must look after yourself. You should take a few days off, it would be the best thing you could do.'

'That I would never do, Monsieur le Commissaire. Right now, Pierre-Louis Pennec needs me.'

Dupin wanted to disagree, but thought about it for a moment and then said: 'I understand. But you should at least relax a little this evening.'

'You're right. I'm exhausted.' She turned to go.

'Just one last question, Madame Lajoux. There was a man who had a conversation with Pierre-Louis Pennec in front of the hotel. On...' Dupin flicked through his notebook, but couldn't find the place, 'in the last few days. Are you sure it wasn't a guest? Or someone local?'

'No, no. It wasn't a guest. I know our guests. And it definitely wasn't anyone local.'

'You had never seen him before?'

'No.'

'What did he look like?'

'That other inspector has already written this all down. He was quite thin, not very tall. But I only saw them out of the corner of my eye. From above, on the staircase. I don't know how long they spoke for, but they seemed to be having a heated discussion.'

'Heated in what way?'

'I can't really say, that's just how it seemed to me.'

'This is very important.'

'They were gesticulating. I… it was just a feeling I had. Does that help?'

Dupin scratched his right temple. 'Thank you very much. That… is very helpful. Good night, Madame Lajoux.'

'I hope you catch the murderer soon. But you've got to rest too, Monsieur le Commissaire. And eat properly.'

'Thank you very much, Madame Lajoux. I will. *Bonne nuit*.' She vanished through the door.

Dupin was alone again. He was reasonably certain Francine Lajoux had known nothing about Pennec's poor health. Pennec hadn't confided in her.

The sound of muffled voices came through the window, which had been closed by the scene of crime team that morning and sealed from outside. Then there was silence again.

Dupin had noticed how tired he was during the conversation, not to mention how hungry. He didn't have a clear idea of what he should be looking for here at the bar. He hadn't promised himself anything specific. Even as a young police officer he had been in the habit of looking at crime scenes a few times. He tried to imagine the way the crime played out in as much detail as possible, sometimes using the latest bit of information about the case and sometimes using nothing but his own imagination. Then he would sit and lose himself in the details. This was how he suddenly came to see significant things. Sometimes. But today, and he was sure of this, he wouldn't see anything at all. He decided to call it a day and go to the *Amiral* for something to eat. It was almost ten o'clock and he didn't have the strength for anything else. He was far from pleased.

Dupin sat in his car and rolled down the front windows, breathing in the gentle evening air and glad to be leaving Pont-Aven behind him. He would be back in his little Concarneau very soon. If someone had told him three years ago that in the not too distant future he would be saying 'my Concarneau' he would have laughed at them. But that's how it had turned out – he loved this little town. He knew of few places in the world where you could breathe so easily or, as silly as it might sound, feel so free. On days like this the horizon was practically endless, as boundless as paradise, everything peaceful and clear. As you drove down the hill along the sweeping avenue de la Gare, lined on both sides by the pretty, immaculate fishermen's houses, you could look right out to the harbour, towards the big, open space, the broad, unspoiled areas that divided the people from the sea. Corcarneau was beautiful, truly beautiful, but the most beautiful thing about the town was the mood it put you in. And this mood – it was the sea itself.

Dupin was well aware that the locals knew the sea in other moods too. Such vastly different moods that on an evening like this you couldn't even picture it: the sea as a monster, cruelly destructive and all-consuming. The powerful harbour and fortress system fended off enemies – but most of all it kept the furious sea at bay.

And yet the town and the Atlantic were too closely intertwined for anything to be able to stand between them when the sea flew into a rage. 'In Concarneau,' went one of the many maxims which the locals repeated over and over so that, at least in words, they could calm the rough seas of their lives, 'the sea is victorious'. It had become clear to Dupin early on that what distinguished the people of the sea from people like him who were tourists and would always remain so, was respect. More specifically, fear. Fear was their prevailing emotion towards the sea, not love. Everyone here knew somebody who had lost someone to the sea, one or more people whom the sea had taken.

This evening however, down here by the harbour, the sea was friendly. The water surrounding the island of the old town was perfectly calm.

Dupin parked his car in the first row of parking spaces, right next to the harbour.

Lily greeted him with a cheerful gesture as Dupin settled down at one of the small tables in the corner of the bar. It was a gesture that showed she knew what a hard day the Commissaire must have had. She came unhurriedly over to his table.

'Tough day?'

'Yes.'

'Huh. Entrecôte?'

'Yes.'

That was their entire conversation.

Quite apart from the fact that it was long enough and was typical of the length of conversation Dupin had with the restaurant-owner, it was all Dupin could manage It was just coming up to eleven o'clock.

He felt sick with hunger. It was true he loved Breton cuisine and the *Amiral* had all of the delicious Breton specialities, but nothing to Dupin's mind, absolutely nothing, could beat entrecôte with chips (the real national dish of the *Grande Nation* – Dupin thought they should be very proud of it). There was nothing like it. Nothing even close after a day like that. And red wine to wash it down, a deep red Languedoc. Rich, velvety and smooth.

Dupin didn't have to wait long until everything was in front of him. Then he ate. And stopped thinking.

The Second Day

It was half past six in the morning. Dupin had been having confusing, unsettling dreams. Even though he had been in bed by half past twelve he hadn't fallen asleep until at least three, and had only slept deeply for the last hour or so. The phone made a dreadful, ear-splitting racket. It was a new phone, the volume of which Dupin had desperately tried to adjust several times through the various menus and sub-menus but had failed miserably. He could see it was Labat. He really only picked up to stop the diabolical noise it was making.

'Somebody removed the cordon from a window in the side passage and bashed in the windowpanes. The window is open.' Labat hadn't even asked if he was through to the right person.

'What? Labat! What's wrong?' Dupin couldn't understand what Labat was talking about.

'Somebody broke into the crime scene last night.'

'Into the *Central*?'

'Into the bar where Pierre-Louis Pennec was murdered.'

'And what did they do?'

'No idea.'

'No idea?'

'Our colleagues from Pont-Aven just rang. All they've done is log it.'

'Somebody forced their way into the crime scene through a window?'

Labat hesitated over his answer. 'Strictly speaking we don't actually know that. Just that someone bashed in a window and that it's now open. The window next to the cast-iron door, so it's further back and towards the bar if I understand correctly.'

'Is anything out of place in the restaurant or the bar?'

'No, there's no damage as far as I know. But that's very much a provisional observation.'

'What's that meant to mean?' Dupin was feeling more and more awake.

'The police on the scene didn't see anything conspicuous, but of course they haven't started any forensic examinations yet. They've informed Salou, which is definitely the most important thing right now.'

'How did they find out about this? The restaurant is cordoned off.'

'The chef.'

'Edouard Lenaff?'

'Yes, Monsieur le Commissaire.'

'Did someone come into the hotel through the bar and restaurant?'

'No, definitely not. The door is intact and locked. You'd need to have had the key, and we've taken in all of them.'

'I'm on my way, Labat. Where are you?'

'At home. I'm leaving now.'

'Okay.'

'Bye.'

Before he did anything else, Dupin needed a coffee. It was still too early for the *Amiral*. He had bought himself a little espresso machine during his last year in Paris. He'd only used it three times since then; he just liked sitting in cafés too much. The machine had cost an eye-watering amount. Dupin hadn't had a clue about espresso machines and the saleswoman with the dark green eyes had been persuasive, assuring him that this was the only sensible option. The beans were probably as old as the machine. It was a somewhat laborious process, but as the last drops dripped into the little cup he felt something approaching pride.

Once he was dressed, Dupin took his coffee and stepped out onto the narrow balcony overlooking the sea. Almost all of the other rooms in this flat, which had come with the job, looked out to sea too. The flat was in a late nineteenth century building, one of the most beautiful in Concarneau. Not ostentatious, but very stylish and painted a radiant white. You could look directly out onto the 'Flaubert Cliffs' as they called them in Concarneau. Apparently Flaubert had always sat there when he was in town. There was just one narrow street separating Dupin's building from the sea. On his right the coast led to the *Sables blancs*, a stunning, long, dazzlingly white sandy beach with expensive villas along it; and to the left was the entrance to the harbour with the little lighthouse and the buoys bobbing sleepily in the gentle groundswell. But the best thing was the view of the vast ocean. Dawn was just breaking above him, the sky and sea still indistinguishable on the horizon. The sun would be coming up any moment.

The beans might have been old but the coffee was strong and didn't taste too bad. Dupin brooded over everything that had happened so far. He was no longer sure whether he should rush over to Pont-Aven. The priority over there was Salou's work; Labat had been right about that. And Salou was conscientious, he would definitely get there quickly, before Dupin would. There was something strange about all of this. Why would someone have broken into the restaurant? Had the murderer returned to the scene of the crime? The forensic evidence from the night of the murder – although there was precious little anyway – had already been collected, unless they had overlooked something yesterday. Whatever way you looked at it, the intruder had taken a huge risk. Breaking into a crime scene the day after a murder – it was madness. There must have been a very good reason for it. It could have been a diversionary tactic – but from what? And why?

It now seemed clear that the case was not about some drama that had developed over a short or even a long time, culminating in murder and thereby drawing to a close. The drama was still playing out, even if they couldn't see it yet. A drama that old Pennec himself might have sparked off with something he did after finding out about his life-threatening illness. Whatever the case, Dupin had to hurry, that much was clear. The pace of events was picking up.

Dupin decided not to drive to Pont-Aven. He would go the police station, have his conversation with André Pennec as planned and wait for the results of the forensic work.

André Pennec was already waiting at the station when Dupin entered the nondescript, rather ugly building near the train station a little after eight o'clock. Purpose-built, eighties, and not even very spacious, let alone comfortable. Dupin couldn't stand the smell of the building either (a unique plastic smell that nobody else really seemed to notice), a smell that all the open windows in the world couldn't alleviate.

'He's sitting in your office.' Nolwenn was already on top of things.

'*Bonjour*, Nolwenn.'

'*Bonjour*, Monsieur le Commissaire.'

'I'll be right with him. Do we have any information yet on who the executor of Pennec's will is? Is it Madame Denis?'

'She's expecting you.'

Dupin had to laugh. Nolwenn looked rather bemused.

'Half past ten at her office in Pont-Aven. Or does the break-in mean you want to go to the *Central* first?'

'No. I just want to be informed whenever there's any news, as soon as anyone has the smallest thing.'

'It's strange though. This case is getting more complicated all the time,' she faltered for a moment, 'and it's complicated enough already. What do you think is going on?'

'I don't know. I really don't know.'

'I have all the other information too; I'll give it to Le Ber. Now you should –'

'Okay, okay.'

Dupin hesitated a moment, and after a token knock on his own door (even though it felt strange) he went inside.

He practically jumped out of his skin. André Pennec was the image of Louis Pennec. It was astonishing. You couldn't tell he had a different mother. The same build, the same facial features. Strange that nobody had mentioned this.

He was sitting in the chair across from Dupin's desk and made no move to stand up, looking Dupin directly in the eye. A light-coloured, very formal, stiff summer suit, his hair somewhat longer than his half-brother's, painstakingly combed back with gel.

'*Bonjour*, Monsieur.'

'Monsieur le Commissaire.'

'Good to see you.'

'I would have expected you to inform me personally.'

At first Dupin didn't know what André Pennec meant, but he pulled himself together again quickly.

'I'm terribly sorry. I was concentrating on the initial stages of the investigation. That's why Inspector Le Ber was given the task of informing you.'

'That's not good enough!'

'As I said, I'm terribly sorry. And I'd like to express my sincerest condolences on the loss of your half-brother.'

André Pennec looked coldly at Dupin.

'Were you close, Monsieur Pennec? You and your half-brother?'

'We were brothers. With all that family entails. What can I say? Every family has its stories. And being a half-brother is probably even more complex.'

'What do you mean?'

'Exactly what I said.'

'I would like to know more, Monsieur Pennec.'

'I don't see any reason to divulge personal details about my relationship with my brother.'

'You were a radical advocate of the Breton nationalist movement *Emgann* at the beginning of the seventies.' Dupin had used one of his favourite techniques, launching straight into a topic without preamble. 'There are rumours you have links with its extremist military wing, the Breton Revolutionary Army.' Dupin paused for a few moments. 'There have been casualties in the struggle against the "French oppressors". Quite a few in fact.'

André Pennec momentarily lost control of his facial features, just for a split-second, but Dupin had seen it. Anger and bewilderment. 'That's ancient history, Monsieur le Commissaire.' André Pennec was speaking in an arrogant, relaxed tone now. 'The sins of one's youth! I never had any links to the Breton Revolutionary Army. None at all. Foolishness is what it was, that army. Good thing they stamped it out.'

'A young socialist, Fragan Delon, publicly accused you of these links at the time. Repeatedly and publicly. The story goes that you refused to take any action against him because you were afraid of the investigations.'

'That is absurd. Delon has always been a lunatic. My brother should have been more wary of him. I was always telling him so.' His voice was still under control, even if his tone had become a little sharper.

'Wary?'

'I mean –' He broke off. 'People choose their friends.'

'Your brother was firmly against *Emgann*, in every way.'

'We had our differences over it.'

'You haven't seen each other much in the last, what, forty years since then? They must have been pretty serious "differences".'

'That's just how it happened to turn out, Monsieur le Commissaire. These old rumours.' Again he hesitated a little. 'We talked on the phone from time to time. Every so often.'

'I understand you left Brittany at the end of the seventies and started all over again in Provence because you were afraid that a political career here could be put at risk at any time by those old rumours.'

'That is also absurd.'

'Your career rather took off in the years that followed.'

'What are you trying to get at, Monsieur le Commissaire? Do you suspect me of murdering my brother? That is grotesque in itself. All because of minor ideological disputes forty years ago? I'm seventy-five now and I'm not going to sit here and listen to any more of this. This is all irrelevant. A joke.'

'You have a significant event coming up. You're going to be receiving the National Order of Merit. That would be the crowning achievement of your life's work as a politician.'

'Very much so.'

'Bad news could ruin everything.'

'Bad news? There is no bad news. I don't know what you're talking about.'

'Where were you the day before yesterday, Thursday, during the day and evening?'

'Is this an interrogation, Monsieur le Commissaire?'

He sounded openly aggressive now. But André Pennec remembered himself straight away and changed his tone. 'Toulon. I was at my house in Toulon on Thursday. I was working all day.'

'And somebody can attest to this of course.'

'My wife certainly can. Then yesterday morning I was in the office when Loic Pennec's call came through. I set out immediately. My wife brought a few things in a little suitcase to the airport for me. Feel free to take a look at my boarding pass. I hired a car in Quimper. And that's all I'm going to say.'

'Did your brother remember you in his will?'

'Excuse me?'

'I just want to know whether you think you're getting anything in your brother's will?'

'No. I shouldn't think so. Unless he changed it again recently, which I'd imagine is highly unlikely. After our differences of opinion he drafted a clause to exclude me from inheriting anything and deposited it with his notary. He told me.' André Pennec was speaking in hushed tones again now. 'I've managed to achieve a certain level of wealth myself you know. I don't need any financial support. And of course you'll have been familiar with the contents of my brother's will for a while by now. You know I'm not mentioned.'

'A politician's reputation is his greatest asset. And his most vulnerable.'

'Monsieur le Commissaire,' Pennec's tone was almost conciliatory now, 'I don't think this is appropriate. I came to find out what really happened to my brother and whether you've got any leads yet. I'm not interested in anything else to be honest.

And then I'll see if I can help Loic and Catherine in some way. Make sure everything's okay at the hotel. My brother considered it his life's work.'

Dupin only just managed to control himself. 'We don't have any significant findings yet, Monsieur Pennec. The investigation is ongoing. I'll be conducting interviews with the suspects.'

'So nothing yet then.'

'Have some faith in the Breton police… So do you have any idea what might have happened, Monsieur Pennec? I'd be interested to hear it.'

'Me? Not at all. How would I have any idea? A robbery? My brother was a good businessman and you can get stabbed for ten euro these days.'

'That would be your theory, then?'

'I don't have a theory. It's your job to solve the case.'

'Were you in touch with your brother recently?'

André Pennec answered without hesitation. 'We spoke on the phone on Tuesday.'

'Tuesday of this week?'

'Yes, two days before he died.'

'That's quite a coincidence, isn't it? You speak so rarely… and then you speak to him just before he dies.'

'What an insinuation! Even more of this disrespect. Whatever it is you're trying to say in your disgracefully vague way, I'm not going to respond.' His harsh words were strikingly different from the quiet, confident way he said them. André Pennec was a master of self-control – and of the strategic, completely nonchalant change of tone as and when he wished. In this too he was ever the politician.

'Can you tell me what this phone call was about?'

'As you already know, I called him from time to time. To hear how he was, how the hotel was, how his son and daughter-in-law were. Just family stuff. For the last ten years at least. I wanted some interaction with my brother, as difficult as that was with our history looming in the background.'

'That's all you talked about for ten minutes.'

'That's all we talked about for ten minutes. And I can tell you now, he didn't say anything out of the ordinary. I didn't notice anything unusual about him.'

'What specific things did you talk about?'

André Pennec thought about it for a moment. 'We spoke about fishing. He was planning to buy a new set of fishing equipment. That was one topic. The sea. Fishing.'

'Yes,' Dupin paused unnaturally, 'yes, then I think we can end our talk there… If you've found out everything you wanted to find out, I mean.'

André Pennec looked momentarily irritated again. 'I take it you will inform me personally as soon as anything happens.'

'We will, Monsieur Pennec. You can depend on it.'

Pennec stood up firmly, held out his hand to Dupin in a professional, polite way and moved towards the door. 'Au revoir, Monsieur le Commissaire.'

'Excuse me, Monsieur Pennec… One last thing. How long are you staying for?'

Pennec was already at the door. He didn't even turn round all the way. 'Until everything is sorted here. The burial and everything else that's going on at the moment.'

'Good. I have your number. And I know where to find you.'

Pennec didn't respond. Dupin waited until he over-heard Pennec leaving the reception. Then he left his office too.

'I'm going to the notary's office, Nolwenn.'

There was a coffee right at the edge of Nolwenn's desk. Dupin smiled. Nolwenn always put it there without a word. He took the cup and drank it in one go.

'Please do. By the time you get there we'll have the official judicial order to inspect the will, just one more phone call. Madame Denis only came back from London at midday the day before yesterday. An extremely impressive woman. Her family goes way way back and she speaks fluent Breton. But she just doesn't have any luck with men.'

Dupin was still preoccupied with the unpleasant conversation he'd just had. 'I've got to call Le Ber.'

'He just called. About the break-in.'

'Good.'

'A horrible man, that André Pennec,' said Nolwenn sadly, 'it's so strange, they look incredibly similar and yet they couldn't be more different.'

Dupin didn't say anything.

'Oh yes, there was another thing. Your sister called yesterday. Nothing specific, she just wanted to speak to you, so I told her you were busy with a complex case. She wanted me to say hello from her.'

Lou. He had been meaning to get in touch with her for ages; she never called his mobile any more.

'Thanks, Nolwenn. I'll call her.'

He really would call her.

He hurried out of the door.

Dupin had left his car in the big car park by the harbour because driving it that last little bit was never worth it. Concarneau was a tangle of one-way streets.

Dupin fiddled with his mobile.

'Le Ber?'

'Yes?'

'Check what time André Pennec left Toulon yesterday – and look into his whole journey. He was in the office beforehand. When did he buy the ticket and where, what flight was he on? Where did he rent the car in Quimper? Everything. Immediately!' He paused for a second. 'What is Salou saying about the break-in at the scene?'

'I... Okay. I'll handle it. On the break-in, Salou says there's nothing to report. So far. He's concentrating on possible traces, footprints, whatever there might be, around the window. To establish whether anyone actually climbed in.'

'You didn't notice anything either? Did you look carefully?'

'Of course, Monsieur le Commissaire. But there was nothing to see, no changes since yesterday in the bar or restaurant. If somebody did go into the room, there are no indications as to what they might have been doing.'

'All right, Le Ber.'

'It doesn't make sense though. Why would anyone take down the cordon at a crime scene and smash in a window? Do you think it could have been some stupid joke?'

'I have no idea, Le Ber.'

'I'll let the Pennecs know. I assume you don't feel you need to do that yourself.'

'Good. I'll see you after my appointment with the notary.'

'My instinct is telling me there's something big here. Something very big is going on.'

Le Ber's grave pronouncement seemed to change the tone of the conversation. There was a long pause.

'What do you mean?'

'I don't know. I don't think *I* even know what I mean.'

'Right… well, then.'

Dupin hung up.

The notary had a beautiful old stone house, a tastefully renovated one, further upstream where the river flowed with quiet grace over its bed of granite. She had her office on the ground and first floors, and she lived on the second floor. In the small, pristine, landscaped front garden stood half a dozen palm trees – ever an attraction for tourists; and you could always hear someone showing off about what everyone knew anyway: 'The Gulf Stream hits Brittany directly which means a mild climate even in winter. There's never any frost in Brittany because of it, it's rarely under ten degrees – ideal weather for palm trees.'

Madame Denis opened the door herself. She was stylishly dressed in a beige shift dress with matching high-heeled sandals. Expensive-looking, but understated.

'*Bonjour*, Monsieur le Commissaire.' She smiled at Dupin without overdoing it, looking him in the eye.

'*Bonjour*, Madame Maître.'

'Please come in. We'll go up to my study.' She gestured

towards the stairs, which led directly upstairs from beside the front door.

'Absolutely.'

Dupin went first.

'Are you well?'

'Yes, thank you. Marvellous.'

'Thank you for making time to see me at such short notice. You must have known Monsieur Pennec very well.'

'I've known him a long time. Since I was a child.'

She was sitting behind her elegant old desk, and Dupin in one of the two, no less elegant, chairs opposite her.

'Monsieur Pierre-Louis Pennec called me on Tuesday morning, he said it was about a personal matter. Nothing to do with the hotel. It was urgent. Initially he wanted to have a meeting at six o'clock on Thursday evening. I'd confirmed it with him, but he called again an hour later wanting to postpone the appointment to Friday morning. He said he was planning to make a change to his will. I thought I should tell you that before we get on to the contents.'

Dupin was startled by her words. He was suddenly wide awake. 'A change to his will?'

'He didn't tell me exactly what it involved on the phone. I asked him whether there was anything I could prepare in advance. But he wanted to talk to me about it in person.'

'Do you have any idea what it might have been? What he wanted to change?'

'I haven't the faintest idea I'm afraid.'

'Is there anything special in the will? Anything

112

surprising, I mean? I take it Loic Pennec will inherit everything.'

'His son will inherit the hotel – although there are certain conditions attached to that, to do with how the hotel is to be run – as well as the house he's living in with his wife. Pierre-Louis Pennec had four properties in total and he left the second one, which was the house he lived in himself, to the art society in Pont-Aven. The third property will be inherited by Fragan Delon and the fourth by Francine Lajoux. Pierre-Louis Pennec also left her a letter, which she will receive now. Monsieur Delon inherits both of Pennec's boats.'

Dupin leaned forwards; he couldn't hide his astonishment. There was no obvious emotion apparent in Madame Denis' face or voice. She reported the stipulations of the will with utter professionalism.

'The last two properties I mentioned are in fact the houses that Madame Lajoux and Monsieur Delon have already occupied for quite a long time. Cash and everything else goes to the son, but we're not talking big amounts. The last I heard was that the liquid assets amounted to about two hundred thousand euro. And that has certain conditions attached to it as well: at least a hundred thousand euro must always remain in the account for potential repairs and renovations to the hotel. Some plots of land in the legacy are going to the son too – seven pieces, scattered all over the region, all of them quite small except for two bigger ones, around a thousand square metres each, with a kind of warehouse on each one. One of these is in Port Manech, the other is in Le Pouldu. None of it is land for building on, it's worthless really, but if you were to get planning permission it would of course be a completely different story. But the strict coastal protection laws prevent that. Monsieur Pennec inherited most of the plots of land himself in the first place… That's the core of the will.'

Dupin had meticulously noted everything down. 'Delon and Lajoux inherit. And the art society too. A whole house.'

This wasn't a question, and Madame Denis didn't reply.

'Three out of the four properties aren't going to the son.'

'Three out of five.'

'Five?'

'The hotel.'

'Yes, of course. It's still a surprise though.'

'I'm expecting Loic and Catherine Pennec at three o'clock today, for the unsealing of the will. I'll be making appointments with the other beneficiaries for tomorrow morning.'

'Does Loic Pennec know? I mean, did Monsieur Pennec ever tell you that his son was aware of these provisions in the will?'

'I'm not sure. We didn't speak about things like that.' Madame Denis thought for a moment. 'He never told me his son was familiar with the contents of the will. But that's not any business of the notary, you know.'

'What do you think though, what does your instinct tell you? If I can put it like that.'

'I really can't say, Monsieur le Commissaire. I don't feel comfortable with the thought that my instinct on this question would play any kind of role in your investigation.'

'I understand, Madame. When does the will date from?'

'Pierre-Louis Pennec made the will twelve years ago. I drafted it for him. And it's never been changed since.'

'Is there only one copy, the one here?'

'Yes, just this one copy. Appropriately stored of course, in the building's safe with all the other important documents.'

'And what kind of letter did he write to Madame Lajoux?'

'I obviously don't know the contents. A personal letter.'

'The Pennecs won't be very happy about the will.'

'There are two more clauses to mention. One of them concerns a shed. There is a large shed, practically a little house, right on the edge of Delon's plot of land. There was a dispute about it once between Pennec and his son, around the time the will was drawn up. The son had set up a workshop for his honey there. You know about Loic Pennec's business, don't you?'

'Not much, just that he once tried to run a small business. He wanted to sell Breton honey, *miel de mer*.'

'That's as much as I know too, Monsieur le Commissaire.'

'Is he still in business? Is he still using that building as a workshop?'

'That I couldn't tell you, unfortunately. I just know that Pennec wanted to allow Delon to use it – it's in his garden after all. How the son even got in there with his honey I don't know. There was an argument, and in the end Pierre-Louis Pennec did give his son the use of the building, but the will stipulates that the building goes to Delon after Pennec's death. What the son really wanted back then was to be given Delon's house so he could turn it into a shop. I only know this because the clause in the will can be traced back to their argument about it.'

'Was it a bad argument?'

'Monsieur Pennec was very determined. It was important to him that this clause be clear and airtight.'

'And the second clause? You mentioned two.'

'The second dates back thirty years. It excludes his half-brother from the legacy. Completely.'

'I've heard about that one. Do you know the exact reason?'

'No. I don't know anything about it. The clause was originally my predecessor's responsibility; it was on file when I took over the case. The clause is in fact very concise. It sets out the exclusion in one sentence.'

Dupin fell silent for a moment. 'Did you know about the state of Pierre-Louis Pennec's health?'

'What do you mean?'

'He only had a short time to live. It was probably a miracle that he was still alive at all. His arteries were completely blocked. He was at Doctor Pelliet's on Monday this week and ought to have been operated on immediately but he categorically refused. He knew that that would mean imminent death.'

Madame Denis shook her head almost imperceptibly. 'No, I didn't know that. I hadn't seen him for some time. And I didn't hear anything about it from anyone else either.'

'He probably didn't tell anyone. As far as we know at this stage.'

Madame Denis's forehead furrowed and she spoke

slowly. 'If I may say so, Monsieur le Commissaire, that sounds extremely strange. Pierre-Louis Pennec finds out he only has a few days left to live, wants to change his will... and is murdered two days later.' She broke off.

'I know.'

After the terrible turn of events, it was true that a coincidence sounded unlikely. But maybe there was another way of looking at everything.

'You mentioned a few conditions just now. Relating to inheriting the hotel.'

'Yes, there aren't many. One was that Madame Lajoux would keep her position as long she lived, and her salary too. Another was that Madame Mendu would become her successor as housekeeper. A kind of hotel manager. Above all, that the hotel cannot be sold or substantially changed from its current design. There is of course a certain vagueness in the wording of these things. Loic Pennec has to consent to these binding conditions in order to come into his inheritance.'

Dupin thought this over.

'At the time, I had the feeling that Pierre-Louis Pennec actually wanted to add more conditions to the list. He hinted at it a few times.'

'Could that have been the reason why he wanted to amend the will or include an addendum?'

'I can't really say.'

'Did Pierre-Louis Pennec mention an amendment or addendum to the will?'

'An amendment.'

Dupin noted the word down, underlining it twice.

'In its current form, what kind of motives for murder might there be in the will? It's not all that spectacular… It is, shall we say, surprising in a few places.'

Once again, he hadn't really asked a question. Madame Denis didn't look at Dupin, staring uncertainly out of the window instead. Dupin followed her gaze.

'Such an incredible blue.'

There was another long pause. Finally Madame Denis made as though to shake herself. 'I don't like to speculate. My profession is about facts and safeguarding facts. Records.'

Dupin didn't fully understand what she meant. He was wrapped up in his own thoughts now and had started to feel rather uneasy, almost impatient.

'Well, this has all been very helpful. That information was very important. Please accept my thanks, Madame Maître. You've been most kind.'

'A pleasure, Monsieur le Commissaire, a pleasure. I hope you'll shed some light on this dark crime soon. It's so horrific, it doesn't bear thinking about, Monsieur Pennec having to die so violently. And at his age!'

'Indeed.'

'I'll see you out.'

'No, no, Madame, don't go to any trouble. I know the way.'

Dupin shook Madame Denis' hand.

'All the best, Monsieur le Commissaire.'

'Yes, all the best. I hope we see each other again soon – under more pleasant circumstances.'

Madame Denis smiled.

'I hope so too.'

Commissaire Dupin knew that he had left Madame Denis' office rather abruptly, but he wanted to take a short walk. Things were getting more and more confusing. Deep down he knew that this was usually a good sign at this stage in an investigation. But it didn't feel that way this time.

He walked back to the hotel, turned right into the little alleyway and then decided to follow the path wherever it might lead, right up the hill. As it didn't go straight to the river, the area wouldn't attract any tourists and he would have some peace and quiet.

The will wasn't all that controversial, but there were still a few surprises. As with his heart condition, it wasn't clear whether anyone had known about the provisions in Pennec's will. Had he ever told the beneficiaries anything? His son and daughter-in-law had denied knowing anything specific about the will, evidently considering the whole thing nothing more than a formality. They felt the entire inheritance belonged to them. But that didn't mean anything of course. And Fragan Delon and Francine Lajoux hadn't given anything away. The crucial point was not the existing will. After finding out he was going to die, Pennec had decided to change the will again, as a matter of urgency. But which part? One part, many parts? Had he wanted to add something new? This information might be the key to everything. And so again the question arose, did anyone know what he intended? Clearly it must have been about this intended change – everything else, the existing will with its conditions didn't seem to be enough of a motive for murder. The issue must have been more divisive than that. Or else the will contained things that he hadn't seen yet, that he wasn't able to see.

Dupin had reached the top of the hill. The view from here really was spectacular. This was how Pont-Aven looked in the painters' work. You could see how hilly the whole area was, how many twists there were to the valley, and how the inlet had developed. He suddenly had an idea. He rummaged around for his mobile and dialled Madame Denis' number.

'Georges Dupin here. Forgive me for bothering you again, Madame Maître. I have another question.'

'You're not bothering me at all, Monsieur le Commissaire.'

'When Monsieur Pennec requested the appointment to change his will on Tuesday, he said it was "very urgent" and then suggested Thursday himself, is that right?'

'Yes, he suggested Thursday.'

'He said it was very urgent and yet he didn't want an appointment on the same day, if it were possible? Or at least Wednesday?'

'Em, no. As I say, he suggested Thursday.' Madame Denis was silent for a little while. 'I see what you mean. You're right. Three days. He makes an appointment for three days later on an issue which is of the utmost importance to him – knowing that he could drop dead at any moment. He...' she hesitated, 'he still had things to sort out before the meeting with me.'

Dupin had been told how astute she was. 'Yes. I think so too.' There was a short pause. 'Thanks again, Madame Denis.'

'I'm sure you'll solve the case soon, Monsieur le Commissaire.'

'I'm not so sure yet. Bye, Madame Maître.'

'Bye.'

Dupin took the steep, narrow path down the hill and found some old stone steps that threaded their way between the villas and gardens, right down to the banks of the Aven. At the bottom of the steps there was a hidden path which branched away from the footpath by the river. Twenty or thirty metres along the path, he discovered a bright red wooden bench, which suddenly appeared from behind a profusion of shrubbery underneath a handful of poplars. It wasn't visible from the path, even though it was no more than half a metre away from the river, just a little higher up. He sat down. There was a rushing sound like a mountain stream at this point of the Aven because of some dramatic rapids and waterfalls. You could hear the sound of the falling water all over Pont-Aven except by the harbour. The sound was there in the background the whole time, especially at night. There was no sign of the sea here, it was a different world. Incredible.

Dupin sat completely still for a few minutes. Then he reached for his mobile. 'Le Ber?'

'Monsieur le Commissaire?'

'Yes.'

'I can't hear you very well.'

'Where are you?'

'In the office, I've just come from Pont-Aven. The connection isn't very good. There's a real roaring noise. Where are you?'

'I'm sitting by the river.'

'You're sitting by the river?'

'That's what I said. Is there any news on the break-in? Forensics?'

'No, nothing yet. Salou would have been in touch.'

'Call him again.'

'But he –' Le Ber stopped himself.

'I want to speak to the chairman of the art society. Do you have an address for him?'

'Labat has it.'

'I'll call Labat then.'

'One more thing, Monsieur le Commissaire. Docteur Lafond called an hour ago, he wanted to speak to you but you were at the notary's, so Nolwenn put him through to me.'

Le Ber knew that Dupin always wanted to speak to Lafond himself.

'And?'

'Four stab wounds, as we already knew. Deep stabs, each one up to hilt. Upper abdomen, lungs, two in the heart area. Docteur Lafond says he probably died very quickly. The knife penetrated the body at a right angle. A very sharp, smooth blade, about eight centimetres long.'

'Which means?' Dupin could never get his head round knives.

'It's an average length of blade for a knife. Could also have been a large penknife. Opinel, Laguiole, something like that. No rust, no dirt. A well-kept knife.'

'When did Pennec die, do we know the exact time yet?'

'Around midnight. Not much later than that. But we can't say to the very minute, as you know...'

'I know, we don't want to force Lafond to make it up and risk his scientific reputation.'

'That's pretty much how he put it, yes.'

'Fine. I'm up to speed. Call me if there's any news.'

Today had turned into another magnificent summer's day. The sky was clear and vast, no sign of the clouds or haze that had been forecast for the evening. Dupin was sure he could see all the signs of a high pressure period that would remain stable for a few days at least.

Labat had had Monsieur Beauvois' address ready immediately. He lived centrally too, in one of the streets upstream where it was always damp. Rue Job Philippe. Like almost all the other houses in this picture book village, it was a very pretty old stone house straight out of a travel guide with huge hydrangea bushes in the little front garden. There was every shade of hydrangea imaginable: pink, purple, light blue, dark blue, red.

Dupin opened the garden gate and was about to ring the doorbell when the door swept open and a short, very round man stood in front of him, squinting dubiously. Not much hair any more and what was left had been cut short to make up for it. Small oval glasses. An oval head.

'Commissaire Georges Dupin. Hello.'

'Ah – Monsieur le Commissaire. Frédéric Beauvois. Delighted to meet you,' he hesitated a little, 'although these are terrible circumstances of course.'

'Is this a bad time?'

'No, no. Not at all. I was just about to go and get something to eat,' he seemed to feel as though he had been caught out somehow. 'I live alone. An old bachelor... I'd be pleased to help. Whatever I can do. Pierre-Louis Pennec, it has to be said, was one of the most important citizens in this town, and his loss is a great tragedy for Pont-Aven. That's the only word for it. Tragedy. He served our village in so many generous ways. And if I may say so, I was his friend. We'd known and worked with each other for three decades. He was a true and wonderful patron of the arts. But do come in!'

'Thank you.'

As with most of the stone houses, it was quite dark inside. Sometimes that could be quite cosy – by the fireside with a roaring, lashing storm outside – but Dupin often found it depressing, especially on such a bright, sunny day.

Dupin hummed and hawed a little. 'You know, I'm hungry too. Why don't we go and get a bite to eat together? What do you think?'

This was a completely spur-of-the-moment idea. But Dupin was now realising just how hungry he was, and he had no desire to sit in semi-darkness in this weather, when it was so bright outside. Monsieur Beauvois looked at the Commissaire with some surprise, but only for a moment.

'That sounds fantastic. Let's go to Maurice's place in the mill. An old friend of mine, and the best restaurant in Pont-Aven – apart from the *Central* of course.' Beauvois smiled in a very friendly way.

'That sounds great, Monsieur Beauvois.' Dupin tried not to seem too eager as he turned round and hurried out the door as quickly as he could.

They walked purposefully through the little alleyways, past the lane leading to the hotel, and towards the old mill, a restaurant called the *Moulin de Rosmadec*, which had been renowned throughout Pont-Aven and the surrounding area for twenty years. As a retired teacher, Beauvois couldn't resist giving Dupin a little tour of the village and a lesson on its history, overflowing with pride and numerous superlatives. Dupin, whose stomach was rumbling, hardly said a word.

Finally they were sitting underneath a magnificent, tall lime tree next to the old mill wheel.

With the water roaring over the stones, it was like a fairy tale. Dupin knew precious little about the many mills in Pont-Aven. Long before the artists, the village had been famous for its mills, a great number of millers having settled here over the centuries, providing flour for the whole region. The flour had been delivered to Nantes and even as far as Bordeaux when Pont-Aven had still been a proper sea trading port, as Beauvois explained with great emotion.

Beauvois and Maurice Kerriou, the over-eager owner of the restaurant, agreed after some extensive culinary discussions – with Dupin simply looking on from the sidelines – on a little *plâteau de fruits de mer*, followed by *filets de rougets*.

'You must have the *fruits de mer* – the *palourdes grises*! The best mussels in all of Brittany. You can't get ones like this in your neck of the woods, up in Paris. They're a real speciality here.'

In fact Dupin loved *palourdes grises* – and he would have liked to have said that he had had them many times in *Lutétia*, his favourite brasserie in Paris, and that they had always been very fresh and that he preferred them to *palourdes roses* because they tasted like a distillation of the whole Atlantic Ocean. He had been eating them whenever they were in season since he'd moved to Brittany. But he didn't say anything. He had just accepted a sympathetic smile: you poor Parisian, you get fobbed off with rubbish that's been travelling for a day, bad mussels from overseas in the first place, and at such extortionate prices! He knew that look.

'Yes please, that's very kind.'

'You'll see, this will be an eye-opener for you. Everything is excellent here.'

'Monsieur Beauvois, you saw Pierre-Louis Pennec just this week, on Tuesday.'

'My God, yes. I can't take it in. On Tuesday. He was very much alive! We mainly spoke about the new brochure.'

'The one about the artists' colony in Pont-Aven and the hotel?'

'Yes, that's right. We had been talking about an expanded edition for a long time. We kept everything very concise in the first edition and it's more than twenty years old now. We know so much more now about the lives of the artists, especially in Pont-Aven. It was a disgrace you know, they had all been forgotten, apart from Gauguin and maybe Émile Bernard. The other artists were only rediscovered two decades ago. There were such stunning talents amongst them, such great artists. We've started to do a lot of research here in Pont-Aven. Who lived where exactly, who painted together where, who ate what where...'

Beauvois smiled mischievously, knowingly. 'And who had affairs with which innocent country bumpkin. They had colourful lives. My, there are a lot of stories there.' He interrupted himself, as though he had to remind himself to concentrate. 'So I brought Pierre-Louis the text for the new brochure. He wanted to be in charge of photographs again. He had a small, but superb collection of photographs, you know. They belonged to his grandmother, Marie-Jeanne. She took a few of them herself.'

'In the hotel? Photos from when the artists were around?'

'Yes. Maybe a hundred photographs. Including a few truly extraordinary ones. All of the artists are there, all the greats!'

Dupin had taken out his Clairefontaine notebook. He made a note. 'Where did he keep them?'

'Upstairs in that little room of his, next to his bedroom. There are a few prints up there too, ones he couldn't find room for in the restaurant after the renovation. He showed them to me once.'

'Could I see the text?'

Beauvois was irritated. 'My text for the brochure?'

'Yes.'

'Of course. I'll send it over to you.'

'Was Pennec in a hurry?'

'With the brochure?'

'With the brochure.'

'He was always in a hurry when he wanted something.'

'You collaborated on many projects, not just on this brochure... if my sources are correct.'

Beauvois sat back a little and drew a deep breath, apparently pleased with Dupin's question. 'Perhaps you should know a little bit more about my work, Monsieur le Commissaire. Otherwise you might misinterpret some things. With your permission, I'd like to explain something, very quickly of course.'

'Go ahead.'

'Without wanting to seem vain – things really have gone marvellously well for the museum under my direction. I started running it in 1985. I founded a permanent exhibition, sorted out what we already had and had it displayed properly at long last. And then bit by bit I also made some significant new acquisitions. We have over a thousand paintings now, a thousand! Even though we obviously can't display all of them. In 2002 the *Ministère de la Culture* officially designated us a *Musée de France* which was long overdue but even so, it was a recognition of my work. And I had Pierre-Louis' support from the beginning. He was a member of every club that I founded, even the first one, the *Association des Amis du Musée de Pont-Aven*, he was vice-president for a while.'

Maurice Kerriou appeared with the seafood, a bottle of chilled Sancerre and a big bottle of Badoit. Dupin was finding this all a little over the top. Everything was laid out beautifully on the table. This was taking a while.

'You were talking about the clubs.'

'Yes, as I was saying, alongside his work in the hotel, Monsieur Pennec found the time to get involved in societies relating to Pont-Aven and the museum.

I should make special mention of course, of the fact that he was the chairman, until last year, of the *Mécénat breton* – an organisation for the patrons of the museum. We have a huge number of prominent donors. Without them we could never have achieved what we have – the town, the region and the *département,* as well as local government, have supported us too of course. With the financial backing of the society we were able to convert the rear section of the *Julia Hotel* into a museum and we were able to commission a respected architectural firm in Concarneau to build it – I'm sure you're aware of that.'

'Yes.'

'And that was the only way we were able to finance our spectacular acquisitions too. You'll be aware of those?' Beauvois was looking expectantly at Dupin.

'I would like to know how much money Pierre-Louis Pennec contributed... and what exactly it went towards?' said Dupin, instead of answering Beauvois' question. He was gradually losing patience with Beauvois' wonderful stories about himself.

Beauvois looked quite disappointed. 'It varied a lot. Sometimes it would be small amounts for putting up exhibition posters, for instance. Other times it would be larger amounts.'

'If you could be more specific?'

'There were two donations recently. Three thousand euro for a series of radio adverts for our new exhibition. We're going to –'

'And the second amount?'

'It was a larger amount of money, for the museum and the exhibition rooms. We need to do some renovation and we need a new air-conditioning system. We don't have any of the truly important paintings here, of course we don't, but there are some interesting ones.'

'What do you mean by *larger*?' Dupin was annoyed.

'Eighty thousand euro.'

'Eighty thousand euro?'

'That's only a fraction of what the air-conditioning system and installation will cost. We had to do some construction work for it. Armor Lux is generously giving us the rest of the money – the Breton textiles company, do you know it? The one with the stripy jumpers.'

Of course Dupin knew Armor Lux, everyone in France knew it.

'Pierre-Louis Pennec knew the owner of Armor Lux, he helped me a little bit with getting the funding. And he wanted to take care of the funding we still needed.'

'This is seriously big money. Do you have any idea how much he's donated over the last few years and decades? Just to the museum I mean.'

'Well it's hard to say. I'll have to think about it.'

Beauvois scratched his nose. Apparently this topic made him uncomfortable.

'Maybe... maybe three hundred thousand in the last fifteen years, that's how long we've had the art society. There was one before that too actually. But so unprofessionally run, Monsieur Aubert had –'

'You think it was three hundred thousand euro?'

'I can't say exactly off the top of my head. About that, I reckon.'

'So they were substantial donations then.'

'Indeed. The individual amounts add up. But the

eighty thousand, if I'm not mistaken, was the highest single amount.'

'And how were the other amounts used?'

'Oh, well that has been documented very carefully, every detail, you're free to take a look at our books.' Beauvois was looking somewhat indignant.

'I meant in broad terms, what kinds of projects were implemented with these funds?'

'Renovation work at the *Julia Hotel*, converting that section of the museum. If you only knew how much sanitation systems in such old buildings cost. A whole new floor in three rooms. The inner insulation, I could –'

'Pierre-Louis Pennec's death must be quite a blow to the art society. I'm sure you can't have many supporters who are quite that generous.'

'Well not many, no. That's true. But it's not like we can complain. We've been able to persuade a huge number of local businesses to get involved, not just private individuals. But yes, it's a great loss to our society. Pierre-Louis was a generous soul!'

'I'm sure that Monsieur Pennec would have wanted to protect your work beyond his death.' His sentence had been awkwardly phrased, Dupin knew that. But he was very interested in finding out whether Beauvois knew anything about the provisions of the will. And when you couldn't ask something directly, bizarrely vague sentences could sometimes come in handy.

'What do you mean, Monsieur le Commissaire? That he remembered us in his will?'

Dupin hadn't reckoned with Beauvois being so direct. 'Yes. I suppose that's exactly what I meant.'

'I don't know anything about that, Monsieur le Commissaire. Monsieur Pennec never so much as hinted at anything like that. Never, not even once. We never spoke about it.'

A mobile with an irritating ringtone went off. Monsieur Beauvois reached into the pocket of his rather baggy dark blue jacket. 'Hello?'

He smiled conspiratorially at Dupin. 'Ah. I see. Go ahead.'

Beauvois listened carefully to the person on the other end of the line for a while. Then his voice suddenly became curt. 'No, that's not how I see it at all. Not in the slightest. I'll be in touch. We'll discuss it. Yes, *au revoir*.' He hung up, smiled at Dupin again and continued smoothly. 'It would of course be very fortunate... in the midst of this catastrophe of course. Very fortunate for our work. But I really don't know anything about it. About any kind of provision along those lines in his will.' He blinked. 'And I'm not counting on it... even though I don't know either way.'

Beauvois was doing this in style. Or else what he said really was true.

'Anything else then?'

Beauvois looked confused.

'I mean, did anything strike you about Monsieur Pennec when you saw him on Tuesday, a change in his behaviour, in his appearance? Whatever it might be, any insignificant detail could be important.'

'No.' The answer came without hesitation.

'Did his health seem to you to be affected in any way?'

'His health?'

'Yes.'

'No... I mean, I didn't notice anything about him in particular. He was very old. You could tell he was feeling his age more in the last few years. But his mind was totally alert and still razor sharp. Did you have anything specific in mind?'

This was exactly what Dupin thought he would say.

'Do you know Pierre-Louis Pennec's half-brother?'

'André Pennec? No. I just know that he exists. He wasn't here very often. I've only been in Pont-Aven for thirty years. I'm from Lorient. I don't know all the stories. André Pennec had already left Finistère by the time I came to Pont-Aven. All I know is there was a serious quarrel. Something very personal I think.'

'And his relationship with his son?'

'I don't think I can really judge that either. Pierre-Louis Pennec was such a discreet person, you know, a man of firm principles. He would never have said anything if the relationship hadn't been all that good. There was a lot of talk about the relationship between father and son. Here in the village I mean.'

'Really? What were people saying?'

'You shouldn't take this very seriously.'

'I won't. But maybe I should at least know what the gossip is, eh?'

Beauvois gave him an amused, knowing look. 'People used to say that the father wasn't too pleased with his son.'

'Really?'

'I can actually imagine, that... Well, one thing was for sure, you know, you could see it straight off. Pennecness, that typical Pennecness, Loic Pennec didn't really have it. The desire for something big. To create something that mattered. Not every generation inherited that.'

'And you think this was obvious? Obvious to everyone?'

'Oh yes, anyone with eyes could see it. It's sad. We'd resigned ourselves to it here in the village. Myself included.'

'Here in the village?'

'Yes. The village is a… a close community. You just don't know it well enough. Don't think about the few weeks of the summer when there are thousands of outsiders here. Think of the rest of the year. We're very much left on our own. So inevitably people are very close to one another. Everyone knows a lot about everyone else, that's just how it has to be.'

'Did they fight? Were there any arguments?'

'Oh no, that wasn't it. Not as far as I know.'

Beauvois' forehead creased.

'Was there much talk about the son?'

'There used to be. Not so much now. At some point it just became clear.'

'What became clear?'

'That he isn't a real Pennec. That's all.'

'And did he know there were rumours going round about him?'

'I'm sure he must have. He felt it. He failed at everything.'

'Then why has his father left him the hotel to run?'

'Has he really?'

'Wouldn't you assume so?'

'Well, absolutely. I certainly would.' Beauvois looked a bit shocked. 'I don't think there was any other option.

134

Pierre-Louis Pennec would never have wanted to cause a scandal under any circumstances. And that would have been a very big thing in every possible sense. If the hotel had gone to someone else, I mean.'

'Who else could have taken over the hotel?'

'Well, nobody. That's what I mean: the *Central* – it just *is* the Pennec family. Family and tradition were sacred for Pierre-Louis. A non-Pennec in charge of the *Central* – that would have been unthinkable. And Pierre-Louis Pennec was clever enough, you know, to have established Madame Mendu in the hotel years ago, and she can run it after Madame Lajoux... exactly as Pierre-Louis Pennec would have wanted it to be run. Under his son's leadership of course.' Beauvois was visibly uncomfortable with this topic now.

'This is all quite complicated.'

'Yes. Very complicated, Monsieur le Commissaire. And I shouldn't be going around talking about all of these things. I think I've probably already said too much.'

'Did you have any other joint projects? You and Pierre-Louis Pennec I mean?'

'We used to discuss so many different things whenever we met. But there was nothing specific recently. No specific plans I mean. Except for the little photography exhibition. Yes, we were seriously considering that. He would have liked to have seen those photos, the ones I mentioned earlier, on display sometime.'

'Did you speak about that on Tuesday too?'

'Yes, briefly. I brought it up but then we didn't go into it. Pierre-Louis Pennec was focused on the brochure on Tuesday, it was very important to him. And the building work in the museum too.'

'Did Pennec request the meeting?'

'Yes, on Monday evening. We always agreed to meet up at short notice.'

'He didn't seem different to you that day in any way?'

'He seemed full of energy. Very impatient.'

If he were honest, Dupin really didn't know where he should be steering the conversation at this point. But he had learnt a huge amount. He thought Beauvois was an odd character; he seemed to be playing some sort of role. Apart from all that, there was something bothering Dupin, deep down. Something vague, all day long, stronger and more urgent now after this conversation with Beauvois. He didn't know what it was, but it was making him uneasy.

They had already polished off the red mullet. It had actually been exquisite, grilled, just the way Dupin liked it. That little hint of bitterness to the pure white, firm flesh, it was simply sublime. Although he found there was never much fish left after it had been filleted. They had also drunk a second glass of Sancerre each, although Dupin really hadn't wanted another.

Beauvois broke the silence that had descended, 'Now, we should be speaking to Maurice about dessert.'

'Oh not for me today. I'm sure they're excellent. But no thank you. I still have a lot to do.'

'You're really missing out, Monsieur le Commissaire.'

'I'm sure I am. But I have to get going. You stay and enjoy your dessert.'

'All right, that sounds like an order.' Beauvois laughed, a frank, relieved laugh. 'I'll stay then. We pensioners have earned this.'

'Thank you, Monsieur Beauvois. You've been really

helpful.' Dupin was glad to be finally getting shot of Beauvois.

'I hope you make progress with your investigation.'

'Thank you. *Au revoir*.'

Dupin stood up, held out his hand to Monsieur Beauvois and was already a few metres away when it suddenly occurred to him that he hadn't paid. He turned on his heel to find Beauvois already smiling at him.

'It was my pleasure, Monsieur le Commissaire.'

'No, I can't accept, I mean –'

'I insist.'

'Okay... yes, well thank you very much then, Monsieur Beauvois.'

'It was a pleasure. *Au revoir*.'

'Have a nice day.'

Dupin left the restaurant extremely quickly.

It was half past three now. The Pennecs would be at Madame Denis' office. Dupin wanted to speak to both of them again but their appointment with the notary wouldn't take too long. He decided he would just drop in on them later. He had time to make a few calls now. He could go to his hidden bench where he would have some peace and quiet. It wasn't far.

The minute he turned off the path there wasn't a soul in sight. He stood in front of the bench right by the water and watched the rapids. Two trout darting here and there. If you forgot for a moment that you were just a few metres away from the Atlantic, this looked just like the village his father came from. It was on the other side of France, in the foothills of the mountains right in the middle of the Jura. This wasn't the first time he had been struck by the similarity. The Doubs was a little river in Orgêt, just like the Aven was here. It had the same atmosphere to it, it really was uncanny. His father, Gaspard Dupin, had loved that little village, even after living in Paris for a very long time and marrying Anna, an upper-class Parisian who could not have been more Parisian if she'd tried and who to this day would rather die than leave Paris. At the age of seventeen Gaspard had left his village and its one hundred inhabitants on the edge of the mountains, gone to the capital and entered the police service there where he had risen quite quickly to the rank of Chief Commissaire. He died of a heart attack aged forty-one; Dupin had been six at the time. He didn't remember much about his father, but he did remember them going trout-fishing together in the Doubs.

Dupin realised his mind was wandering. He got out his mobile. Le Ber was on the line immediately.

'Monsieur le Commissaire?'

'I've just come from a meal with Beauvois.'

'And?'

'I'm not quite sure.'

'An oddball I reckon. And not entirely harmless. The Pennecs would like to speak to you again, I thought you should know. They called late morning and asked to have a meeting with you soon. And the mayor of Pont-Aven was here, Monsieur Goyard. Also the Prefect was trying to get in touch with you, he said it was urgent.'

'What do you mean by "not entirely harmless"?'

'I... I can't hear you. It's loud on your end – are you at the river again?'

Dupin didn't answer, just repeated his question much more loudly.

Le Ber was silent for a long time. 'I don't know.'

Dupin ran his hand through his hair. He knew it was pointless asking any questions when Le Ber spoke like this. But it drove him mad. Every time they were in the middle of a complex case, he would suddenly come up with these mysterious sentences – without any explanation. As much as he wanted to, Dupin couldn't deny that they had an effect on him.

'What about you and Labat, how are your inquiries coming along?'

'We've made some progress with the telephone call lists. With the main line that is, the calls that were made to or from here. We've listed the calls according to destination, distance and region. Two thirds were to Pont-Aven and the surrounding region. Most of those to Quimper and Brest. And we have lots of calls to Paris, mainly private numbers. Probably guests. Most of the guests at the *Central* are from Paris. Then a few other calls to Paris. Three conversations with the Ministry of Tourism. Three to a cake company. Two to the Musée d'Orsay.'

'The Ministry of Tourism and the Musée d'Orsay?'

'Yes.'

'Why?'

'We don't know yet.'

'Try and find out. I want to know who made those calls from the hotel. And why.'

Dupin knew the Musée d'Orsay, rather well in fact.

A girlfriend of his had worked there for a long time; she was in Arles now. He had visited many times and had loved it.

'When were these calls?'

'Both on Tuesday, one at half eight in the morning, the other at half eleven.'

'Okay. I'll be back at the hotel soon. But first I'm going to see the Pennecs. Has Salou said anything else about the break-in?'

'Just that he hasn't found anything yet. Not even traces of footprints. He's pretty much assuming it's a case of someone playing a terrible joke or else some kind of diversionary tactic.'

'Nonsense… Has anyone been in the room today?'

'Nobody. Only Labat and I have the key. And you of course.'

There was a pause. Le Ber knew that the Commissaire sometimes hung up without saying goodbye if he felt the conversation was over. 'Are you still there, Monsieur le Commissaire?'

Dupin again began his answer with a hesitation. 'I want to go into the restaurant again.' Dupin spoke very firmly, although he was really speaking more to himself than Le Ber.

'Is there anything I should be doing?'

Again there was a pause and while Le Ber was asking again whether the Commissaire was still there, Dupin hung up.

'Yes?'

Madame Pennec was standing in the doorway. She was looking Dupin right in the eye, her gaze somewhat reproachful. It occurred to him that he hadn't prepared any kind of strategy for this conversation; he couldn't just ask how the reading of the will had gone.

'Inspector Le Ber tells me you've asked to speak to me.'

Madame Pennec composed herself. 'Yes, of course. That's what we wanted. Do come in. My husband just wanted to have a lie down. He's burnt out. Emotionally I mean. I'll get him, if you could wait in the drawing room.'

Dupin already knew where it was. Loic Pennec appeared on the stairs a few minutes later.

'Monsieur le Commissaire. I'm so glad you've come.'

Pennec looked absolutely awful. His face haggard, his eyes red.

'No problem.'

Pennec glanced at his wife. 'First of all we obviously wanted to know how the investigation is going. Whether you've made progress yet. And how your investigation into what happened last night is going, too.'

'We have made progress, Monsieur Pennec, I can assure you. Although we don't have a smoking gun, as they say, the investigations will continue. The more we know, the more complicated the case is becoming.' Dupin paused. 'And we have nothing new on the broken windowpane and the possible break-in last night.'

'Yes, I can imagine you have a lot on your plate at the moment.' Pennec tried to smile but he couldn't manage it.

'That's exactly it. But this is our job.'

'And the other thing,' Madame Pennec's voice sounded

strained, 'the other thing we wanted to ask is how you foresee your work in the hotel going? I mean all the rooms that are locked up, all of that. I'm sure you can see that this isn't easy for us. The tourist season has started. My husband is responsible for everything now,' she broke off for a moment, 'and he wants to handle this new responsibility properly since he's been landed with it in this terrible twist of fate. I'm sure you understand.'

'Of course, Madame Pennec, I understand completely. If you tell me exactly what you mean then maybe we can help.'

'When will everything be back to normal in the hotel? The tourist season with no restaurant, how's that meant to work? The guests quite rightly expect the *Central*'s restaurant to be open. And normally the restaurant is used as the breakfast room too. The guests always have to come first.'

'Are you asking when we will be finished using the crime scene for our investigations?' Dupin was familiar with this situation. It was always the same. 'It's hard to say. Every murder case I solve takes on a rhythm all of its own.'

Catherine Pennec briefly seemed to be considering carrying on but didn't.

'Does your father and father-in-law's will contain what you expected, I mean, did you expect those conditions?'

Dupin's sudden question surprised them both. Madame and Monsieur Pennec looked irritated. It took a while for them to react, but Madame Pennec was first.

'So you already know what was in the will?'

'Obviously examining the contents of the will is one of the first things police do in a murder case.'

'Of course.'

Madame Pennec looked somewhat abashed, Loic Pennec noticeably calm.

'As I'm sure you can imagine, we... we had expected slightly different provisions, that's not something we can deny... But fundamentally I think it corresponds exactly to our expectations... to what my father and I have discussed time and again for years. I'm taking over the hotel.'

'That is really the core of the will.' Madame Pennec's voice shook a little. But she had herself under control.

'We assumed, and I'm sure this is something you'll be asking about, that all of my father's real estate would be part of our inheritance. I think we were justified in assuming that.'

'Of course. Why were Madame Lajoux, Monsieur Delon and the art society all remembered in the will? I mean, these are high value properties.'

'My father-in-law was a very generous man, a man who really valued family as well as his friends.'

Loic Pennec came to his wife's aid. 'I'm sure you understand what my wife is trying to say. Friendship and of course his work were very important for my father – the hotel, the tradition, the artists, all of that – and so he expressed that in his will. We obviously respect that completely. His will corresponds exactly to his life.'

It was clear from both their faces how upset they were by the will – and also how much they were trying to hide it. But Dupin didn't think the will had come as a shock to them. They looked more nervous than shocked.

'Yes, of course. I understand. So are you still selling honey?' Again the question was abrupt.

'We never really got it off the ground.' Madame Pennec had rushed to answer before her husband could.

'We thought it over for a long time. It could have been a very lucrative business. But we ditched it in the end. It would have been all-consuming, if it were done properly I mean. And after all it was always clear that my husband would one day take over the hotel.'

'But there was already a workshop.'

The Pennecs looked at Dupin in astonishment. 'You mean my father's shed?'

'Yes, on the plot of land where Monsieur Delon lives.' This last sentenced had slipped out of Dupin's mouth very curtly.

'You're right. The shed would have been ideal for setting up a workshop. We actually did consider it.'

'Was there anything your father used to worry about?'

There was absolute confusion on Catherine and Loic Pennec's faces now. The question was as abstract as it was open.

'What do you mean?' asked Loic Pennec.

'Something that was often on your father's mind?'

'I really don't know what you mean, Monsieur le Commissaire. The hotel was my father's life. And it was constantly on his mind. The whole time.'

'I mean other things.'

'Such as?'

'That's what I'm asking you.'

There was silence.

'Did you know about your father's heart condition?'

'Heart condition?'

'A serious one.'

'No. What do you mean? What heart condition?'

'He didn't have much longer to live.'

'My father? He didn't have much longer to live? How do you know?' Pennec's face was ashen, he looked utterly distraught.

'Darling, calm down. It can't do him any harm. He's already dead.' Madame Pennec noticed the black humour in what she'd just said. 'I mean,' she stammered, 'I mean it's simply awful.' Trailing off, she laid a hand on her husband's cheek.

'Docteur Pelliet informed me yesterday. Doctor-patient confidentiality and all that. He examined your father at the beginning of the week and advised him to have surgery straight away. Your father seems not to have told anyone about this.'

'Monsieur le Commissaire,' Madame Pennec beat her husband to it, 'Pierre-Louis Pennec was an incredible person, but also very solitary. He never wanted to bother anyone. Maybe he wanted to spare us unnecessary worry. And lots of old people have weak hearts. You shouldn't be trying to make our grief even worse.'

'Of course, Madame Pennec. I just thought it might be important to you to know something so significant about your father and father-in-law.'

Catherine Pennec looked embarrassed for a moment. 'Of course.'

'Thank you for your frankness, Monsieur le Commissaire. Did my father suffer… I mean, was he in pain?'

'Well how did he seem to you, was his health giving

145

him any trouble? Didn't anything about him strike you as different?'

Pennec still looked extremely distressed. 'No. I mean, I don't know. Nothing in particular. He did seem exhausted sometimes. There was that.'

'But he was ninety-one. If you're ninety-one you're going to feel exhausted sometimes. He was slowing down of course. Had been for the last few years.'

Pennec looked somewhat disapprovingly at his wife.

'That's just what I think. It's normal for a ninety-one year old to get tired more quickly than someone in their eighties or seventies. But he was still in very good shape for his age. And he didn't have any obvious physical weaknesses. Not even towards the end.'

Pennec nodded in agreement with his wife, looking relieved. 'I'm going to speak to Docteur Pelliet sometime. I want to know exactly what was wrong with my father.'

'I completely understand, Monsieur Pennec.'

There was a long pause, a pleasant one, which allowed everyone to get their thoughts in order. Dupin got out his Clairefontaine and leafed through it as though he were looking for something.

'And in the last few days, I want to ask you again, did anything specific strike you about your father? You did see him this week. What did you speak about?'

'Various things, as usual. The fish, the shoals of mackerel, his boat, the hotel. The start of the season was his main topic recently. About how the season was just getting going.'

'Are things getting off to a good start?'

'Yes, thank you, a very good start. My father was

sure this was going to be a great season. Even in the financial crisis we didn't have to deal with any real losses.'

'Only the cheap hotels did, Monsieur le Commissaire, not the better ones.'

'Were you involved in your father's patronage work?'

'I think one can... I don't think he involved anyone in these things. He saw it as his personal mission. And he enjoyed it.'

'Did you know that there had just been discussions about a relatively large sum he wanted to donate? To the art society and the museum. For renovations.'

'Pierre-Louis Pennec was a great patron.' Madame Pennec had spoken in an assiduously solemn tone.

'What kind of sum was being discussed?' asked Loic Pennec in a somewhat cautious voice.

'Oh, I don't know the specific amount. But it was substantial.'

'And you have no idea how much it might have been?' Madame Pennec had leaned forward slightly as she said this.

'I really couldn't say.' Dupin supposed they were now wondering whether this amount would be taken out of their inheritance.

'I'd also like to ask what else you spoke about in your last conversations, Monsieur Pennec?'

'Minor hotel issues.'

'What do you mean by that?' asked Dupin.

'My father used to tell me about hotel issues all the time. What had to be done. He spoke about buying new televisions for the rooms, for example. The ones we have are really very old and he wanted to get in some modern, chic flat screens. He hated televisions but thought these awful contraptions at least wouldn't take up so much room. And of course when you take all of the rooms into account it's a big investment.'

'You spoke about that this week?'

'Yes. Amongst other things.'

'And what do you mean when you say you spoke about it?'

'I don't understand the question.'

'I mean, did he tell you about it or did you discuss it together?'

'He told me about it… and then we discussed it, yes.' He looked enquiringly at Dupin as though wanting to be told he'd given the right answer.

'And was there anything your father was concerned about recently, a big issue?'

Madame Pennec intervened sulkily. 'You've already asked about that. We didn't notice anything unusual.'

'But you've got to keep going over things again and again in your mind. You might forget something when you're so emotional.'

Dupin found himself impressed with Loic Pennec's poise.

'No. I don't know of anything that was particularly worrying my father recently. Although of course I now know that… I'm sure his health was very much on his mind, for the last weeks and months, most of all in the last days of course, since the diagnosis. I can only imagine.'

Dupin had suddenly started to feel uneasy while Loic Pennec was speaking. All at once he caught hold of that shadowy thought that had been going round and round in his head ever since he had spoken to Beauvois.

'I think… we've covered a lot of ground here… you have been very helpful once again, Monsieur Pennec, Madame Pennec.'

Dupin wanted to leave. He wanted to follow up this new lead. The abrupt end to the conversation didn't seem to bother either of the Pennecs.

'That goes without saying, Monsieur le Commissaire. We want to help in any way we possibly can. Please don't hesitate to drop in any time if you think we could help.'

Madame Pennec nodded her agreement, looking perfectly relaxed again. As though in response to some secret signal, all three of them stood up at the same time.

Loic Pennec was speaking again. 'We would like to thank you very much for your hard work. And I would ask that you excuse us if we sometimes react somewhat… emotionally at the moment. We –'

'I totally understand, Monsieur Pennec. The way I see it, I have it on my conscience now, bothering you with all these things in your grief. As I said yesterday, it really is an imposition.'

'No, no, Monsieur le Commissaire. It's the right thing to do.' Madame Pennec had already gone on ahead and opened the door.

'*Au revoir* Madame, *au revoir* Monsieur.'

'*Au revoir* Monsieur le Commissaire. I'm sure we'll see each other again soon.'

Dupin stood in the doorway. 'Oh, Monsieur Pennec?'

Both Pennecs looked enquiringly at the Commissaire.

'Just one more little thing. I wonder whether we

could meet in the hotel, late morning tomorrow? That would be useful. You could show me round.'

'Around the hotel? No problem. And what... I mean, what's this for?'

'Nothing specific. I'd like to go over the whole hotel with you once and take our time over it.'

Louis Pennec looked faintly offended. 'Of course, Monsieur le Commissaire. We have an appointment with the undertaker at eleven, but apart from that I'm free. I have a lot to do in the hotel now anyway.'

'Great, thank you. See you tomorrow.'

'See you tomorrow.'

Labat and Le Ber were already waiting when Dupin got to the hotel. Le Ber was smoking outside the front door. He rarely smoked; Dupin had seen him do it perhaps three or four times in the last few years. Labat was leaning casually against the doorframe in the entrance. He looked decidedly sullen when he saw Dupin coming and made a beeline for him straight away.

'Monsieur le Commissaire, I've got to –'

'I want to go to the restaurant. Alone.'

'There are a few urgent things we need to discuss. I have to inform you that –'

'We'll discuss everything. Later.'

'We've –'

'Not now.'

'But Monsieur le Commissaire –'

Dupin simply walked past Labat. Le Ber followed Dupin with his eyes and took a deep pull on his cigarette, all with minimal movement. Dupin was already in the foyer of the hotel, taking out his keys and opening the door to the restaurant. Labat wouldn't let it go. He was standing right next to Dupin now.

'We've also –'

'Not now, Labat.' Dupin's voice was sharp. He went into the room, closed the door behind him immediately and turned the key twice. He had forgotten Labat within seconds.

All at once there was silence. The insulation really was excellent. The air-conditioning was a faint, low buzzing in the background. It was a constant hum, so you really had to listen out for it. Dupin looked around. He walked a little further into the room and stood still. He let his gaze drift slowly over the walls and ceiling. The air-conditioner, the unit itself, was nowhere to be seen. It must have been in the adjoining room or maybe in the kitchen. Every two metres or so, there were inconspicuous air vents about thirty centimetres long right the way across the entire ceiling in matte aluminium casing. This was where the air was coming out. It must be powerful air-conditioning and it must have required extensive building work.

Dupin walked into the middle of the room, keeping his eyes glued to the walls and the paintings. There were twenty-five of these by his estimation, maybe thirty, by artists from the famous artists' colony such as Paul Sérusier, Laval, Emile Bernard, Armand Seguin, Jacob Meyer de Haan and of course Gauguin, and also some by artists he wasn't familiar with at all. Dupin had heard a great story once. Juliette had told it to him. She had still been a student of art history at the *École des Beaux-Arts*. They had been travelling round Coullioure and Cadaqués. The story she told him was a crazy one, but true. Dupin was moving very slowly, looking at each painting in turn with the utmost concentration.

Dupin had spent three quarters of an hour in this way, going through the restaurant and bar. There had been a few knocks at the door, but Dupin hadn't really noticed them. Then at six o'clock he opened the door himself. Both inspectors were standing across the way at the little reception desk. This time it was Le Ber who came hurrying up to him.

'Monsieur le Commissaire, did something happen?' His voice was agitated. Labat had stayed where he was and he still looked put out.

'Who is the greatest art expert in this town? I mean an expert on the famous painters who used to come here.'

Le Ber looked stunned.

'Art? No idea. Monsieur Beauvois I reckon. Maybe someone who works at the gallery, or the new art teacher at the school here. We would have to ask someone.'

Dupin thought about it. 'No. I want an expert who isn't from Pont-Aven. I want someone from out of town.'

'An art expert from out of town? What's going on?' Labat had come up and was standing in front of Dupin too. 'It would be incredibly helpful if you could keep us in the loop.'

Dupin left the hotel without saying a word. He turned left, then left again and found himself in the quiet little side street. He took his phone out. 'Nolwenn? Are you still there?'

'Monsieur le Commissaire?'

'I need your help. I need an art expert. An expert on the Pont-Aven School. Somebody who knows their work, the paintings. Not someone from Pont-Aven.'

'Not someone from Pont-Aven?'

'No.'

'Doesn't matter where, just so long as they're not from Pont-Aven? And an expert.'

'Yes.'

'Okay. I'll sort it.'

'I need them very quickly.'

'Do you mean immediately? By this evening?'

'Exactly.'

'It's half past seven now.'

'Well then as quickly as possible please.'

'And do you want them to go to the *Central*?'

'Yes.'

Nolwenn hung up.

Dupin stood still for a few moments. He was thinking. Then he went further along the alleyway until it forked. This time he walked straight to the river and across the overly ornate wooden bridge to the other side, to the harbour. And he just stood there. The sea had come in again, the tide had almost reached its highest point, the boats were sitting proud and upright in the water. He watched the seesawing ships' masts as they danced about in wild disarray. The little waves never reached the boats at the same time or in the same way and so each boat had its own rhythm. Each one dancing alone – and yet all together, in chaotic harmony. Dupin liked the sounds they made, the little bells at the very tips of the masts.

He walked a distance along the harbour, his hands

interlaced behind his back. If it was as he suspected, there was something unbelievable at the bottom of all this. A great story. He knew it would sound far-fetched.

Only when he reached the last house right at the end of the harbour, did he turn around and take a circuitous stroll back to the hotel. He thought everything through over and over again.

It took Nolwenn exactly thirty-two minutes to call back. The art historian was called Marie Morgane Cassel. She was from Brest, from the renowned *Université de Bretagne Occidentale*. Nolwenn quoted articles, experts from Paris. She was probably the best. Nolwenn had got Cassel's mobile number via a series of different manoeuvres and through the use of the highest police authority – the homicide division –had reached her immediately. Marie Morgane Cassel had been astonishingly laid back, Nolwenn said, even though Nolwenn hadn't actually been able to tell her even in the broadest terms why she was needed. It must all seem like quite an adventure. Nolwenn had informed her that the police urgently needed her as a consultant on a case and that if she agreed, two officers from Brest would bring her to Pont-Aven that very evening. On a Saturday. Immediately. Madame Cassel had simply asked whether she should pack an overnight bag.

Le Ber and Labat were eating in the breakfast room when Dupin got back to the *Central*. Madame Mendu had been looking after them, feeding them regional specialities: rillettes (scallop rillettes were Dupin's favourite), paté, Breton goat's cheese, various types of mustard, baguettes and a bottle of red Faugères. Dupin sat down and ate with them.

Nolwenn had been speaking to Labat and Le Ber. They knew that the Commissaire was expecting someone and indeed who that someone was. To Dupin's surprise, neither asked any questions; they didn't even make an indirect attempt to get anything out of him, even Labat, who seemed bizarrely cheerful now. Nolwenn must have had a word with them. Dupin didn't think there could be any other explanation for it and he didn't ask. Nobody knew as well as Nolwenn that you just had to leave him alone when things got serious, that's the way he was. But perhaps it was just the calming effect of the food and red wine.

Le Ber reported on his trip to the harbour to see the man who cut Pennec's hair on Monday afternoon. The barber, a Monsieur Lannuzel, had laughed when Le Ber asked what they'd discussed – they had talked very little. They had never talked much and this Monday was no different. Pennec had been occupied by papers, but Monsieur Lannuzel had no idea what kind of papers they had been. Labat was silent during Le Ber's report and then began presenting his own results with little enthusiasm. They had almost finished going through the telephone call lists now. That was important, and Dupin would take a look at them himself tomorrow morning. But his mind was elsewhere for now. And he had eaten a lot.

The police car arrived a little before ten. Dupin had gone into the bar on his own again after dinner. It was perfectly quiet again, although the square was quite busy now. He jumped at a knock on the door. He hadn't locked it. Le Ber came in.

'The professor from Brest has arrived, Monsieur le Commissaire. Marie Morgane Cassel. We brought her upstairs to the conference room.'

'No, no, she's to come down here.'

'Here? To the crime scene?'

'Exactly.'

'As you wish. Nolwenn has organised everything for Madame Cassel. There's a room here at the hotel for her.'

'Good.'

'And one of the local officers finally got hold of Commissaire Derrien just now. It wasn't easy. He's up a mountain somewhere with practically no reception. They could hardly understand him; the conversation kept breaking up.'

'Up a mountain? I thought he was on La Réunion.'

'They're doing a tour of the mountains after the wedding, right up to the Piton des Neiges. It's a volcano, the highest peak in the Indian Ocean. They'll be back in Saint-Denis in two days.'

'What are they doing up a volcano after a wedding?' Dupin sighed. 'What does it matter anyway? We'll cope without Derrien.'

So this is how it would be. It was on the tip of his tongue to ask Le Ber how he came to be so knowledgeable about volcanic islands off the African coast, but he left it.

'I think so too, Monsieur le Commissaire. I'll fetch the professor now.'

A minute later Madame Cassel was standing in the doorway. She was very young for a professor – mid-thirties, he guessed. Long, fly-away, black-brown hair, sparkling blue eyes, a striking mouth, slim. A dark blue, figure-hugging dress.

She stayed in the doorway.

'*Bonsoir* Madame, I'm Georges Dupin, the Commissaire on this case. I'm investigating the murder of Pierre-Louis Pennec. You might have heard about it. I hope my colleagues have already told you a little about what's going on.' Dupin was irritated. What he'd just said was nonsense.

'Actually, I don't know anything at all yet. The two policemen who brought me here were very friendly but they said they didn't know anything themselves. And all their colleague could tell me was that it was about the murder of that hotelier that was in all the newspapers, and that I could potentially help in some way. They said I would be told exactly how when I got here.'

Dupin was glad he hadn't read any newspapers today.

'I'm sorry. That's my fault. It's very rude to let you get into a police car without anyone telling you why, even in the broadest terms. And it's very kind of you to get in and come here anyway.'

There was the hint of a smile on Marie Morgane Cassel's face. 'So what's all this about, Monsieur le Commissaire? What can I do for you?'

'I have a theory. It might be absurd.'

Madame Cassel was smiling broadly now. 'And I can help you with it?'

Now Dupin had to smile. 'I think you can.'

'Good. Let's get started.'

'All right then.'

Marie Morgane Cassel was still standing in the doorway.

'Come in. I'd like to shut the door.'

He locked it and then went to the bar without saying another word. Madame Cassel followed.

'What kind of estimate would you put on a Gauguin of this size?'

Dupin pointed to one of the paintings on the wall, one of three dogs drinking out of a bowl on a table.

'That's a very famous painting of Gauguin's, *Still Life with Three Puppies* – the fruit, the glasses, the bowl, these objects seem so incredibly familiar, but look closely and out of nowhere you start to see how the spatial relationships are fluctuating. You can see Gauguin's typical approach very clearly here... Oh, I'm sorry, that's not what you asked at all...'

'I don't mean this particular painting, it's just an example. I mean the value of a Gauguin of this size.'

'Gauguin often used this format, around ninety centimetres by seventy. But the value is not just a question of the size; it also depends on the period. Most of all it depends on the significance of the painting within his oeuvre and in the history of art. And also of course on how crazy the art market is feeling at any given moment.'

'I'm thinking of a painting that Gauguin did here in Pont-Aven. Not directly after he arrived, a little while later.'

'Gauguin was in Pont-Aven four times between 1886 and 1894, although the length of his stay varied. Did you know that he lived right here? In this hotel?'

'I knew that, yes.'

'By his fourth stay, he wasn't even in Pont-Aven any more, strictly speaking. It had already become too much hassle for him so he lived and worked in Le Pouldu. The critical periods were definitely 1888 and then 1889 to 1891 – his second and third visits, this was when he produced his most important paintings, he...' The professor was in her element. She was clearly a passionate scholar. The information came pouring forth.

'Let's say a painting from the second or third visit. Just hypothetically.'

'There are some paintings approximately this size, which were produced during that time. You'll definitely know a few of them – *The Yellow Christ* of course, *Portrait of the Artist with the Yellow Christ*, or *Portrait of Madeleine Bernard* who was Laval's fiancée as well as being Gauguin's muse and long-term correspondent. Have you got a particular painting in mind?'

'No, no known painting,' he hesitated somewhat, 'I'm talking about a hitherto unknown painting.'

'An unknown large Gauguin from the years 1888, '89 or '90?' It was clear Marie Morgane Cassel was very excited. She was speaking more quickly now.

'Those are the years when he developed his revolutionary approach, which he then applied to everything he did: technique, colour, everything. It meant he was finally able to free himself from his ties to Impressionism. He had returned from his first trips to Panama and Martinique, and was already the leading light in the artists' group. In October he moved to Arles to live and work with Van Gogh –

which only lasted two months and ended in a terrible fight, during which Van Gogh famously cut off a bit of his own ear, you know that of course... Sorry, I'm going off topic again. An occupational hazard I think.'

'Exactly, a painting from those years.'

'It's highly unlikely, Monsieur Dupin. I don't think there are paintings from that time and of that size that we're not aware of.'

Dupin's voice grew quiet. 'I'm aware of one.' Even more quietly, almost inaudibly, he added: 'I think there is one hanging in this room. A hitherto unknown painting by Gauguin. From that time.'

There was a long pause during which Marie Morgane Cassel stared incredulously at the Commissaire. 'A genuine Gauguin? An unknown painting from one of his most important periods? You're insane, Monsieur Dupin. How could a real Gauguin have ended up here? Who would hang a Gauguin in a restaurant?'

Dupin nodded good-naturedly. He took a few steps towards the centre of the room. 'One night,' this was the story that Juliette had told him years ago, 'Picasso had eaten at a restaurant with a group of friends and it had turned into a long, wonderful evening. They ate and drank a huge amount. Picasso was in an extremely good mood and drew and painted all night on the paper tablecloths. When they went to pay, the landlord suggested he sign the tablecloth instead and leave it behind. And in the morning there was a Picasso, a real, large Picasso hanging on the wall of a country inn... Why couldn't a similar thing have happened here in Pont-Aven between Marie-Jeanne Pennec and Gauguin?'

Marie Morgane Cassel was silent.

'I know it sounds ridiculous. But maybe there was no safer place for a painting like this. Where nobody would ever have suspected a thing. Where it had always been and where everyone knew it. And Pierre-Louis Pennec could see the painting whenever he wanted.'

The art historian was still silent.

'Look, this room has an extremely high-tech air-conditioning system, who builds that kind of thing into a restaurant in Brittany? The air-conditioning is completely over the top. For the purposes of the restaurant, a much smaller, simpler unit would have been fine. Pierre-Louis Pennec must have invested a huge amount in it, not to mention the building work it needed. It's the kind of system that you only find in hospitals, massive offices... and museums.'

This was the shadowy thought that had stuck in his mind from the conversation with Beauvois. The thing about the air-conditioning. This was what had so preoccupied him this entire time, without him knowing what it was. And it wasn't just in his conversation with Beauvois that air-conditioning had come up – the unwieldy word was written half a dozen times in his notebook. Who needed it in Brittany at all? And a unit this size? And why only have air-conditioning in this one room? It all fitted perfectly, however ridiculous it sounded.

'So you think this would have been a reliable way of keeping the air humidity and temperature constant and –' Marie Morgane Cassel broke off and seemed to be thinking hard.

Dupin hadn't intended to let the professor in on his thoughts and the case to such an extent. That wasn't his style at all.

'Thirty million. Maybe more. Forty million. It's hard to say.'

Now it was Dupin's turn to be speechless. It was a long time before he could compose himself. 'You mean... thirty million euro?'

'Maybe forty million or even more.' In a casual-sounding voice she added, 'I know that Picasso story. It's true.' She had started moving slowly through the room, her eyes completely focused, scanning every single painting.

Thirty million. Maybe forty million. Or more. Dupin could feel goosebumps on his forearms. This was a motive. A huge motive. When there were sums like this at stake, anything was possible. There isn't much that people wouldn't do for that kind of money.

'A Sérusier, a Gauguin, a Bernard, an Anquetin, a Seguin, a Gauguin, a Gauguin. All copies. Good copies... Marie-Jeanne Pennec must have commissioned some of them herself, they're almost as old as the originals. Or they were given to her as gifts, that happened quite often too.'

She inspected each painting carefully as she moved from the bar, where they had been standing, towards the door. Dupin was watching her intently. Suddenly she stood still. In front of the last painting. Where there were no tables.

'This is ridiculous!' She was absolutely outraged.

'The painter – or the copyist, I should say – has made absurd mistakes here. This is meant to be one of Gauguin's most important paintings, *Vision after the Sermon* or *Jacob Wrestling with the Angel*, another painting from 1888.'

'And?' Dupin had positioned himself next to her and was staring at the painting, transfixed.

'A lot of infelicities have crept in here. The base colour, the red, it's a garish orange here. Overall it's a bit too big. There are more Breton farm women in this painting than there are in the original, and they're closer to the edge here. And above all, the priest is standing in the middle, underneath the tree trunk, do you see? That's wrong too.'

Marie Morgane Cassel was angrily pointing out the relevant parts of the painting as she spoke. 'In the original he's standing right in the corner. Bottom right. The whole perspective in this copy is wrong; it's like a wide-angle lens. You can see some landscape here at the top, a little bit of the horizon. In the other one… in the *real* painting, there's just a red expanse with the branches above it. This one almost has a larger maelstrom. Gauguin loved that maelstrom. But –'

She broke off. Froze, almost motionless. She leaned in as close to the painting as she could, until her eyes were only a few centimetres away from it, then examined it closely, starting from the bottom. It was a few minutes before she spoke again.

'It's astonishing! Just bizarre. An off-the-wall Gauguin… if he'd actually painted it. But he didn't. Even though it does clearly have an imitation of his signature.'

Dupin wasn't following. 'What do you mean?'

'Gauguin never did a painting like this. The painter of this piece has done an improvised version of Gauguin's painting.'

'And who painted it – I mean, who on earth came up with this painting?'

'No idea, any one of the hundred painters who imitated and did versions of Gauguin paintings. And still do. Someone who might also have painted the other paintings here, who knows? They're all very well done, by people who know their craft. They are familiar with Gauguin's style, his paintbrush, his way of working.'

'What you're saying is, you don't know of any such painting by Gauguin. No painting that looks like this one.' Dupin needed her to be absolutely clear on this point.

Marie Morgane Cassel took some time to answer. 'Yes. You're right. Strictly speaking that's all I can say.' Her gaze was still fixed on the painting, concentrating hard. 'An extraordinary piece of work. A fantastic painting. This imitator is very good.'

She shook her head. Dupin wasn't sure what that meant.

'But would you categorically rule it out as a Gauguin? I mean, as being painted by Gauguin himself.'

'Yes I would. Even without spectroscopic analysis, you can see that the paint here is titanium white. It first appeared in modern art in 1920. Gauguin painted with a compound of white lead, barium sulphate and zinc white. And the craquelure is not deep enough or advanced enough to be a one-hundred-and-thirty-year-old painting.'

Dupin ran his hand through his hair. There was still another possibility. He wasn't finished yet. 'Maybe *this* is just a copy. Like the other paintings. And the real painting is in a safe somewhere.'

'And Monsieur Pennec had the expensive air-conditioning system installed for a copied, almost worthless painting?'

Dupin was silent for a long time now. 'In the days leading up to his death, Pierre-Louis Pennec tried to get in touch with the Musée d'Orsay.' Dupin had said this half-heartedly, as though this was a last ditch effort.

'The Musée d'Orsay? Are you sure?'

'Yes.'

'Do you think he would have... if there really had been a Gauguin that is... decided to tell someone about the painting? An expert? I mean, why now? And...' Now Madame Cassel was at a loss.

'At the beginning of the week, Pennec found out that he was terminally ill, liable to die at any moment.' Again, Dupin was astonished at how much he was telling her. His inspectors didn't know a thing about any of this.

'He was terminally ill? And someone killed him?'

'Yes. But please keep that confidential.'

Marie Morgane Cassel's forehead creased. 'Could I have a laptop with internet access please? I want to look up something about this particular year in Gauguin's life. About the *Vision* and the preliminary work and studies for it.'

'Sure, that sounds like a great idea.'

Dupin looked at his watch. It was half past eleven

now. He suddenly felt like he couldn't go on any longer. He was exhausted and didn't know what to do next. He went to the door without a word and opened it.

'Take all the time you need. We've booked you a room. I'll ask one of my inspectors to bring up a laptop for you.'

'That's great, I didn't think to bring mine with me.'

'Why would you? It's almost midnight. I'll see you tomorrow morning then. Shall we meet for breakfast?'

'Let's! Eight o'clock. That way I'll have a little more time.'

'All right then.'

Dupin went out into the foyer. Labat was standing at reception.

'Labat, Madame Cassel needs a laptop. Is there internet access in her room? We need it straight away.'

'Now?'

'Yes, now. It's for important research.' In a more confident tone, he added, 'And I want to see Salou tomorrow morning.'

'Salou called an hour ago wanting to speak to you about the break-in or whatever it was.'

'I'd like to see him. At seven o'clock. Half seven. Here in the restaurant. I want him to bring his equipment with him.'

Le Ber, who had said nothing this entire time, seemed to want to ask something, but decided against it. 'I don't know, it's –'

Dupin calmly interrupted Labat. 'Half past seven.'

Marie Morgane Cassel was standing in the doorway looking a bit lost. Dupin turned to her. 'Thank you so

166

much for everything you've already done, Madame.'

'No problem.' The professor smiled. Dupin was very pleased to see her smile. It had been a long, stressful day. He felt drained.

'I'll see you tomorrow morning then, Madame Cassel. Sleep well.'

'Thanks, I hope you sleep well too.'

'Yes, I should think I will.' And very soon, he hoped.

Labat had taken her bags and was making a show of climbing the stairs to the first floor. Madame Cassel followed him.

Dupin had started to get dizzy again in the last hour but he was going to drive back to Concarneau now. He'd be glad to be home.

Le Ber was standing in front of the hotel smoking when Dupin headed out into the night. Dupin looked at him just once, very briefly. He looked worn out too.

'*Bonne nuit*, Le Ber. See you tomorrow morning.'

'*Bonne nuit*, Monsieur le Commissaire.'

Dupin had parked his car on Place Gauguin itself, to the right of the hotel.

The journey home would take no more than fifteen minutes and he chose not to look at the speedometer. The streets were deserted. He had opened the huge sun roof on his XM to let in as much of the beautiful, mild summer's air as he could and to see this incredible starry sky. The Milky Way beamed bright and clear. He wanted to be closer to all of it. It helped, a little.

The Third Day

Salou was already there when Dupin walked into the *Central*. He was alone, no team with him. He was standing at the end of the bar and looked shattered. Dupin walked over to him.

'What's the news? What's going on?' asked Salou.

Dupin had expected Salou to take a more aggressive line with him. He had been convinced Salou would consider it an affront to be called in at this hour for no apparent reason. Not that Dupin was overly upset about having called him in so early. But Salou actually looked more nervous than anything else. Dupin had to focus, this was important.

'I want you to tell me how long the painting over there by the door has been hanging in comparison with the others. Or have they all been hanging here for the same length of time? Is there any trace evidence on this painting or the frame?'

'How long the painting has been hanging here? You want to know how long this cheap copy has been hanging in this room? That's what I came here for?'

Dupin walked over to the wall very calmly and positioned himself in front of the painting. 'I'm talking about this painting in this frame in comparison to the others. And yes, I want to know whether this painting has been hanging here as long as the others.'

'You've already said that. I have no idea what you're trying to get at. What's your hunch?'

Salou deserved an answer. But Dupin had no desire to give away even the slightest bit more. 'I want to know whether this painting here could, potentially, have been hung in the last few days. Surely that's not too difficult. This place must be dusted on a regular basis. Since the last dusting all of the paintings must have a certain –'

'I am quite familiar with how to do my job. Nothing in this room changed between yesterday and today. Nothing at all. And apparently not for a long time before that either. We compared the current room with photographs from recent years. We looked at the paintings too. They're hanging in the same arrangement as they have been for the last few years at least.'

'I know. No, I mean very specifically this painting.'

'And why do you want it compared to all the others? This is a nonsense task.'

'One or more paintings might have been replaced in the last few days.'

'I still don't know what you're driving at, particularly as this is the most idiotic of all the paintings here. Gauguin never painted a piece like that; some amateur came up with it. It doesn't get much more stupid than that. A mangled imitation of the *Vision after the Sermon*.'

Dupin couldn't hide his surprise at Salou's knowledge of Gauguin. 'So you know a lot about art?'

'Gauguin is my great passion, the whole artists' colony movement, I –' Salou broke off. He seemed to be asking himself why he was telling Dupin this. 'That's really neither here nor there of course. I'm asking you this formally and officially: is it essential for the Pennec murder case to know whether this painting was hung here for the first time a few days ago?' He was confrontational again.

'Absolutely, this question is of the utmost importance.' Dupin was sure that Salou wouldn't accept that from him and would take the way he'd phrased it as a further provocation – but it was true. That's exactly what it was.

'Then we'll get to work immediately, I'll call my team.'

Salou had excellent self-restraint, Dupin had to admit that.

'You don't know of any painting like this painted by Gauguin either?'

'No. As I said, the imitator has made ludicrous mistakes. A complete misrepresentation.'

'But overall. In theory. What do you think, couldn't this be a painting by Gauguin?'

'That question doesn't make any sense.'

'I know.'

Salou looked the Commissaire in the eye. He thought about it. Then he said: 'Well in a way, I suppose it's possible he painted it. It looks like a Gauguin.'

Now Dupin was confused. He felt very awkward – he had been readying himself for an attack. 'Thanks. I mean, thank you for sharing your opinion.' He cleared his throat.

'All right then. I'm going to call my colleagues now.' Salou reached into his jacket pocket. Without another word he left the room, clutching his mobile in his hand. Dupin didn't say anything either.

Dupin walked into the breakfast room a little before eight. He had asked that the other guests not be allowed in until half past. Marie Morgane Cassel was already sitting at one of the little tables, right in the corner by the window, a *grand crème* in front of her. There was a big basket on the table full of croissants, pains au chocolat, brioches and baguettes, along with various jams and butter. There was also a whole *gâteau breton* with its distinctive taste – extremely salty butter and a lot of sugar. There was even a huge basket of fruit and some yoghurt. Madame Mendu had made a real effort. In the midst of all these delicacies lay an open laptop.

'Good morning, Madame Cassel. Did you sleep well?'

The professor smiled pleasantly at Dupin, her head tilted slightly to one side. Her hair was still damp; she must have just come out of the shower.

'Good morning. I'm not a good sleeper actually, never have been.' She shrugged her shoulders. 'But it's not too bad. It was a very quiet night here, if that's what you mean. I was able to do my research in peace.'

Marie Morgane Cassel didn't look at all tired – on the contrary, in fact. She looked wide awake.

Dupin sat down at her table. 'Did you find anything?'

'There are no indications of a second *Vision after the Sermon,* a second painting that dealt with this theme, or even that Gauguin had worked on a different version.' She was really on top of things. 'But, in theory, it's not impossible.'

'What do you mean?'

'For one thing, Gauguin certainly did occasionally undertake multiple studies of a single subject if it was something that preoccupied him. Sometimes he did several paintings of one subject, which varied in certain things, motifs or viewpoints. There's a huge number of sketches, studies and even smaller preliminary studies for most parts and motifs of the *The Vision*. Many elements were varied across these. I've looked at everything again very carefully and found something quite astonishing.' She was beaming now.

'Look at this. I found something in the special archive of the Musée d'Orsay. A scientific databank, they scanned in all of Gauguin's material recently, a lot of the personal stuff too, which had been unknown or little known.'

She turned the laptop around. Dupin looked at the screen. There really wasn't much to see in the image.

'This is a sketch, fifteen centimetres by twelve. The quality of the scan isn't very good here. But you can see everything that matters.'

There were patterns all down the left hand side and along the bottom of the painting. They looked three-dimensional but were in fact just flat and white, heavily contoured in black. Right in the middle there was a tree trunk looming steeply upwards, with a few hints of branches along the top towards the right. But the most striking thing about this sketch was the colour. The whole background was a garish orange, as though it were the base colour of the piece of paper.

'He tried it out. Gauguin tried out this orange. It's unbelievable.'

Dupin wasn't sure what Madame Cassel meant.

'Now that I've seen this, a painting like the one hanging here in the restaurant – I mean a potential original of this painting – has become a bit more, how should I put it, more conceivable.'

'A lot more conceivable?'

Suddenly there was a loud knock. Dupin wanted to respond with a grumpy 'Not now', but Labat was already standing in the room. He was completely out of breath and deathly pale. His voice shook strangely.

'There's,' he gasped for breath, 'there's another body.'

For a moment neither Dupin nor Madame Cassel knew whether to laugh. Labat's entrance had looked like a bad scene in a bad play.

'You've got to come immediately, Monsieur le Commissaire.'

Dupin leapt up in the same theatrical and absurd way that Labat had burst in, and still didn't know what to say. 'Okay, yes. I'm coming,' he murmured.

The corpse was in bad shape. The arms and legs stuck out unnaturally from the body; the bones must have been broken in many places. His trousers and jumper were ripped in some places, tattered, like his skin and the flesh on his knees, his shoulders, his chest. The left hand side of his head had caved in. The storm-tossed cliffs were treacherous at this part of the coast. Towering upwards, thirty or forty metres above sea level and dropping away steeply, so rugged, so sharp-edged and cavernous with so many interlocking crags that even a short fall was disastrous. Loic Pennec must have hit a few of the narrow ledges before eventually landing on the huge rocks right at the breakwater.

Nobody would ever know whether he had survived the fall, spending hours and hours simply waiting for help to come. The heavy rain and the storm had swept away the blood and everything else along with it. The sand was dyed red between the large stones.

The wind came in brutal gusts, whipping the rain in front of it over and over again. It was half past eight but not yet light. The sky was a dramatic black, and huge clouds swarmed above the surface of the sea. Pennec was lying perhaps two hundred metres from Plage Tahiti, Dupin's favourite beach, with its two small islets just off the coast like a landscape painting. The beach was around ten minutes from Pont-Aven by car. Just yesterday holiday-makers had been enjoying a perfect summer's day, children playing in the calm, blue-green water and on the fine, dazzlingly white sand. In good weather it looked just like a bay in the South Seas. Today it looked like the End of Days.

A small path led up through the cliffs from the east end of the beach and then wound along the coast in crazy loops (an old smuggler's path as the locals so proudly claimed), to Rospico and on to Port Manech. The area was sparsely populated, a nature reserve zone. A breathtakingly beautiful path. Dupin sometimes came for walks here.

Salou and Dupin had come straight here. They had taken Dupin's car. Le Ber and Labat had followed in a second car and arrived at almost the same time.

A jogger had found Pennec and called the police. The two officers from Pont-Aven had set out immediately and had been first on the scene. They were now securing the path above, which you could barely make out any more from down here, the clouds were so low in the sky. Monfort had waited for Dupin in the car park and led them to Loic Pennec's body.

There were four of them standing around the body. Le Ber, Labat, Salou and Dupin, already soaked through after the walk from the car park. It was a gruesome scene. Salou was the first to say something. 'We should secure the forensic evidence on the path now. We can look for traces of a second person straight away.'

'Yes we need that confirmed as soon as possible.' Dupin had to admit Salou was right. Everything depended on whether there had been a second person.

'We have to hurry. Most of the evidence will have been swept away already, if it wasn't stamped right down into the ground. I'll have my team come down.'

Salou turned around and skilfully, but with evident care, began climbing back up over the rocks. The rain and the spray had made everything extremely slippery. Le Ber, Labat and Dupin stayed by the body, silent again, just standing and looking as they had before, as though they were holding some strange vigil.

Labat was the first to snap out of it. He made an effort to sound professional. 'You should inform Madame Pennec of her husband's death, Monsieur le Commissaire. That's definitely the most important thing.' He looked vaguely upwards, to the spot where Salou had disappeared. 'We should cordon off this whole area.'

'Fucking hell.' Dupin had been talking to himself, but very loudly. He ran his hand right through his horrible hair, which was wet and plastered to his head. He needed to be alone. To think. Things had taken a serious turn. Not that it had been an innocuous case before, but now it had gone from being a backwater affair – which had initially seemed to be about inheritances or maybe serious illnesses – to being a violent case. A case of completely different proportions. Especially with this fantastical sum, the forty million which might be the basis of the case. And the second death. If Dupin had felt that everything in some vague way had become strangely surreal in the last two days, this bizarre murder in this perfect summer idyll, everything had taken on a sudden, inescapable and brutal reality with this second body.

'I'm going to make a few calls. Stay here at the scene. Both of you. And get in touch straight away if there's news.'

Not even Labat protested. Dupin had no idea where he was going, especially not in this rain. He clambered a short distance across the rocks along the shore, which was impossible to do without looking ridiculous. It wasn't easy to stay upright on the slippery rocks and stones, but he had no desire to take the direct route up and meet his colleagues again. Only at the next big rock ledge did he climb up onto the coastal path. Then he walked a bit further and turned left when the path forked, the right fork leading to the car park, the left towards the deserted beach below.

Even when he strained his eyes, the other end of the beach and the islets that lay so picturesquely off the coast were only dimly visible. His jacket, his polo-shirt, his jeans, everything was saturated and water was running into his shoes. The rain was being blown sideways by the storm coming off the sea and mixing with the bursts of spray. Powerful waves, three or four metres high, rolled relentlessly onto the beach, breaking on the sandbank with ear-splitting crashes. Dupin had gone so close to the water that the waves were lapping his shoes. He took a deep breath and started walking slowly along the beach.

Was it murder or suicide? Loic Pennec was dead. Two days ago someone had murdered his father. And now the son too? Dupin had to think clearly. He had to concentrate now. Concentrate fully. Take things step by step and not let himself get confused. Not by the second death. Not by the commotion that would break out now. Whether this was an accident, murder or suicide, there was going to be a huge scandal and he didn't even want to think about what would happen when word got out. He had to know the reason. What had set everything off? He had to work quickly. Had there really been a genuine Gauguin hanging in the restaurant? That was the first question. He had to *know*. Know for sure. But how could he find out? And if it was a genuine, undiscovered Gauguin, then the question was who would have known about the painting? About the forty million euro? This was the crucial question. Who did Pennec tell? And when? Sometime in the last few days when he knew he was going to die? Or years ago? Decades ago? Had he even told anyone? His son must have known. And Catherine Pennec too. Or had the son not known anything either? It was obvious old Pennec hadn't had a very close relationship with his son, however much Loic Pennec tried to hide it. And what about Madame Lajoux, his – Dupin was sure of it – lover? And Fragan Delon? And

Beauvois who had advised him on all things art, whom Pennec seemed to have trusted? And the question was an even broader one. What about André Pennec? Or might an outsider have recognised the painting as an original? And what had set everything off *now*, at this specific point in time? The single unusual thing that had happened in the last week was that Pennec had found out that he was likely to die in the near future.

Dupin had almost reached the other end of the beach, where a small road became a slipway for launching boats into the water. On the right hand side, a little higher up amongst the old dunes was a pretty little hotel called the Ar Men Du; for Dupin's money, it had the best restaurant on the coast. This was a special place. Here, in Finistère, there were a few spots where you could really feel it: the edge of the world. Yes, this is where the world ended, on this craggy, wild ledge. There was nothing but the endless ocean in front of you, an expanse so large that you couldn't see it all – but you could definitely feel it. Thousands of kilometres of water, the open sea, not a scrap of land, nothing.

Dupin urgently needed to make a quiet phone call. It wasn't possible out here, but in this weather nobody would be in the Ar Men Du. He could sit in the bar; the hotel guests had their own breakfast room. He would make his call and drink coffee.

The owner of the Ar Men Du was Alain Trifin, who had been running it for some years now. It used to be a dive but Trifin had seen its potential and made something of it. Dupin liked him a lot; he had a dignified, intelligent, laconic manner, and his conversations with Dupin were short but genuine.

Dupin rarely went to the Ar Men Du, but whenever he did it struck him that he should do so more often.

Trifin smiled when he saw Dupin coming in, soaked from head to foot and dripping. Dupin stood in the doorway while Trifin disappeared into the kitchen without a word and emerged with a towel a moment later. He was tall with thick, short hair and prominent, well-defined features, a very good-looking man.

'Dry yourself off first, Monsieur Dupin. Coffee?'

'Thanks – yes please.'

'I take it you'd rather be alone.' Trifin pointed to the table in the corner, right by the big window.

'There are a few calls I need to make. I –'

'Nobody will disturb you here.' He glanced out at the lashing rain as though by way of explanation.

Dupin dried his head and face, took off his jacket, ran the towel over his clothes once and laid it on the chair before he sat down. A little puddle had formed in the spot where he had been standing. Trifin signalled to one of the two waiters.

A moment later Trifin was standing at the huge espresso machine. A very young waiter brought the coffee, trying to be as discreet as possible. He moved as though his greatest ambition was not to be noticed by Dupin.

Dupin dialled Le Ber's number and it rang for a long time before he picked up. At first the only thing Dupin could hear was a horrible hissing sound. Then he heard Le Ber's distorted voice which was almost impossible to understand, even though he was shouting.

'Hang on, Monsieur le Commissaire, hang on,' nothing for a few seconds and then Le Ber was back,

'Monsieur le Commissaire, I've come a bit closer to the rocks, but that's not helping either. The wind is coming off the sea. I'll go back to the car.' He hung up before Dupin could say anything.

Dupin looked out the big window towards where Le Ber would now have been visible, had the weather been better. It was even darker now, and water was running down the window panes in steady streams.

The coffee was wonderful. If it hadn't been for this tragedy, this brutal crime, this whole case, it would have been extremely cosy, being warm and dry in here while the storm raged outside. But he couldn't appreciate it right now.

It took much longer than he had expected for Le Ber to call back. This time Dupin could hear him loud and clear.

'I'm sitting in the car. I've spoken to Salou again. He has been able to pinpoint the place where Loic Pennec fell. Salou thinks he probably wasn't alone.'

'He wasn't alone?'

'There are potential traces of a second person. Salou says it's incredibly difficult to make out, and the rain has already washed away a lot of the trace evidence.'

'Can we assume this information is reliable yet?'

'No.'

'Tell Salou to let me know as soon as he is sure.'

'He will.'

'Le Ber, I want to know who painted the copies that are hanging in *Central*, especially the painting next to the restaurant door. We need the name as soon as possible. This is the only thing we should be concentrating on right now.'

'What do you mean?'

'Exactly what I just said.'

'You want to know who painted the copied paintings in the restaurant?'

'Yes, that one in particular.'

'Now? You mean right now?'

'Now.'

'And the second body? Within the space of three days, somebody murders Pierre-Louis Pennec and then they probably murder his son. Almost wipes out the whole family. The forensic –'

'I need the painter who did those paintings.'

'Shouldn't I stay here? At the crime scene?'

'We also urgently need to get hold of the member of staff Monsieur Pennec spoke to at the Musée d'Orsay.'

'He's on holiday until the end of next week. Labat spoke to his secretary yesterday but she wasn't able to reach him. Apparently, Pennec spoke to the secretary on the phone when he rang the Musée d'Orsay last week, but the secretary doesn't have a clue what it was about or what Pennec wanted, she just transferred his call.'

'We've got to find him. What's his name?'

'Labat knows.'

'It doesn't matter for the moment. What's important is that we find him as soon as possible. And I want to see Madame Cassel.'

Le Ber seemed confused. 'Madame Cassel? Now?'

'Get me her mobile number. That's enough to be going on with. I forgot to make a note of it.'

'Who is going to give Madame Pennec the terrible news? You should do it, Monsieur le Commissaire.'

'Labat can do it. He should get going immediately, right now. I'll drive over to Madame Pennec later. Tell him to let her know I'll be coming.'

'There'll be trouble, you know.'

'He should get going straight away. She shouldn't just find out any old way. And of course we've got to know as much as possible about Pennec's walk. When he set out, where he was going – and why? Was he on his own?'

'I'll let Labat know. But it's going to be difficult, I mean after delivering news like this –'

'Call me as soon as you have anything. The most important thing is to locate the man from the museum... And the copyists.'

Dupin hung up. The rain had eased off all of a sudden. To the west, way out over the sea by the towering black cliffs (the *Men Du* from which the area and the hotel took their name), a crack had opened in the clouds. A sun beam fell theatrically through it, tracing a dazzlingly bright, perfect circle on the otherwise deep black sea.

So there were vague indications of a second person. Dupin hadn't bought the idea of an accident in any case. There was more to it than that. He felt around for his notebook, which had been some-what protected in his breast pocket. He dried it as best he could with a napkin, but it hadn't got too wet. He made a few notes.

His mobile rang; Le Ber again.

'Yes?'

'The name of the man from the Musée d'Orsay is Charles Sauré. He's the director of the collection. I just spoke to his secretary again – we managed to get her personal number. Monsieur Sauré has a house up in Finistère, in Carantec.'

'In Brittany? He has a holiday home here in Brittany?'

'Exactly.'

'Isn't that a strange coincidence?'

'I don't know about that, Monsieur le Commissaire – lots of people from Paris have holiday homes in Brittany. Especially these intellectual types.'

'True. And he's staying there at the moment?'

'That's what his secretary thinks.'

Dupin knew Carantec, a very pretty village on the north coast. A bit gentrified but not unpleasant, not too chic. He had been there twice, the last time was the Easter before with Adèle – her grandmother lived there.

'Do we have his number?'

'Just a landline. His home number.'

'Have you tried it yet?'

'No.'

'Call it out to me.'

'0-2-9-8-6-7-4-5-8-7.'

Dupin made a note of the number in his notebook.

'What does "director of the collection" mean?'

'No idea.'

'I've got to speak to Madame Cassel.'

'0-6-2-7-8-6-7-5-6-2.'

'Have her brought to the Ar Men Du.'

'You're in the Ar Men Du? In that restaurant over there?'

'Yes.'

'And you want Madame Cassel to come and see you there, in the Ar Men Du?'

'Exactly.'

'Okay. I'll arrange it.'

'I'll wait here. Oh yes, I've got to see Madame Lajoux this afternoon. And old Delon. And André Pennec, in the hotel. And we might need a few police officers for searches. Find out who's on duty.'

'Searches?'

'We'll see.'

'Monsieur le Commissaire.'

'Yes?'

'You should be keeping us in the loop.'

Dupin hesitated. 'You're right. I will. As soon as I can. Is Labat at Madame Pennec's?'

'He should be there by now, I reckon. He... he protested very strongly.'

'I know... I mean, I can imagine.' Dupin added pensively, 'I'll go and see Madame Pennec myself later.'

Dupin hung up.

He motioned to the waiter to bring a second coffee. The waiter had understood immediately, just as he was beginning to make the signal. He had to speak to Charles Sauré. It could be very important. A few large raindrops had fallen from his hair onto his notebook, a few lines had run and then he had smudged them with his fist. He had trouble deciphering the numbers; his notebooks always looked pathetic after two or three days on a case – even without rain.

Dupin dialled Sauré's number. A woman answered.

'*Bonjour*, Madame. This is Commissaire Georges Dupin from Concarneau.'

There was a short pause before the woman's voice answered quietly and very cautiously: 'Oh my god. Has something happened?'

Dupin knew all too well the fear it caused when the police called out of the blue and didn't immediately say why they were calling.

'I'm so sorry to be calling like this, Madame. No, nothing has happened. Nothing at all. There's no reason to be concerned. I just have a few questions for Monsieur Charles Sauré. It's not about him at all, it's just that he might be able to help us with certain information.'

'I understand.' Her voice sounded noticeably relieved. 'I'm Anne Sauré, Charles Sauré is my husband. He's not at home at the moment. But he'll back soon. By twelve at the latest.'

'Do you know where he is right now?'

'In Morlaix, picking up a few things we needed.'

'Does your husband have a mobile?'

'Could you tell me what this is about first?'

'He was… well, it's complicated. It's about his museum, an issue in connection with the museum. I just need some information.'

'Well he doesn't have a mobile. He hates all that kind of thing.'

'Hmmm, I see.'

'Feel free to call again at twelve. Let's say half past to be on the safe side. He'll definitely be back by then.'

'Thank you very much, Madame. And I'm sorry to have given you such a fright earlier.'

'*Au revoir*, Monsieur le Commissaire.'

'*Au revoir*, Madame.'

The gap in the clouds had long since closed up and the storm and the rain had started again.

Dupin made yet another signal to the waiter. 'Another coffee, please.' He knew it was his sixth today. But now that he was on a case, this really wasn't the time to cut down on coffee (although he had been intending to do so for years and Docteur Pelliet had strongly recommended it). 'And a croissant.' He was thinking about his stomach again. They had left the *Central* in such a rush.

His wet clothes clung to his skin. It would take them hours to dry. This was what he got for steadfastly refusing to buy one of those ugly waterproof jackets that almost all the locals had... Nolwenn liked to tease him that it was very unbreton of him. Dupin stared out at the rain, lost in thought. A dark-coloured car came up the sandy path to the hotel car park and stopped right at the entrance. He recognised the policeman. It must be Madame Cassel already. That was quick.

Marie Morgane Cassel got out, looked around, spotted Dupin through the glass and headed for the hotel.

She shook the rain off her coat as she stood in front of his table. 'What's happened?'

'Pierre-Louis Pennec's son fell from the cliffs... fell or was made to fall, we don't know which yet. Over there.' Dupin pointed in the direction of Plage Tahiti.

Madame Cassel turned pale. She placed her hand to her right temple. 'How awful! I don't envy you.'

'Thanks. I mean, yes. It's a terrible thing. And it's going to cause such an uproar, it's absolutely dreadful.'

'I can believe that. Did you want to talk about the painting a bit more? Is that why you wanted to see me again?'

'I wanted to ask you whether you would have time to come with me to an interview? I have to go to Carantec

186

to see the director of the collection at the Musée d'Orsay.'

'The director of the collection? You mean Charles Sauré?'

'He was the one who spoke to Pennec. We haven't managed to interview him yet so we have no idea what they discussed. I want to hear it from Monsieur Sauré myself.'

'And how can I help you?'

'What does the director of a museum collection do?'

'They're responsible for its artistic direction... the question of what paintings the collection has, buys, sells. All in close cooperation with the president of the museum of course.'

'Would Pennec have gone to him in connection with this painting? If it were a genuine Gauguin, I mean.'

'Why would he have gone to him if he knew it was genuine? I mean, it wouldn't have been to verify it.'

'That's just it.'

'And so that's what you're trying to find out?'

'Yes and I need your help to do it. The whole art thing –'

Marie Morgane Cassel seemed to be thinking it over. 'I have no idea how I could be of any help to you. And I need to be back in Brest by five. There's a big conference for art historians all weekend. It's not really my type of thing, but I'm giving a lecture today.'

'I would really appreciate it... Charles Sauré is going to tell me things I don't understand. I *have* to know whether it's a genuine Gauguin – that's the most important thing at the moment. We need some solid facts here. And we can make sure that you get to the university by five, that won't be a problem.'

Madame Cassel moved towards the door. 'Shall we take your car?'

Dupin had to laugh, just like he had last night. 'Yes, let's take my car.'

It had been an exhausting, nerve-wracking journey. The type of journey Dupin hated. In 'this weather' the tourists obviously hadn't gone to the beach. They'd decided to go on 'day trips' instead, spending the day in the city doing sightseeing, grocery shopping, souvenir-buying. This was why there was such overcrowding on the N165, the southern section of the legendary *route nationale* that went right the way round the wild, rugged half-island. Brittany had no motorways after Rennes although the *route nationale* was a sort of motorway, with its four lanes and a speed limit of 110. The traffic was 'slow to halting', which was the technical term used by '107.7', the national traffic broadcaster. Everyone trusted it implicitly, from the Canal Coast to Champagne, from the Côte d'Azur to Brittany. First the traffic was halting until Quimper, then halting until Brest. And then halting to Morlaix. For the entire journey.

Under normal circumstances (so for ten months and twenty days of the year) the journey would have taken a good hour, but today it took two and a half. They arrived a little before one o'clock. Marie Morgane Cassel and Dupin hadn't spoken much. Dupin had had to make a string of phone calls. Le Ber twice, Nolwenn once (she was already up to speed; Dupin was always baffled as to how she managed it) then Labat and Guenneugues (it was as excruciating as ever; Dupin had claimed the connection was bad a minute in, said 'I can't hear you any more, can you hear me?' a few times and then hung up). Labat had been at Madame Pennec's house. It had been a depressing conversation according to Le Ber. She hadn't heard the news so he had to break it to her. She collapsed and as a precaution Labat had called for help; her GP had come to the house and given her a sedative. What time Loic Pennec had set out, whether he had been alone, whether he had met up with anyone, there was no way to ask any of these questions under the circumstances. Nolwenn's had been the only cheering phone call – she had found out Charles Sauré's exact address. Dupin didn't want his visit to be announced.

Dupin didn't like the north coast very much. It rained all the time. The weather was considerably worse than on the south coast, where you often had high pressure areas coming in from the Azores. Like a good 'southerner', Nolwenn recited the numbers for him on a regular basis: 2,200 hours of sunshine per year in southern Finistère versus just 1,500 in the north. On top of that, the coast was rugged and stony for the most part and even where there were sandy beaches these tended to be narrow. And low tide revealed kilometres of grey-brown rocky ground covered in seaweed so that the beaches turned into ludicrously narrow strips of sand marooned in gigantic wastelands of seaweed. It was impossible to get to the sea, impossible to go swimming. Carantec was one of the exceptions in the north – it had a marvellous beach, even at low tide, dozens of islets just off a wide, placid bay. The whole village had atmosphere, it was authentic. There was an old town, a lovely little section of the headland with narrow, winding alleyways which somehow all led to the sea, even if people sometimes wondered how that could be possible. The Saurés' house lay in the centre of the little village, near the little harbour and two or three wonderfully unpretentious restaurants (Dupin had fond memories of the entrecôte in one of them). They parked on the main square and the house was a stone's throw from there. The storm still hadn't died down and it was raining, just as it had been for the whole journey, nowhere had been spared. Dupin's clothes were still damp. He was well aware he didn't look like your average commissaire at the best of times, but he looked the part less so than usual right now.

He rang the doorbell twice, quickly and firmly. A short, thin man opened the door, mischievous, intelligent eyes, thick, unkempt hair, a large faded blue shirt, jeans.

'*Bonjour*. Monsieur Sauré?'

Sauré's tense face spoke volumes. 'And to whom do I owe the pleasure?'

'Commissaire Georges Dupin, Commissariat de Police, Concarneau. And this is Professor Cassel, from Brest.'

Sauré's demeanour became more conciliatory, if only a little bit.

'Ah yes, the Commissaire. You spoke to my wife on the phone. Weren't you going to call me? My wife said you were going to call half an hour ago.'

Dupin hadn't given a moment's thought to how he would explain that he was suddenly standing at the door without warning and hadn't phoned as arranged, so he just glossed over it. 'We have some important questions and your knowledge could really help. As we understand it, you spoke to Pierre-Louis Pennec on the phone on Tuesday. I'm sure you've heard about his murder.'

'Yes, it's terrible. I read about it in the paper. Please do come in, we can continue our discussion inside.' Monsieur Sauré stepped aside, let Madame Cassel and Dupin in, and quietly shut the door.

'It's along here. We'll go into the sitting room.'

The house was much bigger than it looked from the outside and very tastefully and expensively furnished. Modern, but not clinical. Old and new confidently combined, everything in the colours of Brittany, the dark blue, the light green, the radiant white – the Atlantic colours. Cosy.

'You must excuse me for not welcoming you more politely. I wasn't expecting your visit and as I said, my wife told me you would be getting in touch by phone. She's doing the shopping at the big *Leclerc*, we're having guests tonight. But I could always offer you something – would you like a coffee, a glass of water?'

'I would love a coffee, thank you.' Madame Cassel had answered before Dupin could react. He would have preferred to get right down to business.

'And you, Monsieur le Commissaire?'

'The same for me. Thanks very much.' He might as well have a coffee now; he hadn't had one for hours anyway.

'Do sit down, I'll be right back.' Sauré pointed to the low sofa and the two matching armchairs, everything arranged to face the incredibly large windows that

191

framed a view that was breathtaking, even in this weather.

Madame Cassel had chosen one armchair, Dupin the other. They were sitting far apart.

'It's spectacular. I would never have thought the sea was so close.' Dupin gazed into the distance, to the black horizon, almost invisible now. They sat in silence, staring out of the window.

Sauré came back with a pretty little wooden tray.

'Madame Cassel is a professor at the University of Brest, an art historian. Gauguin is one of her specialities, she –'

'Oh, but I know who Madame Cassel is, Monsieur le Commissaire.' Sauré practically sounded offended. He turned to Madame Cassel.

'I am of course familiar with some of your publications, Madame Cassel. Excellent. You are very well regarded in Paris. It's a great pleasure to be able to make your acquaintance finally.'

'The pleasure is all mine, Monsieur Sauré.'

Sauré had sat down exactly in the middle of the sofa, so that he was equidistant from Dupin and Madame Cassel.

Dupin decided to be direct. 'What did you think when you heard about the existence of a second version of the *Vision*?'

He spoke very calmly. Marie Morgane Cassel's head still whipped around in his direction. She looked at him in astonishment. Charles Sauré stared at Dupin, his expression unchanged, and answered in a relaxed, clear voice.

'You know about the painting... Of course you

know about the painting. Yes, it's stupendous; I can't believe this has happened. A second *Vision*.'

Now Madame Cassel's head whipped around to Sauré. She looked absolutely flabbergasted. 'There's a second version of *Vision after the Sermon*?'

'Yes.'

'A second painting? A large Gauguin that nobody has known about until now?' You could see the goosebumps on her skin.

'I saw it. I don't mind telling you that in my opinion, it is even more wonderful than the painting we know about. Grittier, bolder, more radical. The orange is like one huge block. It's incredible. Everything that Gauguin wanted, everything that he was capable of – it's all there. The struggle is at once more clearly a vision and more realistically an actual event, just like the nuns who are standing there watching.'

It took a moment for Dupin to grasp what Sauré had just said. 'You did what? You saw the painting yourself?'

'Yes, I've seen it. I was there. On Wednesday. Pierre-Louis Pennec and I met in the hotel that afternoon.'

'You've actually seen the painting?'

'I stood in front of it for half an hour. It's hanging in the restaurant, right behind the door. It's hard to get your head around it, a genuine Gauguin, a completely unknown painting –'

'And you're sure that it's real? That it's really by Gauguin?'

'I'm confident it is. Of course it's going to have to undergo a string of scientific tests, but in my view that will just be a formality. There's no doubt in my mind that the painting is genuine.'

'The painting that you saw is definitively not a copy?'

'A copy? What do you mean? Where did you get that idea?'

'I mean the painting is not the work of an artist painting in Gauguin's style? Like all those imitators?'

'No, absolutely not.'

'How can you be so sure of it?'

'Monsieur Sauré is a luminary. There's nobody in the whole world better qualified to judge, Monsieur le Commissaire.'

Sauré couldn't hide a flattered smile. 'Thank you very much, Madame.'

Dupin had decided not to mention anything about the copy that was hanging in the restaurant right now. Madame Cassel seemed to have caught onto this.

'Why did Pierre-Louis Pennec call and ask you to come? What did he want? Could you talk us through what happened, from the very beginning?'

Sauré leaned back. 'Of course. Pierre-Louis Pennec called me for the first time on Tuesday morning. Around half past eight or so. He asked whether he could have a confidential conversation with me, it was about a rather important issue. That's how he put it. Absolute confidentiality was very important to him. I was on the way to a meeting so I asked him to call me back late morning. And he did.'

'So he called you back, rather than vice versa?'

'Yes. Late morning. He came to the point very quickly: that his father had left him a Gauguin, one which art historians had known nothing about up till now, that he had kept it for decades, but that he wanted to leave it to the collection at the Musée d'Orsay. As a gift.'

Dupin sat up straight. 'He wanted to leave the painting to the museum? Just donate it?'

'Yes. That's what he wanted.'

'But the painting was immensely valuable. We're talking thirty, forty million euro.'

'Indeed.' Sauré was completely calm.

'How did you react?'

'At first I wasn't sure what to make of the whole thing. It sounded fantastical of course, but then again it was too fantastical to be made up. Why would someone make up a story like that? Worst case scenario, I said to myself, someone just wants a bit of attention. Monsieur Pennec wanted to meet as soon as possible.'

'Did he say why this had to happen so quickly?'

'No. He was actually rather formal, which I found agreeable, and I thought it inappropriate to ask him personal questions. We have dealings with a lot of very strong-willed people in the art world. And a straightforward donation to the museum is fairly normal.'

'But surely the value of this donation is not normal. Surely the museum doesn't get a donation like that every day.'

'Monsieur Honoré must have been dumbfounded,' Madame Cassel chimed in.

Charles Sauré looked a little disapprovingly at her. Turning back to Dupin, he added: 'The president of the museum. One of the most renowned and influential figures in the art world. I haven't spoken to Monsieur Honoré yet, I haven't found the right moment. I didn't want to jump the gun; that would have been a reckless thing to do. I thought I should take a look at the painting first, make sure that this really was a genuine Gauguin. And there was so much to discuss first, the donation, the timing, the conditions. Everything.'

'So you agreed to meet the next day then?'

'My wife and I had decided to come here for the weekend anyway and were considering staying for a few more days. Pont-Aven isn't directly on our way, but it's not too far. It suited us quite nicely.'

'And so you met in the hotel itself?'

'Yes. My wife walked around Pont-Aven for an hour, and I went into the hotel. He was already waiting for me downstairs at reception. He had asked me to come between three and five so we would have some peace and quiet in the restaurant. He came straight to the point in the meeting too. He had already made an appointment with his notary to include the donation in his will. He wanted to hand over the painting the following week. In Pont-Aven, he didn't want to go to Paris. He had already written a short text for the plaque next to the painting, telling the history of the painting and also the history of the hotel, his father, and of course the great Marie-Jeanne Pennec.'

'He wanted to make the history of the painting public?'

'Absolutely. In a humble way. He didn't want any fuss at the handover, no press release, no official unveiling, nothing like that. Just the little plaque. I told him you can't just go along one morning and hang a painting like that in a museum like ours without any explanation. The existence of this painting is a miracle, and everyone would ask where on earth it had come from, the academics, the press, the public.

Everyone. He wanted to reflect on these things with me one more time.'

Dupin had made a few notes in his Clairefontaine. Sauré looked rather appalled by the sloppy-looking notebook. Dupin simply carried on. 'Did he tell you the history of the painting?'

'Some of it. He said his grandmother, Marie-Jeanne, had got it from Gauguin himself. He gave it to her during his last visit in 1894 to thank her for all she'd done for him. Gauguin had always stayed at her hotel, never at Mademoiselle Julia's. But above all, Pennec said, it was to thank her for looking after him for nearly four months after the fight in Concarneau, when someone seriously insulted his young Javanese girlfriend. He was quite badly injured at the time, but Marie-Jeanne nursed him with love and devotion, day after day, until he recovered. It's been hanging in that spot in the restaurant ever since... It's unbelievable when you think about it. Amazing.'

'You were very close to the truth, Monsieur le Commissaire.'

Marie Morgane Cassel looked very pensive as she spoke. She gazed wide-eyed at Dupin, who couldn't suppress a quick smile.

'Did it never occur to you, Monsieur Sauré, that all of this might be extremely relevant to the police investigation... I mean when you later heard that Pierre-Louis Pennec had been murdered?'

Charles Sauré looked at Dupin in genuine astonishment. 'I'm accustomed to working with the utmost discretion. Monsieur Pennec had asked me to remain utterly discreet at all times. And that's not unusual for the art world. The majority of things in our world are, how should I put it, very private. Of course I was irritated when I heard what had happened. But even then I felt the most appropriate thing would be to maintain confidentiality. It's our most important asset. Perhaps the heirs of the painting will appreciate this discretion. It's an entirely private matter, owning a painting like that with that kind of value, as is the decision to donate. We have a strict code.'

'But –' Dupin broke off. It made no sense. It was clear that Charles Sauré didn't find any of this at all strange, either at the time or now. Neither the fact that he had seen Pierre-Louis Pennec just two days before his murder, nor that he had learned of the existence of a painting worth forty million euro, which – it didn't require much imagination – could quite clearly have been a motive for the murder he heard about later.

'When was the handover due to take place?'

'We were planning to arrange a time over the phone. But as he was walking me out, he was definitely talking about the beginning of next week. He wanted to get it sorted quickly.'

'I take it Monsieur Pennec didn't tell you the reasons for his donation?'

'No.'

'And that he didn't tell you anything else that could be significant – or that seems significant to you now after his murder?'

'It was all about the painting and the plan to donate it. The procedure. I didn't expect an explanation from him anyway, or a story. I didn't ask him any questions at all. It wasn't my place.'

'I understand. And nothing about Pierre-Louis Pennec struck you in any way? He wasn't overly anxious... did anything cross your mind after the meeting?'

'No. The only thing that was clear was that he didn't want to waste any time. But he didn't seem rushed or hasty, just determined.'

Dupin's enthusiasm had vanished. Not that this was all that rare for him, even in the most important interviews and interrogations. But he knew what he wanted to know now.

'Thank you very much, Monsieur Sauré. You have been extremely helpful. We need to be getting back now, I'm needed in Pont-Aven.'

Charles Sauré looked bewildered at this abrupt end to the conversation. 'I... yes, well I don't have anything else to tell you. They weren't long telephone calls and it wasn't a long meeting.'

'Thanks very much... thanks again.' Dupin stood up. Marie Morgane Cassel seemed just as surprised by the sudden end to the conversation as Sauré did. She jumped up too, somewhat embarrassed.

'There's something I'd like to know myself, Monsieur le Commissaire.'

'Of course.'

'Who will inherit the painting? I mean, who owns it after the... the death of Monsieur Pennec? I read something about a son in the paper.'

Dupin saw absolutely no need to inform Monsieur Sauré of the events of that morning. 'We'll see, Monsieur Sauré, I don't want to comment on that right now.'

'I assume that the heirs will continue with the donation, it was the owner's greatest wish after all... it's only right... a painting like that should belong to the whole world.'

'I can't comment on that.'

'Surely he managed to write his wishes about the donation into his will in time? He seemed to be treating it as very urgent.'

That was no doubt about it. Dupin understood what was going on here. 'I'll be in touch if you can be of assistance to us again.'

It took Sauré a while to respond. 'Yes, please do. That would be great. You can reach me here till the end of the week. We're not planning to head back until Saturday.'

Sauré walked them to the door and bade them a very formal farewell.

At least it had stopped raining, even though the sky still hung low, a dark grey. Dupin needed to go for a little walk, but he wanted to get back to Pont-Aven as quickly as possible.

'Shall we walk once round the block? Maybe we should walk back to the car a different way.'

'Good plan.'

The professor still seemed a little stunned.

They turned right onto a little path that ran past Sauré's house. They could still catch glimpses of the house through the thick, metre-high rhododendron bushes as they walked down towards the sea. They didn't speak until they'd reached the cliffs.

'It's unbelievable. Do you know what this means? This story is going to spread round the world. An unknown Gauguin has been discovered in a restaurant in the middle of nowhere in Brittany. It hung there unnoticed for over a hundred years and is among the most important works in his oeuvre. Its estimated value: forty million euro. Minimum, I would say.'

'And two deaths. Two so far.'

Marie Morgane Cassel looked ashamed. 'Yes… you're right. Yes. Two deaths. I'm sorry –'

'I understand your enthusiasm. They're two very separate things. You know, in my job I always see the other side too. The other side of things, the other side of people. That's what I'm there for.'

They stood there in silence for some time, side by side. Dupin was feeling uncomfortable about what he'd just said. 'What do you think? Did it sound plausible, what Monsieur Sauré said?'

'Yes, absolutely. It's an accurate insight into, how should I put it, the little *conventions* of the art world, his attitude, his approach. His whole personality. It's a very peculiar world.'

'You don't think Charles Sauré murdered Pierre-Louis Pennec?'

Marie Morgane Cassel looked at the Commissaire, momentarily thunderstruck. 'Do you think he could have done it, Commissaire?'

'I don't know.'

She was silent.

'But do you think we can now assume that the painting is definitely genuine? Charles Sauré couldn't have got it wrong?'

'No. I mean, in theory he could have, of course. But I would trust his judgement – and his instinct. As I said, you won't find a more knowledgeable expert in the whole world.'

'Good. I... I trust *you*.' Dupin smiled, which seemed to please Marie Morgane Cassel.

'So we're dealing with two deaths and the theft of a forty-million-euro painting then. A painting that, officially speaking, does not exist. We only have Sauré's... let's say, *appraisal*, that there is an original and that what's hanging in the restaurant right now is not just something a copyist dreamt up.'

Dupin paused. His smile had vanished. 'What proof do we have that the painting that's hanging in the restaurant isn't the only one there is? The quick appraisal by Sauré, his confidence that what he saw was an original? That's not enough. Not enough for a court anyway. Whoever has the painting now, they must be feeling pretty confident. He stole a painting that doesn't exist – so long as we don't have it in our hands and scientific experts can't confirm that it is a Gauguin.'

'Who actually owns the painting now?'

'Madame Pennec. It's all hers since this morning. It's a very simple inheritance. The hotel belongs to her now and, as there are no other provisions, everything that is in the hotel too. Pierre-Louis Pennec didn't manage to change the will in the end.'

'So the donation is invalid?'

'That will be up to Madame Pennec to decide.'

Dupin's mobile rang. Labat. 'I have to take this call. Let's go back to the car.'

'Okay. Would it be best for me to go straight to Brest from here?'

'I'll give you a lift part of the way... Labat?'

'Yes, Monsieur le Commissaire. There are a few urgent matters here. Where are you?'

'I'm standing by the sea in Carantec.'

'Carantec? By the sea?'

'Indeed.'

'What are you doing in Carantec?'

'What's going on, Labat?'

'You have to get in touch with Salou. He wants to speak to you in person again. As does Docteur Lafond. Both of them are expecting your call... soon.'

Labat waited in vain for Dupin to say something.

'When will you be at the hotel? We've asked Madame Lajoux and Delon to be on standby. We haven't been able to reach André Pennec or Beauvois yet. Who do you want to see first after your visit to Catherine Pennec?'

'I need a car,' Dupin thought for a moment, 'at one of the big roundabouts in Brest, at the first roundabout if you're coming from Morlaix, no wait, the Océanopolis would be best. That's the simplest. The car is for Madame Cassel to get to the university.'

Dupin had been to the Océanopolis in Brest many times and knew it very well. He'd always loved big aquariums, especially the penguins... and the Océanopolis was amazing.

'Is Madame Cassel with you?'

'She's got to be at the university by half four.'

'You've got to bring me and Le Ber up to speed on the progress of the investigation, and soon.'

'You're right, Inspector Labat. You're absolutely right. Speak to you soon.'

They had made good time on this journey because the holiday-makers were still sitting in the crêperies. It took thirty minutes to get to the Océanopolis. The same policeman as yesterday, the one from Brest, was waiting for Madame Cassel in the same car. Madame Cassel and Dupin hadn't managed to speak all that much this time either. Dupin had been on the phone for most of the journey, just like on their way there. Docteur Lafond, who was working on Loic Pennec's autopsy, hadn't said much as usual; but he had confirmed that Loic Pennec died last night, not this morning, that – as far as the evidence went – the fall had been the cause of death, and that, so far, there was no indication of violence against or injuries to Pennec before the fall.

Salou noted that there were footprints within Pennec's vicinity that were 'reasonably likely' to belong to a second person, especially right next to the lethal precipice. But he couldn't confirm it. The storm and the heavy rain had more or less washed everything away; there was a danger it wouldn't be possible to confirm the footprints even after further investigation. Dupin didn't think things sounded half as positive as they had sounded in his first conversation with Le Ber – or else the great star forensic scientist had just been trying to make himself seem important.

So far no members of the public had been in touch to report seeing anything suspicious, either yesterday evening when it happened, or this morning. The officers from Pont-Aven had begun a systematic questioning of all the locals, but hadn't turned up any leads yet. Dupin hadn't expected anything else here; this wasn't a case which would be solved by anything as banal as fingerprints, footprints, textile fibres or random eyewitnesses.

Dupin parked his car down by the harbour a little before four, very close to the Pennecs' villa. This wasn't going to be an easy conversation.

It took a long time for Madame Pennec to come to the door. Catherine Pennec was clearly in a bad way; her eyes were glassy, her expression frozen, even her hair, which had been so painstakingly done yesterday, was a complete mess.

'Excuse me if I'm intruding, Madame Pennec, but I'd like to speak to you if possible. I know this is terrible, it's a real imposition to be bothering you like this.'

Catherine Pennec looked at Dupin blankly. 'Please come in.'

Dupin stepped inside. Catherine Pennec went on ahead without saying a word, and Dupin followed. He sat in the same armchair he had sat in only yesterday and the day before.

'I've been given some medicine. I don't know if I'm in a position to have a proper conversation.'

'First of all, I'd like to express my deepest condolences, Madame Pennec.'

This was the second time in forty-eight hours that he was offering his condolences to the same person. It was eerie.

'Thank you.'

'This is a great tragedy. Either way.'

Madame Pennec raised her eyebrows enquiringly.

'We don't yet know whether it was an accident or if your husband was pushed. Or... or whether your husband... whether he –'

'Jumped?'

'We might never be able to say with absolute certainty what happened. We don't have any eyewitnesses yet. It's impossible to find any significant forensic evidence at the scene now. You saw the rain that came down last night. Everything is tentative so far.'

'I just want to know whether it was murder. And, if so, you have to find the murderer, you've got to promise me. If it was murder, it must be the same person who killed my father-in-law, mustn't it?'

'I don't know, Madame Pennec. We can't say anything yet. You shouldn't concern yourself with that right now.'

'I really hope you make progress soon.'

'I won't impose on you for too long. But there are a few things I have to discuss with you. Please tell me about yesterday evening, what time did –'

'My husband left the house just before half nine. He wanted to go for a walk. He often drives to the coast in the evenings, sometimes to his boat at Plage Tahiti and sometimes he just goes for a walk here in the village. He likes walking, has done for years. He –' Her voice cracked. 'He liked the route from Rospico to Plage Tahiti. And in summer, in the tourist season, he would always go walking late at night. He's obviously been in a bad state since the day before yesterday, and he was hoping it would calm him. He couldn't sleep the night we heard the terrible news. Neither of us could.'

'Was he on his own yesterday?'

'He always went for walks by himself. Even *I* never went with him. He took his car.' Her voice became even more solemn. 'It took him ages to find his car keys.

And then he was saying "see you later" at the door.'

'How long would he usually be gone for?'

'Two hours perhaps. We left at almost the same time yesterday, that's why I know exactly what time he left the house. I drove to the all-night pharmacy in Trévignon; my doctor prescribed sleeping tablets for us, both of us. We needed to sleep. We would usually never take anything like that.'

'You did the right thing. There's no need to reproach yourself.'

'I went to bed when I came back; I put his tablets on the bed in his room. They're still there.'

'You have separate bedrooms?'

Catherine Pennec looked at Dupin indignantly. 'Of course. Otherwise I would have noticed straight away that my husband wasn't back this morning.'

'I understand, Madame Pennec.'

'There was absolutely nothing unusual about the situation last night, Monsieur le Commissaire. The walk, the time, the route, nothing out of the ordinary, it was like always... apart from what happened of course.' Madame Pennec sounded almost like she was pleading with him, beseeching him.

'I understand. This is so terrible. I won't impose on you any longer with all of these things. There's just one more important issue we have to speak about – everything depends on it and you haven't brought it up yet.'

Madame Pennec looked the Commissaire in the eye. Dupin thought he saw uncertainty in her gaze for a moment, but he might have been mistaken.

'You mean the painting. You know. Of course. Yes,

that bloody painting. It's all about the painting, isn't it?' Her voice was confident.

'Yes. I think so.'

'It's hung there happily for over a hundred and thirty years. And now?' She broke off for a moment. 'Nobody ever spoke about the painting, we weren't even allowed to. You've got to understand, it was taboo in the Pennec family. Everything depended on this secret, the whole family depended on it. It had to be kept secret, whatever else happened. Even after Pierre-Louis Pennec died, do you understand? It's a disaster. That much money is a disaster. They were probably right to keep it so secret. Fate only took its course after Pierre-Louis Pennec had made the decision to donate it to the Musée d'Orsay. You must know about that too?'

Now it was beginning. Dupin knew this stage in every case. At a certain point the first real stories came to light. Up until that moment everyone tried to present seamless, impenetrable fronts so as not to give away anything of real significance. And everyone had their reasons – not just the perpetrators.

'Yes. We're aware of your father-in-law's intention.'

'He discussed it with my husband just this week.'

'Pierre-Louis Pennec told your husband about it?'

'Of course. It's a family matter, after all.'

'And how did he react? How did you react?'

She answered very clearly. 'It was his business. Not ours.'

'The painting belongs to you now, Madame Pennec. It's part of the hotel which you and your husband inherited. And now it's just yours.'

Catherine Pennec didn't say anything.

'Will you follow through with the donation to the Musée d'Orsay? It was Pierre-Louis Pennec's final wish after all, even if he never managed to arrange it legally-speaking.'

'I'd say so. Right now I'm not able to think about anything beyond today. I'll deal with it in the next few weeks.' She looked exhausted.

'Of course not. I've already asked too much of you. You have been extremely helpful. Just one last question: who else knew about the painting?'

Madame Pennec looked at Dupin with some astonishment. 'I couldn't say exactly. I thought for a long time it was just me and my husband. But my husband was sure Frédéric Beauvois knew about it too. And I sometimes suspected Madame Lajoux knew. Maybe he told her about it once.' She paused. 'I never trusted her anyway.'

'You never trusted her?'

'She's a fraud. But I shouldn't say things like that. I'm just so worked up. I shouldn't make comments like that.'

'What makes you think Madame Lajoux isn't sincere?'

'Everyone knew they'd been having an affair for decades, and her swanning around as hotel manager. We knew she was getting money from him. To this day. And that she sent some of the money to her son in Canada. He was a waster whom she spoiled.'

Her voice had hardened for a moment. Dupin took out his notebook.

'Can you say for sure that they knew about the painting?'

'No… no, I don't know. I really shouldn't be saying anything anyway.'

'And what about Pierre-Louis Pennec's half-brother, André Pennec, did he know about the painting?'

'My husband was sure he did. He once said Pierre-Louis' father told André. The painting was the great family secret of course. How could he not know?'

Dupin wanted to say that this was exactly why it would have been very helpful for the investigation to have been informed about the painting directly after the murder of Pierre-Louis Pennec – so they would know the motive. He also wanted to tell her how much time they had wasted because of it. And the even more serious issue: that her husband might still be alive if someone had told Dupin about the painting. But it was pointless.

'And Monsieur Beauvois?'

'He's the worst of the lot. My father-in-law was a fool not to see through him, he –' She stopped herself.

'Yes?'

'He's a pompous idiot. That ridiculous museum. So much nonsense in one man's head! When you think about how much money he wheedled out of Pierre-Louis Pennec. All that renovation work at the museum. Why? It's ludicrous. The museum is third rate and is going to stay that way. Provincial.' She looked utterly exhausted after this outburst.

'I really will leave you in peace now.'

Madame Pennec heaved a deep sigh. 'I hope you find out what happened to my husband soon; it doesn't make any difference, but it would still help me.'

'I hope so too, Madame Pennec. I really do.'

She made as though to stand up.

'No, no, don't get up. Please. I'll see myself out.'

Madame Pennec seemed to find it difficult to accept this offer, but she managed it. 'Thank you.'

'If you need any help or if you think of anything else that could be relevant... please don't hesitate. You've got my number.' Dupin had stood up.

'Thank you, Monsieur le Commissaire.'

'*Au revoir*, Madame.'

Dupin left the gloomy room in a hurry.

Outside again, a warm beam of sunlight fell on Dupin's face; the sky was a blazing blue, not a cloud to be seen. Although he had experienced it many times in his nearly three years in Brittany, Dupin was always fascinated by how abruptly the weather could turn. It was a sight to behold. An entirely innocent, warm, sunny day, when you would swear that the summer had finally decided to maintain a stable, high pressure front for weeks, could turn into an autumnal day in the space of half an hour, threatening rain and storms, and then you'd bet anything that this was a solidly low pressure front and it was going to plague you for days – and vice versa. It was as though the previous weather had simply never happened. Dupin sometimes thought that he had never known what this thing called 'weather' really was before moving to Brittany. And that he had only really understood it for the first time here. It was no wonder the changeable weather was a constant topic of conversation in Brittany. And Dupin was deeply impressed with how accurately some Bretons could predict it – over thousands of years the Celtic inhabitants had made a great art of it. Even Dupin had started trying his hand at this art form. In some ways it had become a little hobby of his (although so far he had only impressed himself with his successes).

Dupin stood outside the door for a few moments, took out his Clairefontaine, and made a series of notes. There were a few things he needed to do urgently. He took his mobile out of his pocket.

'Le Ber?'

'Yes?'

'I'm on my way to the hotel now. I want to speak to Madame Lajoux, then you and Labat. No, you and Labat first, then the others. Did you manage to get hold of Beauvois and André Pennec?'

'No, neither yet. Beauvois doesn't have a mobile and Pennec is driving, probably in Rennes on business. His voicemail is turned on. We've left him multiple messages asking him to get in touch with us immediately.'

'Fine. I need to speak to him today no matter what. Same goes for Beauvois.'

'We're doing all we can.'

'One more thing. Check whether Madame Pennec was at the all-night pharmacy in Trévignon last night and if so, when. I need the exact times. I want to know what she bought, how she seemed, everything. Speak to the person who served her.'

'Is she under suspicion?'

'I get the feeling nobody has been telling us the truth so far.'

'We need to discuss things urgently, Monsieur le Commissaire.'

'I'm on my way.'

Labat, Le Ber and Dupin sat in the breakfast room for half an hour discussing everything very carefully. Dupin had brought the inspectors up to speed. He told them about the forty-million-euro painting that had hung in the same place for over a hundred years but had now been stolen. Labat and Le Ber were silent for long stretches. Dupin could see from their faces that the scale of the case was dawning on them now. And it was clear to both of them that there was one thing they absolutely had to do. They had to find the stolen painting – as proof that it had been stolen in the first place. Maybe it would lead them to the perpetrator. Not even Labat complained when Dupin stood up half an hour later and went to speak to Madame Lajoux.

Madame Lajoux was standing at reception when Le Ber, Labat and Dupin came down the stairs. She looked somewhat intimidated when she saw the three of them.

'*Bonjour*, Madame Lajoux. Thank you for making time for us.'

'It's so horrible, Monsieur le Commissaire. Now Loic. There's no end to the tragedy. These are difficult times.' She spoke in that halting, pained way again.

'Very difficult times indeed. We still don't have anything to report about Loic's death. I've got to speak to you again, even if it's not easy for you. Would you mind if we went into the restaurant?'

She looked uncertain. 'Into the restaurant? Back into the restaurant?'

'I want you to show me something.'

The uncertainty in her gaze was growing. 'I'm to show you something?'

213

Dupin took out the key and unlocked the door to the restaurant. 'Follow me.'

Madame Lajoux followed slowly, haltingly. Dupin closed the door behind them. They went towards the bar and just before the bend in the L-shaped room, Dupin stopped. 'Madame Lajoux, I wanted –'

There was a loud knock at the door. Madame Lajoux flinched.

'What on earth?' Dupin was annoyed but he went to the door and unlocked it again. Labat was standing there.

'Monsieur le Commissaire, Madame Cassel is on the phone. Your mobile is off. She was trying to get through to you.'

'I'm in a meeting, you know that. Tell her I'll call her back as soon as I can.'

There was a peculiar look of satisfaction on Labat's round face. He turned around without a word and went back to reception. Dupin hesitated.

'Labat... hang on. I'm coming. If you could excuse me for a moment, Madame Lajoux. I'll be with you again very soon, this won't take long.'

'Of course, Monsieur le Commissaire.'

Dupin left the restaurant. Labat was holding the phone out to him at reception.

'Madame Cassel?'

'Something else occurred to me. I should have told you it immediately in fact. About the painting, the copy. You wanted to know who copied the paintings, didn't you? I mean, who painted the copy of the second *Vision*... Is that still significant?'

'Of course.'

'It's just a possibility, but still. Copyists sometimes immortalised themselves in the paintings, in very subtle ways. They hid their signatures somewhere. It was a game really. You might just be lucky.'

'Interesting.'

'That's it.'

'Thanks. I'll definitely be in touch again, if we find anything I mean.'

'I'm always here.'

'*Au revoir.*'

Dupin hung up. Labat had been standing behind him the entire time. Dupin hated it when people did that. 'Labat?'

'Yes, Monsieur le Commissaire?'

Dupin came right up to him. 'We've got to take a closer look at that painting this minute. Let Le Ber know.'

'A closer look at the painting?'

Dupin couldn't be bothered discussing it all again with Labat. In fact he had just realised he didn't have the faintest idea how they were going to do it. How and where should they be looking for the name? He should have asked Madame Cassel.

'We'll talk later. I'm going back to Madame Lajoux... I don't want any more interruptions, Labat. If there are any, I'll hold you personally responsible.'

It almost seemed as though Madame Lajoux had been standing stock still the entire time Dupin was gone. She was standing there exactly as she had before.

'I'm sorry, Madame Lajoux.'

'Oh no, it's completely understandable. The police investigation takes priority.'

'I wanted to ask that you, I'd like to ask you –' He

began to stammer. 'I wonder if you would excuse me again briefly, Madame Lajoux. This is very rude, but I've got to make one more urgent call – I'm sure we'll have some peace and quiet for our conversation then.'

It was clear Madame Lajoux felt uncomfortable. She didn't know what to say.

'I'll be right back.'

Dupin went around the corner to the end of the bar. He fished his mobile out of his trouser pocket.

'Madame Cassel?' He was speaking very quietly.

'Hello, Monsieur le Commissaire?'

'Hello. Listen, I need you. You've got to help us with the hidden signatures. I have no idea where or how I'm meant to find them. We don't have the... tools for it.'

Dupin could hear a soft laugh at the other end of the line.

'I thought you would call again. I think I should have offered straight away.'

'I'm so sorry, Madame Cassel, I – we are being guided entirely by your art expertise in some aspects of this case, I know you're at your conference, I'm –'

'I need five minutes to get ready. I can leave right now... I'll drive my own car, if that's okay.'

'I'm so grateful to you for doing this. We'll be expecting you. It's now,' Dupin looked at his watch, 'it's quarter past seven now. So... well, we'll be expecting you.'

'See you soon, Monsieur le Commissaire.'

Dupin went back to Madame Lajoux.

'You have my full attention now, Madame Lajoux. I really must apologise.'

'As I said, your investigation is the most important thing, Monsieur le Commissaire. We all want you to catch the murderer as quickly as possible. He's been free to walk around for three days. That's not right.'

Her voice had taken on the same mournful rhythm which Dupin recognised from their previous conversations. He waited a few seconds, then he spoke firmly. 'You can tell me now, Madame Lajoux.'

Madame Lajoux flinched, avoiding his gaze.

'I... I don't know what you mean. What can I –' She broke off, a resignation in her face and in the way she held herself. It was some time before she could look Dupin in the eye again. 'You know, don't you? You know.' She almost burst into tears and for a moment she seemed to be in danger of losing control completely.

'Yes.'

'Monsieur Pennec wouldn't think it right, any of this. He would be so unhappy. He didn't want anyone to know about the painting.'

'Madame Lajoux, we're talking about more than forty million euro. About the probable motive for Pierre-Louis Pennec's murder.'

'You're wrong,' she sounded incensed now, 'we're not talking about more than forty million euro – we are talking about someone's unequivocal final wish, Monsieur le Commissaire. The fact that the painting is hanging safely here, without anyone knowing about it. It belongs to the hotel and its history –'

'He wanted to present the painting to the Musée d'Orsay as a gift. With a donation plaque making the story of the painting public.'

Madame Lajoux looked aghast. Either she was an extremely good actress or her true emotions were revealing themselves. 'What? He wanted to do *what*?'

'To give the painting to the Musée d'Orsay. He got in touch with the museum last week.'

'That's... that's –' She broke off.

'Yes?'

Her features hardened. 'Nothing... it's nothing. If you're sure it's true. We should just go along with what he thought was right.'

'Does it seem – how should I put it – *inappropriate*, to you?'

'What?'

'The museum thing. The donation.'

'No, no. It's just... oh, I don't know. In many ways it was the secret at the core of everything. It's all so strange, so wrong. I don't know.'

'How long have you known about the painting?'

'Thirty-five years. Monsieur Pennec let me in on it early. In my third year.'

'Who else knows about the painting?'

'Nobody. Just Beauvois – and his son of course. Monsieur Beauvois was Monsieur Pennec's art expert you know, Pierre-Louis asked his advice on everything to do with painting. I told you that already. Monsieur Beauvois advised him on the renovations here too and answered all his questions to do with the air-conditioning. So that the painting would be kept in ideal conditions. A man of great integrity, with high ideals. He takes all of this to heart, all of the tradition. Not because of the money. Monsieur Pennec knew that.'

'And why did Monsieur Pennec have the Gauguin hanging here all those years?'

'Why?' Madame Lajoux looked appalled, as if this question was somehow improper. 'Marie-Jeanne Pennec hung it there. Oh yes. The Gauguin always hung there. That's where it belongs. Pierre-Louis could look at it every evening when he was at the bar. It embodies the entire legacy. Pierre-Louis would never have dreamed of keeping it any other way, or of removing it from the hotel, not in a million years. This was the safest place for it, right here.'

This was the answer Dupin had expected and Madame Lajoux was, however strange it sounded, probably right. Quite apart from the sentimental reasons for this location, maybe it really was one of the most inconspicuous places for something like this.

'And who else knew about the painting?'

'His half-brother. I don't know whether he confided in Delon, I don't think so. It was a genuine secret.'

Dupin almost laughed; this was too funny. Pierre-Louis' son, his daughter-in-law, André Pennec, Beauvois, Madame Lajoux… and the painter who made the copy that was hanging there now, maybe Delon… that meant that in Pierre-Louis Pennec's inner circle, everyone had known. And then there was Charles Sauré too.

'At least seven people, perhaps eight, knew about the painting and that it was worth forty million euro. Most of them could see the money hanging there every day.'

'Well when you put it like that it sounds awful. As if one of those people murdered Pierre-Louis… is that what you think?' Madame looked like she was preparing to be outraged again.

'And who knows who those people told, in confidence... who knows who else knew all about this?'

Madame Lajoux looked sadly at Dupin. There was a hint of mistrust in her gaze. 'You've got to admire the way Pierre-Louis Pennec dealt with the difficult mission his father entrusted him with, and how he dealt with the hotel and the painting. He did it all in the most wonderful, impressive way. That much money can destroy absolutely everything. Bad things can happen.'

It was on the tip of Dupin's tongue to ask what could be worse than murder or probably even two murders. 'What do *you* think happened then, Madame Lajoux? Who murdered Pierre-Louis Pennec? And who murdered Loic Pennec?'

Madame Lajoux glared at Dupin for a few moments, openly hostile, her whole body ominously tense, as though preparing to attack. But then she looked away and her shoulders fell in resignation. She walked very slowly over to the painting and stood in front of it. 'The Gauguin. After the break-in I was so afraid that it had been stolen. All would have been lost.'

Dupin didn't fully understand her last comment, but he had a vague inkling of what she meant. Initially he had decided he wouldn't mention the theft of the painting, even if this was ridiculous in many ways, something which Labat had – strongly – argued. And it was ridiculous, because they were throwing away an important point in the interviews. But he just had a feeling about it.

Madame Lajoux was still standing there, motionless. 'Do you know who I don't trust, Monsieur le Commissaire? André Pennec. He's an unscrupulous character. I think Pierre-Louis Pennec hated him. He would never have said it, but I could sense it.'

'It can't have been easy for him, being excluded from the inheritance by his own father and seeing Pierre Louis-Pennec inherit it all – especially the Gauguin obviously. And then his brother excluded him from the inheritance in the same way.'

'We basically never saw him. He only ever phoned. But I can believe it, oh yes. Even his dodgy lawyer friend couldn't help him.'

'What do you mean by that?'

'Don't you know? André Pennec had hired a lawyer who was supposedly going to call the provisions of their father's will into question. It infuriated Pierre-Louis. They didn't speak for ten years after that.'

'When was that? What year?'

'Oh it's a long time ago now. I can't be certain when it was any more. It was around the time they had a political dispute, or just afterwards.'

'So do you think the dispute had less to do with politics?'

'Well not quite. Monsieur Pennec hated the whole *Emgann* thing. It was definitely a bit of both.'

'Do you believe André Pennec to be capable of murder?'

Madame Lajoux hesitated, an inscrutable expression on her face. 'I don't know. Perhaps it's cruel. I don't think... I don't think I should be commenting on this matter, Monsieur le Commissaire. I hardly know him personally.'

'You yourself have come into an impressive inheritance, Madame Lajoux.'

Madame Lajoux looked shocked. 'You know about that? Is it okay then, is it decided? I feel very awkward about all of this, you know.'

'Our concern is the murder, Madame Lajoux.'

'Yes... Yes... Does anyone else know?'

'My inspectors. But you needn't worry. It's their job to remain silent.'

'This really isn't easy for me.' She was pale. 'Do you know about the letter, too?'

'Yes.'

'Have you read it?' Her voice shook.

'No, no. Nobody has read it. That's beyond the remit of the police. I would need to get a judicial order. But I...'

'You... you know about... about our relationship?' Her eyes filled with tears, her voice so faint it was almost inaudible.

'Yes.'

'Where, how could you, I –'

'It's okay, Madame Lajoux. It's your life. It's not my business or anyone else's. Only insofar as it is relevant to the case. I only need to know about the nature of your relationship with Pierre-Louis Pennec to build an overall picture for myself.'

'It wasn't an affair, not one of those nasty little relationships. I loved him. From the beginning. And he loved me, even though it was impossible for us to be together properly. He didn't love his wife, not any more. Perhaps he never did. I don't think he did. They were so young when they met and married. She was never interested in the hotel. Not in the slightest. But he never blamed her for it. He was a noble man.

We could never be seen together, do you understand? Never. Everything was… it was utterly pointless.'

'All of that, Madame Lajoux, that's your own business.' Dupin had said this more harshly than he had intended, but Madame Lajoux didn't notice at all. 'How was your relationship with Loic Pennec?'

'*My* relationship with him?'

'Yes. What did you make of him?'

'Me? Pierre-Louis Pennec always wanted his son to take over everything, to become a great, powerful hotelier like himself, like his father and his grandmother. He didn't like Catherine, he –'

'So you've said… but what did you think of the relationship between father and son?'

'He might have been a little disappointed in his son, I suppose. Loic had it easy. I couldn't understand it. His path was sketched out so beautifully. But it takes real strength to carry out a duty as onerous as running the hotel. You have to make it your entire life's work.' Her voice had become bitter. 'You have to be worthy!'

'Worthy?'

'Yes. Worthy of living up to a calling like that.'

'Did you and Loic often speak to each other?'

'No.' The answer came very brusquely.

'But he was often here.'

'Yes. But he only spoke to his father. He wasn't part of the hotel, you know. He was an outsider here.'

'Is it true that Monsieur Pennec sometimes gave you certain sums of money, over and above your monthly salary?'

Madame Lajoux was looking indignant again. 'Well yes. Listen, I've sacrificed my whole life for him and

223

the hotel. Those weren't favours, it wasn't because I was his lover. I put everything I had into this hotel. Everything. What are you implying?'

'What kind of sums were they?'

'Ten thousand euro, usually. Sometimes less. Once or twice a year.'

'And you transferred this money to your son in Canada?'

'I… Yes, to my son. He's married. And he's self-employed. He's building up his business at the moment. I… I supported him, yes.'

'All of the money?'

'Yes. All of the money.'

'How old is he?'

'Forty-six.'

'How long have you been transferring these sums of money?'

'Twenty years.'

'And you have absolutely no idea what happened to either of the Pennecs?'

Madame Lajoux seemed relieved that Dupin had changed the subject. 'No. Emotions always run high here, but murder…'

'Why do you think that the donation wouldn't have been the right thing to do?'

She looked very unhappy again. 'He didn't say anything to me about it. I didn't know. He should have –' She broke off.

'I have to ask you another question. And I ask that you don't take it personally, this is police procedure. We can't leave any stone unturned at this stage.'

'I understand.'

'Where were you yesterday evening?'

'Me? You mean where was I personally?'

'Yes.'

'I worked until half seven, there was a lot to do, you know, it's all a terrible mess. Someone has to keep their eye on everything. The guests are worried. I think I was home by around eight o'clock. I was absolutely exhausted and went to bed soon after. I showered, brushed my teeth...'

'That'll do, Madame Lajoux. When do you usually go to sleep?'

'For the last few years I've been going to bed early, around half nine. I have to get up very early after all. Half five every morning. I had a different rhythm when I used to sleep at the hotel.'

'Thank you, Madame Lajoux. That's as much as I need to know. Did you see anyone as you left the hotel?'

'Madame Mendu, I think. We bumped into each other briefly downstairs.'

'All right. You should be getting home now.'

'There's still a bit to do tonight.' Something seemed to be making her very self-conscious. 'I –' She broke off again.

Dupin understood. 'I'd like to assure you again that everything we've discussed will remain between us, Madame Lajoux. Please don't worry. Nobody will hear anything about this.'

She seemed somewhat relieved. 'Thank you. It's very important to me. People could get the wrong idea you know. That would be unbearable, especially when I think about Monsieur Pennec.'

'Thanks very much again, Madame Lajoux.' Dupin went towards the door. They left the restaurant together, Dupin locked up again and they said goodbye.

Labat and Le Ber were nowhere to be seen. He needed one of them. Madame Lajoux had almost disappeared up the stairs by the time he realised there was one question he still needed to ask.

'Excuse me, Madame Lajoux – I have one last question. There was that man you saw in front of the hotel on Wednesday, who was talking to Pierre-Louis Pennec... do you remember?'

Madame Lajoux turned around with astonishing speed and sprightliness. 'Oh yes, of course, your inspectors asked me about that too.'

'I would like you to look at a photo and tell us whether it's the same man.'

'Absolutely, Monsieur le Commissaire.'

'One of my inspectors will show you the photo.'

'They'll find me in the breakfast room.'

'Thanks again.'

She disappeared up to the first floor.

Dupin stood outside the main door and took a few deep breaths. It made for a jolly scene, the square and the narrow streets were glittering with tourists. Dupin turned right, heading for his little alleyway. There was nobody around.

It was eight o'clock. He had lost all sense of time, which always happened to him when he was on a case, but today it was also because daylight hadn't really started until the afternoon. It was so hot now that it seemed as though the sun was trying to make up for what it had missed out on that morning. He had a feeling this was going to be a long day. His third long day.

Dupin walked to the end of the road without thinking, then turned right in the direction of the river and crossed the bridge to the harbour. This had already become something of a ritual for him. That's how it always was – without meaning to, he returned to the places he liked. He dialled Le Ber's number.

'Where are you?'

'At the chemist in Trévignon, I'm just leaving.'

'And?'

'Madame Pennec was here yesterday evening, around quarter to ten, she bought Novanox. Nitrazepam. She had a prescription for a high dosage. She was in the chemist's for about ten minutes. She was served by a member of staff called Madame Kabou, who was there this evening too. I've just spoken to her.'

Dupin managed to get out his notebook with his left hand. 'Good. Now we need to know what time she got back.'

'To her house?'

'Yes.'

'How are we meant to find that out?'

'I don't know. We probably won't... There are still a few more things to be done, Le Ber. Find out what time Madame Lajoux left the *Central* yesterday. Make sure you speak to Madame Mendu.'

'Okay.'

'I really need to see Monsieur Beauvois. Have you found him?'

'Yes, he was in the museum. There was a long art

society meeting there today and he had other things to do, too. Phone calls, something to do with donors.'

'Okay. I'll visit him later; I'm going to see Delon first. Tell Beauvois nine o'clock or thereabouts at the hotel. We'll give him a call. Has André Pennec turned up again?'

'We got through to him in Rennes, via his office. He'll be back late. He knows that you want to see him urgently.'

'Call him again. Set up a meeting. Is Labat at the hotel?'

'Yes.'

'Tell him to look up the Musée d'Orsay online and show Madame Lajoux a photo of Charles Sauré. I've already told her about this.'

'The director of the collection?'

'Yes. I want to know if he was the man she saw talking to Pennec outside the hotel.'

'I'll let him know.'

'One last thing. Madame Cassel is just about to arrive at the hotel. I want you to go into the restaurant with her if I'm not there. She may need your help. She has to take a look at the painting.'

'The copy of the Gauguin?'

'Yes. We may be able to find a clue to the copyist. She's already on her way.'

'Fine, no problem.'

'Speak to you soon.' Dupin hung up.

A group of kayaks came into the harbour and stopped on the far side, underneath one of the big palm trees. Loud, cheerful voices and exhilarated people; a merry mixture of colours, the boats yellow, red, green and blue.

The quickest way to get to Delon's house from here would definitely be just to walk diagonally over the hill, but Dupin still found the labyrinth of little streets quite daunting. He took the route past the *Central*, even though it meant he had to push his way through the crowds.

Dupin knocked on the heavy old wooden door. The little window next to it was wide open.

'Please come in. The door isn't locked.'

Dupin opened the door and stepped inside. It seemed very cosy, just as it had the last time he was here. The ground floor of the pretty old stone house was one big room – sitting room, dining room and kitchen all in one. It wasn't unlike Beauvois' house, perhaps a little smaller, and yet it seemed completely different. The atmosphere was different.

'I was just about to eat.'

'Oh I'm sorry. I've come at an extremely inconvenient time. I didn't even let you know I was on my way.'

'Won't you join me?'

'I just have a few questions; I don't want to keep you too long.'

Even Dupin himself didn't know whether that meant yes, I'll sit down with you, or no, I'd rather stand, I'm not staying long anyway. He sat down. On the old wooden table, almost exactly in the centre of the room, lay a plate of langoustines, a dish of scallop rillettes, some mayonnaise and a bottle of Muscadet. Next to these was a baguette (a 'Dolmen', Dupin's favourite kind). He noticed all these details because he suddenly felt ravenous.

Delon had gone over to the old cupboard next to the stove and fetched a second plate and glass without a word, placing them on the table in front of Dupin, who was very grateful. He hadn't even needed to say anything. He took a little bread and some langoustines and began to peel them.

'Pierre-Louis came here too sometimes. We'd sit just like you and I are sitting now. He liked being here like this: a baguette on the table, a few simple things.'

Delon laughed fondly, affectionately. In comparison to his taciturn behaviour the day before yesterday he seemed positively talkative.

'I take it you know about the painting?'

Delon answered in the calm way he had been speaking all along. 'It never interested me. He was glad it didn't.'

Dupin had been expecting this answer. So seven people, at the very least, had known about the painting.

'Why didn't it interest you?'

'I don't know. Everyone flitted around him because of the painting.'

'What do you mean exactly?'

'Everyone saw the money. That some of it could belong to them one day, or even the whole painting… I think he could see it sometimes. That much money changes everything.'

'What did he see?'

'That they all wanted the painting.'

'And who wanted the painting?'

Delon looked at Dupin in astonishment. 'Everyone. His son, his daughter-in-law, Lajoux, I don't even know who else knew. Beauvois did for sure. So did his half-brother.'

'But he never intended to sell it.'

'No, but it was there, always there, do you understand? And everyone thought to themselves: who knows? Who knows?' Delon sounded mournful all of a sudden.

'And do you think one of them could turn out to be the murderer?'

Again Delon looked shocked, but spoke in an even tone. 'I think any of them could.'

'You believe all of these people to be capable of murder?'

'How many millions is the painting worth?'

'Forty, maybe more.' Dupin looked at Delon and waited for a response. Delon reached for the Muscadet and filled both glasses.

'There aren't many people I could honestly say would never become a murderer for that kind of money.' There wasn't a trace of cynicism or resignation in his voice; he acted like he was just calmly stating an established fact.

Dupin essentially agreed.

'They were all waiting for him to die at last. They were all thinking about this day, the entire time. No doubt about it.'

There was a long silence. Both of them ate.

'Everyone wanted the painting... and nobody was going to get it. Did you know about Pierre-Louis Pennec's plan to present it to the Musée d'Orsay as a gift?'

Delon hesitated a little for the first time. 'No. So that's what he was planning, eh? It's a good idea.'

It was on the tip of Dupin's tongue to say that it was

precisely this good idea of Pennec's that might have triggered the events culminating in his murder. When he found out about his serious heart condition, he had turned to the Musée d'Orsay immediately... and somebody must have known exactly what he had done, someone who wanted to prevent the donation being made. Someone who had to act before it came to that.

Dupin was silent. Delon was absolutely right. In itself, it was a good idea.

Delon looked serious now. 'He should have done it before. The donation. No doubt about it. I was always afraid that even more people would find out about the painting. If more than two people know something, eventually everyone will know it.'

'That's true.'

'Pennec was never afraid. It was odd. He wasn't afraid of anything.'

'Can you think of anyone who might have had a motive – a particularly strong one I mean?'

'When that much money is involved, doesn't everyone have a particular motive?'

Dupin felt as though any of Delon's comments this evening might have come straight out of his own mouth. 'What did you make of the relationship between father and son?'

'It was all so tragic.' Delon topped up their glasses. 'A great tragedy. Everything. What happened between them, and now his death. He had a sad old life.'

'What do you think –' Dupin's mobile rang and at an offensive volume. Le Ber's number. He picked up rather reluctantly.

'Monsieur le Commissaire?'

'Yes?'

'You've got to come and take a look at this right now.' Le Ber was practically falling over his words in excitement.

'What's happened?'

'We've taken the painting out of its frame, Madame Cassel and I. She brought special tools with her. We've found a signature on the copy.'

'Yes?'

'Frédéric Beauvois.'

'Beauvois?'

'The one and only.'

'So he did the painting? He copied it?'

'Yes. We found the signature in the tree, up in the branches, very well hidden but still clear. We've compared this signature with the one on some invoices he gave Pierre-Louis Pennec. There's no doubt about it.'

'Does he paint then?'

'Apparently. Madame Cassel thinks it's an excellent piece.'

'I know.'

'It seems… I mean, I don't have a good feeling about this.'

'Are you absolutely sure?'

'About my feeling?'

'That it's Beauvois?'

'Whose signature it is? Yes. Madame Cassel is completely sure. Frédéric Beauvois is the copyist behind this painting.'

'I'm on my way. Let's meet at the hotel.' Dupin thought for a moment. 'No. Let's go straight to Beauvois' house. I'll leave now. See you there.'

'Okay.'

Delon had calmly continued eating during the phone call, remaining thoroughly unconcerned.

'I've got to go, Monsieur Delon.'

'So I thought.'

Dupin stood. 'Don't get up.'

'No, no, I should.'

Delon walked Dupin the few metres to the door.

'Thank you for the excellent meal. And for taking the time to speak to me too, of course.'

'You didn't eat much.'

'Next time.'

'*Au revoir.*'

Dupin tried to get his bearings. It couldn't be that far to Beauvois' house, but he found the narrow, crooked little streets and alleyways of the old town confusing. Dupin decided to go down the main street instead. It took him five minutes. When he arrived, Le Ber was already waiting for him, standing a few metres down the road from the house. The door to the front garden was closed.

'Ring the bell.'

Nothing happened. Le Ber rang a second and third time.

'Let's go to the museum.'

'Are you sure he's there?'

'We might as well try it. Where's Madame Cassel?'

'At the hotel. I asked her to wait there.'

Dupin smiled. Le Ber looked at him in bemusement.

'Is there something wrong, Monsieur le Commissaire?'

'No, no. Nothing at all.'

They hurried back down the lane, past the *Central*

234

and Place Gauguin and up the road to the museum. It was less than a hundred metres from the hotel. The entrance was in the modern part of the building, an ambitious, ugly, white, concrete-steel-glass construction which had been built onto the old *Julia Hotel*.

The door was locked. Le Ber knocked loudly. Nothing happened. He knocked again, more firmly this time, but still nothing happened. There was no doorbell. Le Ber took a few steps back. To the left of the museum was an art gallery, the first in a whole string of them, one gallery after another – perhaps ten or fifteen crammed together, stretching the whole way down the little street. A few steps to the right of the entrance was another door in a gloomy, concrete alcove. This one was heavy and made of steel – it looked like it might be the door to the technical hub of the museum.

'I'll try this one.'

Directly beside the door – strangely low down – there was a very plain doorbell that they might easily have missed. Le Ber held it down three times in a row. A few moments later there was a loud noise from the museum. It sounded like a door banging.

'Hello? Police! This is the police. Please open this door!'

Le Ber was yelling. Dupin almost laughed.

'Please open this door immediately.'

Dupin was just about to tell him to calm down when the door opened, just a crack at first, but then in one swift motion it was thrown open wide. Frédéric Beauvois was standing in front of them, smiling and friendly.

'Ah – the Inspector and the Commissaire. *Bonsoir,* Messieurs. Welcome to the Pont-Aven Museum.'

Beauvois' remarkable friendliness threw Le Ber off. Dupin took over the talking.

'Good evening, Monsieur Beauvois. We'd like to have a word.'

'Both of you?'

'Yes.'

'Well then it must be important. So many police VIPs. Shall we go to my house? Or to the hotel?'

'We'd like to stay here in the museum. Do you have a room where we could chat for a little while?'

Beauvois seemed irritated for a split second, but immediately composed himself again. 'Of course, yes, there is a conference room; we can sit there. I'd be delighted. We use it whenever one of our clubs has a meeting. It's along here. Up the stairs.'

Le Ber and Dupin followed Beauvois. Le Ber hadn't said a word yet.

The stairs led to the first floor. They went along a long, narrow corridor which led to an equally narrow door. Beauvois opened it with a flourish and went into the room. Even inside, the new part of the museum was not particularly attractive. The design was very functional but the room was surprisingly large, a good ten metres wide. Some battered-looking desks were set out in a big U-shape.

They sat at one of the desks in the corner.

'What can I do for you gentlemen?' Beauvois was leaning back in his chair. He looked completely at ease.

Dupin's forehead creased. A question had already crossed his mind on the way to the museum, and he couldn't stop thinking about it. Why had Beauvois signed the painting, thereby running the risk of incriminating himself? What was that about? He was an intelligent man. It didn't make any sense. It seemed to indicate that Beauvois might not even be guilty, despite his name clearly being on the copy.

'We have a search warrant, Monsieur Beauvois.'

Dupin had spoken in an icy tone. Le Ber looked incredulously at the Commissaire. Of course they didn't have a search warrant, but Beauvois was too wrapped up in his own thoughts to check. He ran his hands through his hair several times and shook his head a little, pursing his lips. He seemed to be thinking hard. A minute passed before he spoke in an extremely friendly way.

'Come, gentlemen. Come with me.'

He stood up, waited for Dupin and Le Ber to do the same (which they did after a moment's hesitation) and then briskly retraced his steps. Along the corridor, down the stairs. He opened a door that Le Ber and Dupin hadn't noticed before, opposite the main door, directly to the left of the stairs. It led to the basement of the museum. Beauvois turned on the light. He was still leading the way with determined strides.

'This is our storeroom, gentlemen. And our workshop.'

They entered a very large room.

'Some of the members of our societies are passionate painters...and, I can say this in all modesty, some of them are very talented. There are some remarkable pieces here. But come along.'

In the far corner stood several long, narrow tables. Le Ber and Dupin had to work to keep up with Beauvois' pace. He stood in front of one of the tables. They positioned themselves on either side of him without even thinking about it.

Beauvois reached for one of the switches dangling from the ceiling. Powerful spotlights came on and it was a few moments before they could see properly again.

The first thing they saw was the garish, almost blinding, orange. Then the rest of the painting. It was right in front of them. They could have reached out and touched it. Intact. And overwhelming.

It was another few moments before Dupin and Le Ber could grasp what they were looking at. Le Ber murmured so quietly it was almost impossible to understand: 'I knew it.' And then after another little pause, 'Forty million euro.'

But before either of them could say anything else, Beauvois had reached for a knife lying in amongst the wild profusion of thick pencils, various paintbrushes, scrapers and other painting tools – and thrust it into the middle of the painting. Dupin tried to grab hold of Beauvois' arm at the last second, but it was too late. It had all happened incredibly fast.

Beauvois deftly cut a little square out of the painting. Then he held the square of canvas up to the harsh light.

'Gilbert Sonnheim. A copy. Do you see? An insignificant painter from the artists' colony, from Lille, less gifted, a syncretist. But by Teutates, he was a good copyist! An excellent piece.' Beauvois seemed manic.

Dupin's thoughts were racing at a monstrous pace, darting here and there – he felt dizzy. Beauvois held up the piece of canvas as if he were taking an oath, his eyes blazing.

Dupin was the first to find his tongue again. 'You replaced a copy with a copy. I think you wanted to steal the painting and replace it with your copy so that nobody would notice it was gone. But it had already been stolen – it had already been replaced with a copy. There are two copies.'

The confusion on Le Ber's face seemed to grow as Dupin went on – then all of a sudden comprehension dawned.

Beauvois put the piece of canvas back into the painting with meticulous precision. 'I enjoyed doing it, in fact I was proud to do it.' His voice was charged with smug, ridiculous emotion. 'Pierre-Louis Pennec would have been in complete and utter agreement with what I did, he would have welcomed it. He would be spinning in his grave if his son had inherited the painting – Loic would have sold it at the first opportunity. He was waiting for this exact moment. His whole life he was just waiting for his father's death! The museum was so close to Pierre-Louis Pennec's heart. This was all so important to him, Pont-Aven, its history, the artists' colony. That's the truth, gentlemen!'

'It was you who broke into the hotel the night after the murder. You swapped the paintings and hung up the copy,' Le Ber paused a moment, 'you hung up your copy and then you took down the other copy that was there and kept it. That's this painting here, the one you cut a piece out of.'

'Very likely, Inspector. I fell for it. Me, Frédéric Beauvois! But it was dark in the restaurant, almost pitch black. I just had a little torch... and it's an excellent copy. Not as good as my painting, if I may say so. Up there, in the branches, the brushstrokes aren't quite right.'

'When did you do your copy?' Dupin's voice was very calm and focused.

'Oh, decades ago now. Almost thirty years ago. After Pennec took me into his confidence. I became his expert. He was a hotelier you know, not an art scholar, not an art historian. No. But he had a monumental artistic and historical inheritance to look after; there was the hotel of course, but also this exceptional painting. A marvel. It's Gauguin's most daring painting; believe me, nothing matches it for sheer boldness. I don't mean that...'

'And why did you make a copy?'

'I wanted to study it out of admiration. Out of pure fascination. I took photographs of it and then painted from them. I don't know if I've mentioned it but painting is my great passion and always has been. I know my limitations, but I have a certain amount of skill. I –'

'And your signature on the painting, that was the pride of an artist?'

'Youthful nonsense, yes. A little vanity.'

It was plausible, thought Dupin. Everything was plausible, as far-fetched as it sounded – and indeed was.

'Did Pierre-Louis Pennec know about your copy?'

'No. I've kept it to myself all these years. I was the only person who kept looking at it again and again. To see Gauguin and the fantastic power of this painting, its infinite spirit. It defies everything.'

'Did you know there might be another copy?'

'No. Never.'

'And Pierre-Louis Pennec, did he ever say anything about a copy?'

'No.'

'How did this one here come about?'

'I can only speculate, Monsieur le Commissaire. When Gauguin left Pont-Aven for good and moved to the South Seas, it was by no means the end of the Pont-Aven School. Many painters stayed here for years, as did Sonnheim. Obviously more and more artists of little significance came here. Maybe Marie-Jeanne herself commissioned Sonnheim to do the copy. That wouldn't have been unusual. She had paintings by so many artists hanging in her restaurant, originals at first, but then she gradually replaced them with copies, just like Mademoiselle Julia did in her hotel. Perhaps Marie-Jeanne was intending to keep the original somewhere safe and needed this copy to replace it. But I'd like to emphasise this is all pure speculation.'

'So this copy is over a hundred years old too? It's almost as old as the painting itself?'

'Absolutely.'

'Where was it kept all this time?'

'Again, I really couldn't say. Pierre-Louis may have inherited it along with the original. There's that little room next to his one at the hotel with the photo archive in it, Pierre-Louis kept some copies there because there wasn't space for them in the restaurant; we spoke about those copies a few times, he was considering leaving them to the museum. He always talked about there being a dozen of them. I've never seen them, but perhaps he kept this copy there too. Or else it wasn't in the hotel at all... and someone else had it?' Beauvois paused. 'Maybe even he didn't know about this copy, that's a possibility too. Who knows?'

'Indeed, who knows? But somebody had it... or knew about it and could get their hands on it.' Dupin was irritated now, and sounded very determined.

Beauvois was still thinking everything through. 'The murderer must have swapped it for the real painting the very night they committed the crime.'

Dupin was sure Beauvois was right. That's how it must have been. Sauré had seen the original hanging in the restaurant just the day before the murder, in the same spot it had occupied for the last hundred years.

'What did you intend to do with the painting, Monsieur Beauvois?'

Beauvois' voice rose dramatically again. 'It would have benefited the museum and the society – every last penny of it.' He hesitated for a moment. 'I need hardly add that none of it would have been for me, for my own purposes. That money could have achieved something. A proper museum expansion, a new centre for contemporary painting. So much could have been achieved! Pierre-Louis Pennec didn't want the painting to go to his son and daughter-in-law. Pierre-Louis was intending to give the painting to the Musée d'Orsay as a gift.' He presented this last sentence as his trump card.

'We know about that, Monsieur Beauvois.'

'Of course you do. He had been considering it for a long time but not actually doing anything. Then last week he asked me how to go about it. All at once, out of the blue. He was very determined. And he wanted it taken care of quickly. I recommended Monsieur Sauré to him, a brilliant man, the director of the collection at the museum.'

'Did you introduce Monsieur Pennec to Charles Sauré?'

'He had no idea what to do. He always relied on me in these matters.'

'And did you speak to Monsieur Sauré also?'

'No, I just gave Pierre-Louis his name and number; I offered to speak to him, but Pierre-Louis wanted to do it himself.'

'Did you know that he and Sauré met up? That Sauré was in the hotel and saw the painting?'

Beauvois looked surprised. 'No, when was Monsieur Sauré here in Pont-Aven?'

'Wednesday.'

'Huh.'

'What does that mean?'

'Nothing. Nothing at all.'

'Where were you last Thursday evening, Monsieur Beauvois? And yesterday evening?'

'Me?'

'Yes, you.'

Beauvois leapt up from his chair and then sat back down again, his back ramrod straight and his tone of voice abruptly altered. He spoke sharply, but still very smugly. 'That is grotesque, Monsieur. You can't suspect me. I've done nothing wrong.'

Dupin recalled the short phone call Beauvois had had during lunch yesterday, and how coldly he had spoken all of a sudden. 'I decide whom we suspect, Monsieur Beauvois.'

Dupin was sick of this. Everyone in this case saw themselves as the selfless protector of Pierre-Louis Pennec's wishes, as some noble hero. That's what whoever murdered him would be claiming too. And everyone had lied outright in their initial interviews. They had been keeping the most important fact from him this whole time. Everyone had known about the painting and had been aware that other people knew too. But everyone pretended that this somehow wasn't relevant.

'What are you basing this ridiculous suspicion on?' ventured Beauvois.

Dupin looked amused. 'Perhaps you were also in possession of a second copy? And thought up a very cunning trick. Steal the painting and cover it up with some story about replacing a copy with another copy.'

For the first time Beauvois looked genuinely uncertain. He stammered. 'That's absurd. I've never heard anything so absurd in my life.'

Le Ber laid it on thick now: 'Quite apart from any other suspicious activity, you have committed burglary, Monsieur Beauvois. This isn't some trivial matter. You smashed in the window of a restaurant, got inside in a remarkably professional way and intended to steal a painting worth forty million euro.'

Dupin was very pleased with Le Ber's contribution. Beauvois was so sure he had the moral high ground that even the break-in didn't seem to matter to him.

'This is all utterly ridiculous, Inspector. So what exactly did I do then? All I have is this worthless copy here, nothing more. What kind of crime is that? Attempted serious theft?'

'So, Monsieur Beauvois. Where were you last night and Thursday night?'

'I'm not going to answer these questions.'

'Obviously that's up to you, Monsieur Beauvois. You can call in a lawyer.'

'I will. This is a disgraceful turn of events. I was well aware the police can be seriously lacking in tact sometimes, but –'

'Inspector Le Ber will accompany you to the station in Quimper. We're going to do this by the book.' Dupin's mood had darkened.

'You can't be serious, Monsieur le Commissaire!' Beauvois was becoming more and more frantic.

'I'm completely serious, Monsieur Beauvois. And I find it ridiculous that you would doubt it.' Dupin turned firmly on his heel. He had to get out of here. 'I'll have a car sent for you, Le Ber.' He was already on the stairs and hadn't looked back.

'Monsieur le Commissaire, there will be serious –'

'I'll ask the officers to send the car very quickly, Le Ber. It won't take long.' Dupin could still hear Beauvois' muffled complaints. But he was already upstairs, opening the heavy main door and going outside.

The sun had just set behind the hills, the sky a deep pink. Dupin was exhausted. He still didn't know what to make of Beauvois. Not even now, after this whirlwind of events. A horrible man, but that didn't matter. Did he know the whole truth now? Or had Beauvois just spun them some ridiculous story? A story that was intended to cover up a different one? Beauvois was on a sacred mission... and he was cunning. Nothing in this case was as it seemed, that was the rule.

It was all so difficult. Anything was possible, he had to think creatively. The murderer had been in possession of a copy of the painting, a copy that was painted only a few years after the original and which had been unknown until now. But Dupin hadn't asked anyone about a copy yet, and nobody volunteered information around here. Nobody.

But what worried Dupin most of all was the shadowy thought playing on his mind again, something from the conversations he'd had that day. Something wasn't right. Something crucial. He hadn't the slightest idea what it was, however hard he thought. But maybe it was just because of the bewildering whirlwind of events that day or how tired he was. And he was still hungry; he really hadn't eaten much at Delon's.

Dupin hadn't taken the most direct route back to the *Central*, choosing to walk through the streets of galleries instead, turning right, going down the steps, along the narrow lanes and up to the top of the hill. He leafed through his Clairefontaine over and over as he walked along, almost tripping a few times. Nothing had caught his eye that was able to relieve his shadowy feeling of unease, nothing at all. So he called Labat and explained what had happened (Labat always remained unimpressed by incidents like this). They had sent Le Ber a car from Pont-Aven; Monfort was driving. Beauvois was on his way to Quimper, there was a chance he would talk there.

Labat had given Dupin a quick update on the latest news. Madame Lajoux had identified Sauré as the man whom she had seen speaking to Pennec in front of the hotel. No matter how much Labat pushed him – and this was the type of thing Labat usually excelled at – André Pennec would not confirm what time he would be back from his 'official business' in Rennes that evening. Labat had informed him that they would be waiting for him at the hotel and assumed that he would arrive before midnight. Dupin had tasked Labat with checking out Pennec's entire stay in Rennes and reconstructing his day exactly, down to the very minute. And Madame Cassel wanted to speak to Dupin again, Labat didn't know what about.

Dupin wanted to be alone for a while longer so he went down to the harbour and just stood there, staring at the boats without really taking anything in. Then he walked to the hotel, spoke briefly to Labat again and went upstairs to the first floor. Madame Cassel was sitting in the breakfast room, in the same place as this morning; it seemed like days ago to Dupin.

'*Bonsoir*, Madame Cassel. We are very grateful for your help, the lead you gave us was significant. We've been able to clear up the break-in at the crime scene.'

'Really? I'm so glad. What happened?'

Dupin hesitated.

'Sorry for asking such nosy questions. My curiosity is of course less important than police confidentiality.'

'I –'

'I understand. Really. I'm glad that I could help.' Madame Cassel looked tired; she too had been 'on duty' for twenty-four hours.

'Well… you know, I… you should know, you could –' Dupin felt he owed her an explanation or two.

247

Marie Morgane Cassel looked at the Commissaire in amusement.

'Are you hungry, Monsieur Dupin? I'm starving.'

'Hungry? Yes, to be honest, I am hungry, very. I didn't manage to eat today, I... I have to wait for someone anyway and they're not going to be here before midnight.' He looked at his watch, 'There's an hour and a half to go.'

'There was something else I wanted to tell you. It's to do with the painting and Charles Sauré.'

'Sounds good. Let's talk shop and eat something while we're at it.'

'Great. I'm sure you know where to go around here.'

Dupin thought about it. 'Tell you what. Do you know Kerdruc? It's only two or three kilometres down the river, five minutes by car. There's a pretty little harbour and a fantastic, very traditional restaurant; you sit right beside the river.'

Madame Cassel seemed a little surprised at how enthusiastic Dupin was. He hadn't the slightest desire to set foot in one of the touristy restaurants again, and the same went for Beauvois' mill. He wanted to get out of Pont-Aven.

'Wonderful. I can't stay long, I have a lecture tomorrow morning at nine. But it would be great to eat something. And that sounds lovely. Kerdruc.'

'We'll take my car.'

Marie Morgane Cassel stood up and they walked over to the stairs together.

Labat was standing at reception. 'You're going out again?'

'We still need to discuss something, Madame Cassel and I. Call me as soon as André Pennec gets here.'

Labat looked glum. 'André Pennec could turn up early, Monsieur le Commissaire.'

'Then call me when he's here.'

The landscape became more and more enchanting as the narrow little streets at the edge of Pont-Aven gave way to thick woodland. The trees were dripping with mistletoe and ivy, overgrown and moss-covered. Some of the trees here had entwined as they grew, forming a long dark green tunnel. Now and then the Aven shimmered between the trees on the left hand side as though it were electrically charged, a pale silver colour. The last of the day's light bathed everything in its glow, lending the landscape even more of a fairytale atmosphere. By now, Dupin knew this landscape and this atmosphere very well (Nolwenn called it the 'Breton Aura'). He always thought that if you were to meet a dwarf or an elf or some other mythical creature in this kind of light, you wouldn't even bat an eyelid.

Kerdruc was picturesquely situated where the flat hills along the Aven fell away; the streets wound right down to the river. Some beautiful old stone houses and even a few imposing villas were scattered amongst the lush greenery. Palm trees, dwarf fan palms, larches, pines, lemon trees, rhododendrons, beeches, hydrangeas, high beech hedges, bamboos, cactii, laurels and bushy lavender shrubs all grew in wild profusion. The plants could not have been more typically Breton. Just like in Port Manech down by the mouth of the Aven, you felt like you were walking into a botanic garden. The Aven lay wide and majestic in the valley, halfway to the open sea.

The street turned into a pier. A dozen coastal fishermen had moored their traditional colourful boats here; a few of the locals had left their motor launches and a few holiday-makers their sailing boats. The tide was coming in, the water already high, the waves long and flat.

Dupin parked at the pier. There was space for maybe ten cars here, but no more. The little restaurant's tables and chairs were right at the harbour and some were alarmingly close to the water. A dozen old sycamore trees lined the little quay. It was quiet now.

They sat down at one of the tables by the water. A waiter appeared immediately, wiry, short, quick as lightning – Dupin liked that in a waiter. The kitchen was about to close. They ordered straight away, without much discussion. Belon oysters harvested from the river a few hundred metres away, followed by grilled monkfish with *fleur de sel*, pepper and lemon, washed down with a chilled, very young red wine from the Rhône valley.

'It's beautiful here, insanely beautiful.' Marie Morgane Cassel let her gaze wander.

Dupin thought it felt a bit surreal to be sitting here like this; neither the setting nor the food could be more beautiful, more romantic – and this was the evening of a day that had seen a second death and an arrest in the midst of a tortuous murder case. But she was right, this truly was beautiful.

Madame Cassel tore him from his thoughts. 'I got a call this evening from a journalist friend in Paris. Charles Sauré went to a friend of hers whom he apparently knows very well. He told him about the Gauguin. It's going to be an exclusive in *Le Figaro*.'

'What?'

'Yes. They'll probably run it tomorrow. An article and an interview.'

'As a lead story?'

'Presumably. I did tell you this would make international headlines. Every newspaper is going to be writing about it. Could you… suppress it?'

'Do you mean could we, as police, prevent the newspaper reporting it?'

'Yes.'

'No.' Dupin propped his head against his hand. Now there was the press too. The only thing that had been missing. He had sunk so deep into the strange world of this strange case. But it was obvious; as soon as anything about the existence of the painting and its incredible history was leaked, it would make for sensational news, especially in connection with a murder, or maybe even two. That was just the bare bones of the case and things didn't come much more thrilling than that. 'What on earth is he going to say?'

'No idea. That's as much as my friend knew.'

Dupin was silent for a few moments. 'Why? Why is Sauré doing this? This afternoon he was talking about discretion the whole time. He said he didn't even go to the police when he heard about Pennec's murder in order to maintain confidentiality.'

'It's a huge coup for Sauré, probably the biggest of his life. He is the person who discovered an unknown Gauguin, perhaps the most important painting of the artist's whole oeuvre. What's in it for him? Kudos, fame, honour. It's about his career. You know that.'

'Yes. You're right.'

She really was. By now the food had arrived. Everything looked wonderful. Dupin felt positively sick with hunger. They stopped talking and began to eat.

Madame Cassel was the first to break the silence: 'This is going to make everything more complicated for you, isn't it? The whole world will be watching your investigation.'

'I hope Sauré will keep the "case" out of it as much as possible. But yes, it is going to make everything more complicated. I prefer it when it's not clear who knows what.'

'I know what you mean.'

'How do you sell a painting like that anyway?'

'You've got to know the right people... or get to know them. After that it's much easier than you'd think.'

'And where are these people? Who are they?'

'Well, they're private collectors. Crazy, powerful, rich. They're all over the world. They belong to a loose circle of collectors, although officially it doesn't exist, of course.'

'And they would never associate with the police.'

'There's a lot of illegal stuff going on in that world. For a passionate collector, it's basically immaterial where a painting came from or how it became available. Everything is done very "discreetly".'

'We've got to find the painting before it comes onto the market. It's our only chance.'

'Definitely. Do you think it's still here... I mean in Pont-Aven or this general area?'

'We saw a second copy of the painting this evening.'

'What? A second copy of the second *Vision*?'

'Yes, painted by an imitator from the artists' colony. Gilbert Sonnheim. The copy was probably made just a few years after Gauguin painted the original.'

'I know Sonnheim. It wasn't unusual for "students" to copy large paintings by their masters in order to study them. Even in the artists' colony.'

'And people commissioned copies too.'

'That wasn't unusual either. People who owned a painting like that often had copies made.'

'We just don't know yet.'

'And who had this copy?'

'We don't know that either. Probably the murderer. On the night when...' Dupin gave up.

He had been about to tell her the whole story, beginning with their visit to Beauvois, but he had no idea what or how to tell her. He was no longer capable of speaking concisely or coherently tonight. It all seemed absurd, even to him.

Marie Morgane Cassel looked at her watch. 'Leave it. Another time. It's almost midnight. I've got to get back to Brest. For my lecture tomorrow morning. I've still got to prepare a few things. The *Fauves*, Matisse and the whole gang –'

'I'll just pay quickly.' Dupin stood up and went into the restaurant.

When he came back Madame Cassel was standing at the edge of the pier, looking down at the Aven. The tide was already in and it was extremely dark. The silvery surface of the Aven had shone as brightly as ever until the last scrap of light disappeared but now the silver was gone, replaced by an endless mass of black. One minute there was a silvery sheen and the next minute it had vanished. Above the river and out at sea, all that was left was a darkness you could almost reach out and touch as it swallowed everything in its path.

'This is a special place.'

Yes, thought Dupin. In a way, he was like a collector of 'special places', places that were extraordinary in some way. He'd been doing it for a long time, ever since he was a child and he had made lists of them over the course of many years; now Kerdruc was one. One of those special places.

A few minutes later they were back at the harbour in Pont-Aven and Dupin was parking his car right next to Marie Morgane Cassel's. Madame Cassel seemed to be flagging. They parted without saying much. Dupin waited until she had turned off onto the rue du Port and was driving away at an impressive speed.

Then he walked back to the hotel. Labat hadn't been in touch which meant that André Pennec still wasn't back. He wasn't surprised. He wouldn't have expected any less of André Pennec. But even aside from the interview with Pennec, there really was a lot to do. The most important thing was to inform the Prefect personally about the article in *Le Figaro*. He could picture it now; he knew exactly how tense that conversation would be. 'How is it that every Tom, Dick and Harry of a journalist knows how the investigation is going and I don't? What kind of investigation are you running, with every little detail of the case getting leaked to the press?' The Gauguin was too big an issue. He hadn't been keeping the Prefect

– or any of the top brass – 'sufficiently informed' of late. He was pleasingly indifferent to such things this evening. He didn't want to do any more this evening. He couldn't.

Labat was standing in the entrance to the hotel, staring out into the night. 'Monsieur Pennec hasn't arrived yet. He's not keeping to our agreement at all.'

'We'll sort it out tomorrow, Labat. We should all be off to bed now.'

'What?'

'We need to go and get some sleep.'

'But –'

'Tomorrow, Labat. *Bonne nuit.*'

Labat made as though to protest again, but he was probably too tired himself. 'Okay, Monsieur le Commissaire. I'll call Monsieur Pennec's mobile and let him know.'

'Leave it. I'll call him tomorrow morning myself.'

'He will think it wasn't important to us –'

'He's going to find out exactly what we think is important.'

'I'll just get my things.' Labat disappeared in the direction of reception. Dupin followed him.

'Did you know about the little room upstairs next to Pennec's, where he kept his archive and a few paintings?'

'Yes, of course.'

Dupin thought it over. 'No, no… we'll leave everything till tomorrow. Let's call it a day.'

Labat actually looked quite relieved. 'I'm going to head off, Monsieur le Commissaire. Kerbrat can take over the watch tonight.'

'Kerbrat?'

'Yes, he's an officer from Pont-Aven. One of Monfort and Pennarguear's colleagues.'

'All right.'

'Good night.'

They both left the hotel. Labat turned right, Dupin to the left.

Dupin parked his Citroën in one of the side streets near his flat a little before half twelve. The big car park was already closed because of the *Festival des Filets Bleus* which would be starting tomorrow. He walked down the street to the waterfront, keeping his house on his left. He stood by the solid quay wall that surrounded the new town for a few moments, looking out at the infinite black of the Atlantic by night. You couldn't see the sea of course, but you could feel it. In the west was the *Phare de l'Ile aux Moutons* from the Îles Glénan, a sharp, powerful beam of light, moving in swift but unhurried circles as it pierced the fabric of the night sky.

A quarter of an hour later, Dupin was asleep.

The Fourth Day

Dupin ordered his third coffee, the first two having had no discernible effect. He was exhausted and he'd only been up for an hour. It was quarter past seven now. Even the bracing breeze that had blown right through him on his way to the *Amiral* this morning hadn't helped. He had woken up at half past three, and hadn't really been able to get back to sleep. He had a vague sense of misgiving; the interviews from yesterday kept going round and round his head. He had missed something. For a few moments, his instinct told him, he had been very close to the truth. But he had let himself get confused. And he hated when that happened.

He was still hopelessly tired. And furious. *Le Figaro* had run the story. Oh yes. 'Sensation: Unknown Gauguin Discovered!' That's how the headline across the front page put it. 'For over a hundred years the painting hung unnoticed on the wall of a restaurant,' according to the sub-head. The story was summarised in a few lines and then banished to page three. Half of it consisted of an interview with Charles Sauré and a photo of the man himself, the other half of a longer version of the story and a large reproduction of the familiar painting.

Charles Sauré had put an interesting spin on the story. Naturally the world had Sauré himself to thank for this painting; a provincial hotelier – admittedly that's not exactly what was written, but that's what was implied – had left it hanging on a wall for a hundred years. Apparently he'd had no idea of its significance, which meant it had been criminally neglected. And of course it was now 'probably the central work of Gauguin's epoch-defining oeuvre – and what's more one of the key paintings in the history of modern painting'.

It was disgusting. Sauré reported that he had seen the painting in the hotel, and that it was 'potentially involved in the murder case of the hotelier who owned the painting'. That was in the editorial too, but not in any more detail. 'The police investigation is currently ongoing', was the editor's brief comment. At least there was no question of much speculation on this point, and there was no mention at all of Loic Pennec's death, potentially a second murder.

So it was public knowledge now. Dupin had noticed the regulars whispering animatedly when he'd walked into the *Amiral*, but he hadn't paid much attention because of how tired he was. Even Lily must have read everything already, but she had left it at 'It's really something!' and a cheerful 'It'll work out' while serving the first coffee.

What Sauré was really hammering home was Pierre-Louis Pennec's intention to donate the painting. 'During our conversation, Monsieur Pennec showed his great generosity in wanting to make the painting accessible to the world. He wanted to leave it to the Musée d'Orsay as a generous gift. That was his firm wish.' He managed to say this in three different ways during the interview and the journalist was also most emphatic on the point a number of times. At first Dupin hadn't known exactly why, but then, suddenly, he understood: Sauré was cunning, and he wanted to make sure the painting would go to the museum even after Pennec's death. That even under the – admittedly dramatically – altered circumstances the donation would still be made. More specifically, he was putting subtle pressure on the heirs, even though he didn't know anything, not even who was going to inherit the painting or whether Pierre-Louis Pennec had officially written the donation into his will or not. He wanted to make sure, manipulate, pull the strings. He had to in fact, or his whole campaign would be for nothing. He risked making himself a laughing stock if there were no donation now. Dupin smirked. It was the first time he'd felt good all morning. If he knew Catherine Pennec at all, she wouldn't be the type to let pressure of this kind get to her, or of any other kind for that matter. And although Sauré couldn't have known it, the situation was absolutely absurd and looked set to stay that way. There was no painting, just two copies of it. Sauré didn't have the faintest idea that the original had been stolen.

There was a report about Loic Pennec's death on page one of *Ouest France* but it was vague and confused; it seemed to Dupin that nobody had really taken any interest in it at all. The author didn't dare speculate. The death was briefly noted to have occurred 'just two days after the murder of his father'. And it was stated that a police investigation was underway. At least it did say at one point that 'this old Breton family has found itself struck by great tragedy twice in such a short space of time'. Oddly enough, there was no speculation on any possible link between the two events. Someone was nervous, waiting for more information, or at least some small nugget of verified fact. For the local press these were daunting events. Dupin didn't know the editor; he must have been new. The editorial department at the *Ouest France* in Concarneau was in one of the storm-swept old fishermen's houses right by the harbour, just a hundred metres away from the *Amiral*. He knew the whole gang, some of them quite well.

So that's how things stood as far as the news was concerned – it was going to take up Dupin's time today and throughout the coming days. Everyone would have read it or heard about it. To be on the safe side he put his phone on silent, and after leaving his money on the plastic saucer as usual he saw that he had been right. Six missed calls in the last hour. He had no desire to see who had called – he could figure that out without checking – and his mood was already black enough. He had to get going.

Dupin had been so exhausted last night that he couldn't remember the exact place he'd parked his car. It wasn't something he was good at remembering at the best of times. It had driven him crazy in Paris sometimes, having to spend endless hours looking for his Citroën. He walked hopefully through the streets he thought it might be on and found it on the very last one, not all that far from his house in fact. He had simply been walking in the wrong direction.

Dupin drove at top speed. He fumbled around with the car phone.

'Le Ber?'

'Monsieur le Commissaire, the Prefect wants to speak to you. He is very... upset. He's been trying to reach you and he's called Labat twice already. Nolwenn too.'

'Where are you?'

'I'm at the hotel, I just got here.'

'How did it go with Beauvois?'

'It was an unpleasant journey. They kept him overnight. "Reasonable cause." But it wasn't easy. He has an odious lawyer. It took a while to get the judicial order, it was a close one.'

'When will we be able to question him?'

'Right away, this morning in fact. Are you going to drive over?'

'No, I'm staying here.'

There was one thing Dupin wanted more than anything: to find out what was troubling him, giving him that deep-rooted feeling of unease.

'You drive over.' Dupin thought about it. 'No wait, I need you. Send Labat. Is he there yet?' Labat was more aggressive in interrogations; besides, Dupin would rather have Le Ber with him.

'Yes, we spoke just now. He wanted to see about the room upstairs next to Pennec's. We'd already looked at it, but I assume he's after something specific now.'

'Go upstairs, I want to speak to him.'

'Who, Labat?'

'Yes.'

'Okay.'

Dupin could hear Le Ber climbing the stairs.

'I want you to take over the search from Labat. Go over the little room again carefully. But the most important thing I want you to do is to question Madame Lajoux, and also Madame Mendu, Madame Galez and the rest of them. We've got to know whether there was a copy of the second *Vision* there.'

'I'll take care of it.'

'Then I'd like the museum searched. Especially the basement.'

'For what?'

'For anything out of place – the original painting, who knows? – and for any further copies. Most of all I want Salou to take a look at the painting, that copy of it I mean. I want him to look for fingerprints on the copy that Beauvois claims to have stolen from the restaurant. If what he says is true, then the murderer hung it there.'

'I'll call Salou straight away.'

It occurred to Dupin that he had clean forgotten to tell Salou yesterday that his examination of the frames had been rendered pointless by his conversation with Sauré. Salou would surely have read about the Gauguin in the paper this morning and would be assuming that the restaurant work was to do with the actual painting. He didn't know anything about a copy. And even though he must have spent most of his time on the forensic evidence at the cliffs yesterday, he certainly wouldn't be overjoyed.

'And tell Salou that he can forget about examining the frame. That we've received some new information… No need to tell him any more than that.'

'Okay.'

'And then I want to see André Pennec in the breakfast room in… in twenty minutes.'

'Okay. I'm standing beside Inspector Labat now. I'm handing him the phone.'

'Labat?'

'Yes. I've –'

'Listen, I'm giving you a special mission,' Dupin was sure Labat would like the sound of that. 'I need you to drive to Quimper right now and question Beauvois. Le Ber will tell you everything that happened last night. I want you to be *very* aggressive in the interview, do you understand? I want to know what he's been doing recently, every little detail. Everything. I want him to name possible witnesses for every alibi. Insist on it. Have him tell his story two or three times. Pay attention to the details!'

There was silence on the other end of the line for a moment. 'Understood.'

'This is extremely important, Labat. Make sure we know everything, and I mean *everything*, that Monsieur Beauvois has to say this time. Every last thing.'

'You can count on me. You should call Prefect Guenneugues straight away though, he's already called me twice. He was angry he had to find out about the painting from a newspaper.'

'Hang on, Labat, this cannot be happening, this is unbelievable…'

Dupin could see he had no choice but to overtake, but it wouldn't be easy. He was behind a tractor with a trailer of manure on the winding, blind-cornered street between Trégunc and Névez. It was doing thirty at the most. It smelt foul.

'What do you mean, Monsieur le Commissaire?'

Dupin accelerated hard and pulled ahead of the tractor, only just managing to get back in his lane in the face of an oncoming vehicle.

'Labat?'

'I'm here.'

'We've got to make some progress.'

'I'll get going.'

'Pass me back to Le Ber.'

He heard the telephone being passed back.

'Le Ber?'

'Yes, Monsieur le Commissaire?'

'Take the phone to Madame Lajoux.'

Dupin knew this was a strange situation. Le Ber didn't answer, but Dupin could hear him walking back down the stairs whose loud creaks and groans betrayed their hundred years. Then he heard Le Ber explaining the situation to Madame Lajoux – which clearly took some time – before finally handing her the phone.

'Is that you, Monsieur le Commissaire?'

'*Bonjour*, Madame Lajoux, I hope you've slept well.'

'Me? Yes, thank you.'

'I just have one question, Madame Lajoux. I would like to know whether you knew of a copy of the Gauguin? Did you ever hear about one?'

'A copy?'

'Yes.'

'No. There was no copy.'

'We're aware of two copies so far, Madame Lajoux.'

'Two copies? Of the *Vision*?'

'I thought one of these two copies may have been kept in the little room upstairs next to Pennec's room.'

'Monsieur Pennec never mentioned a copy. It's very unlikely there's any copy.'

'There are two.'

'No. There aren't two either.'

Dupin was sure this could have been a dialogue in an absurdist play. But he had found out what he needed to know. 'Do you know the paintings that are up there?'

'No. I mean, yes. I know which paintings weren't hung up again after the renovation work, of course, and that these were then kept there.' She hesitated. 'But maybe there were some that were there before that.'

'But you never saw them yourself?'

'No, no, I didn't. I can't look after everything.'

'I just wanted to check.'

'I would be surprised if there were a copy. He never mentioned it.' She seemed to be speaking more to herself than to Dupin.

'You can hand me back to Inspector Le Ber, Madame Lajoux, many thanks again.'

'Absolutely, Monsieur le Commissaire.'

'Le Ber?'

'Yes?'

'I'm here now. I mean I've just arrived in Pont-Aven.' Dupin was actually already at the first roundabout. He really had made good progress.

'Good.'

'First, André Pennec. We can get started soon.'

'I'll let him know right now.'

André Pennec was already sitting in the breakfast room wearing a perfectly tailored, expensive-looking, dark suit, a white shirt and a ridiculous red and yellow patterned tie. He looked defiantly nonchalant, having settled himself in the exact chair where Madame Cassel had been sitting earlier. He looked up when Commissaire Dupin came into the room, making a show of the effort it cost him. His superior gaze alighted briefly on Dupin.

'Where were you yesterday, during the day, evening and night?' Dupin didn't wait for an answer. He didn't want to keep his anger under control. He didn't see any reason to any more. 'I'd like precise statements, not vague ones.'

It was clear Pennec was very close to retaliating, given Dupin's tone and aggression. Dupin was practically counting on it. For whatever reason, Pennec decided otherwise.

'I decided to make use of my stay here in Brittany so I met with some party colleagues to discuss a number of issues. Members of various national committees, of which I am also a member on behalf of my *département*. I can have a list of everyone I spoke to sent to you, if it makes you happy. That lasted from nine in the morning until nine in the evening, practically non-stop apart from lunch. In the evening I had a long dinner with Gilbert Colloc, the Chairman of the Union for the whole of Brittany, the opposition leader. An old friend.'

'I want the list immediately.'

'We didn't finish up until half twelve, we were sitting in La Fontaine aux Perles. I'll gladly give you that address too. But moving on to more important matters, how's your investigation going? One of the most valuable paintings in the world, a Gauguin that has lain undiscovered until now, a story that is making international news involving two deaths in as many days. Have you caught the perpetrator? Arrested a suspect? When are you going to convict them?' Pennec was enjoying taunting Dupin and made no effort to hide it.

'Where were you on Saturday evening?'

'I would love to bestow this information upon you too. I had certainly hoped you would devote your time to more important things. But it's your investigation. I was at a dinner given by the mayor of Quimper. There were ten guests in our party, all of whom could see me the entire evening, you'll be pleased to hear. It went on until around one in the morning. I assume Loic Pennec's time of death was before one o'clock and I couldn't have been with him before two.'

'I'm very pleased to hear there are witnesses, Monsieur Pennec. Truly. And I'd be most obliged if you could perhaps furnish us with a blow-by-blow account of all that you have done since you arrived here in Brittany. You are supporting our police work tremendously, it really is exemplary. Worthy of a public servant.'

André Pennec was perfectly composed. 'So was it murder? The death of Loic Pennec I mean?'

'We can't say yet.'

'Of course not, no. Are you aware that two members of a great Breton family have met with their deaths in the space of two days?'

'Thank you for the concise summary, Monsieur Pennec.'

'And the break-in at the crime scene? Which you didn't mention during our last conversation, even though it had happened only a few hours before. Have you been able to make any headway on that one?'

'Regrettably I can't reveal any information in connection with that matter.'

'I assume that the painting remained unscathed during the break-in at the scene?' André Pennec knew this was the crux of the matter, and had pre-empted Dupin's questions about the painting.

'Correct.' Dupin was annoyed that he hadn't brought it up himself.

'And you've made sure that the painting is the original?'

'What do you mean?'

'Well that would be a cheap trick wouldn't it? Replacing the painting with a copy. But surely you'll have long since excluded that possibility.'

Dupin didn't react. 'How long have you known about the painting, Monsieur Pennec?'

'Since my father told me. And Pierre-Louis and I, we used to be very close. It was a family matter so of course we spoke about it.'

'So you've always known about the undiscovered Gauguin?'

'Yes.'

'The painting was a part of your father, Charles Pennec's legacy. He excluded you from the inheritance in his will however.'

'That's just how it was. It's a known fact. And the painting belonged to the hotel.'

'You began legal proceedings to fight the provisions of your father's will. You were hardly indifferent.'

'What are you trying to get at, Monsieur le Commissaire?'

'And your brother categorically excluded you from his will in the same way, a full thirty years ago, once and for all.'

'I have no idea what this conversation is about.'

'You never had a chance to inherit the painting – or at least a part of it.'

Pennec didn't answer.

'If the provisions of your half-brother's will hadn't excluded you too, you would have inherited a considerable sum of money three days ago, somewhere in the millions.'

'Look, you've said it yourself: I don't gain anything from my half-brother's death. And quite apart from having an airtight alibi, I'm also utterly lacking in motive.'

'In your disappointment and anger you might have thought of other ways to get hold of the painting.'

'You can keep wasting your time if you like, that's completely up to you of course. You're heading up the investigation, you're the Commissaire. I tell you though, everyone's patience is wearing thinner by the hour; just yesterday someone in Rennes asked me why there weren't any results yet.'

'Thank you... this has been a very fruitful conversation, Monsieur Pennec. You have been most helpful.'

Pennec's reply came after just a slight hesitation, he was very quick. 'No problem, no problem at all. It's a pleasure and as you say, clearly a civic duty. A duty I'm especially keen to discharge as a public representative.'

Dupin stood up. He'd had enough. '*Au revoir*, Monsieur Pennec.'

André Pennec made no move to stand up. 'I wish

you the best of luck with your investigation. Seems like you need it.'

Dupin walked out of the breakfast room, down the stairs and straight out of the hotel. He needed to get out into the fresh air. Take a little walk. He was sick of this, of everything, and the day had only just begun. He couldn't go on like this. He detested André Pennec. Neither of them made a secret of what they thought of each other. And yet… it wasn't him. He wasn't the murderer. Or he didn't commit the murder himself, anyway.

Dupin walked down rue du Port. The streets were still quiet as the galleries and shops wouldn't open until half ten. He walked to the harbour and stood there for a little while in the place where he always stood, right at the beginning of the pier. Then he walked on, along the western bank of the Aven, further downstream than he had been before.

Here, where the harbour came to an end, Pont-Aven actually looked a little like Kerdruc or Port Manech. The hills on either side of the Aven were less steep here, sloping gently upwards from the banks. Plants grew between the undulating hills like in a botanic garden. There were palm trees every few metres, including the tall, thick ones Dupin liked so much, which always grew in little groups and towered high overhead. Huge rhododendron bushes, gorse and camellias. It smelt like morning, like the sea and the seaweed-slick ground of low tide. The handful of houses on the very outskirts of the village were almost hidden amongst the greenery, with their rambling, rolling gardens. Real villas. The street ended here, in fact the whole village ended here; after this point there was just a muddy little path. This was where the river began – the inlet began its meandering, alternately widening, narrowing, forming streams, pools, big sandbanks. But above all this was where the woods began, the thick, enchanted forests of oak and beech, full of mistletoe, moss and ivy. The legendary *Bois d'Amour* was held in great esteem by the artists at the end of the nineteenth century and appeared in dozens of their paintings.

Without really thinking, Dupin had started following the path into the wood. It forked now and again but he stayed close to the river. His mobile kept vibrating with numbers he didn't recognise or that he didn't want to answer. Guenneugues called twice.

Dupin had been walking for almost three quarters of an hour. He hadn't meant to walk this far at all. He hadn't taken in much of the landscape around him. His thoughts had been swirling aimlessly around his head and his mood had darkened even further. Bizarrely, he felt even more tired in the fresh air. The walk hadn't helped at all. What he very urgently needed now was more caffeine; he should have gone to a café. This walking around seemed preposterous now – he had found himself at a desperate juncture in a difficult case and had upped and gone for a walk through wild Celtic woods.

The narrow path led directly back to the bank. Dupin stood still. He should go back the way he had come. The Aven was a small river here at low tide, flowing gently in its channel right down to the sea. His phone vibrated again. Dupin saw Nolwenn's number. This time he picked up.

'Yes?'

'Where are you?'

'I'm standing in the *Bois d'Amour*.'

'Ah.'

'Yes.'

'And what are you doing there?'

'I'm thinking.' Dupin knew it sounded silly. And it was. But he also knew that Nolwenn was used to this.

'Good.'

'You'd like to tell me the names of all the people who've got in touch as a matter of urgency and absolutely have to speak to me. And also that there is a lot going on.'

'Are you making progress?' Nolwenn knew it wasn't a good sign when he didn't get in touch himself.

'I don't know. I don't think so.'

'Don't lose hope; I'll smooth things over as much as I can. You know Brittany rests on very old and very solid landmasses.'

This was one of Nolwenn's mantras. Their significance in any given situation usually remained a complete mystery to him but Dupin thought it was a good saying nonetheless.

'Very solid landmasses. And granite on top. Massive blocks of granite.'

'Exactly, Monsieur le Commissaire.'

The saying had an undeniably calming effect on him.

'I have to call that cranky old Prefect, don't I? And I'm on the point of being kicked out of the force?'

'I think you should call him, yes.'

'I will. I just want to –' Dupin didn't finish his sentence. He stood there motionless for a moment. 'Oh shit.'

He smacked his forehead and ran his hands through his hair over and over. It had come to him. It had come to him, the thing that had been dimly running through his head all day yesterday and all night too. The thing that hadn't been quite right. The point in the conversation where he had let himself get confused.

'Hello? Monsieur le Commissaire? Are you still there?'

'I'll call you right back.'

'Please do.'

Dupin hung up. This was it. If he wasn't mistaken. Thoughts were racing through his head now and the pieces were beginning to fall into place.

He had to act now.

If he walked quickly, it might only be half an hour to his car. He contemplated whether Le Ber might be able to pick him up somewhere. But by the time he had got to somewhere Le Ber could pick him up, he would long since have reached his own car.

The first thing would be to find out exactly where he needed to go. He leafed through his notebook as he walked along; he knew he had written it down. He found what he was looking for, a scribble at the edge of a page he had scrawled all over. Then he scrolled through the dialled numbers on his phone's tiny screen. He wasn't absolutely sure whether it was the number for the notary but he hadn't dialled many numbers in Pont-Aven. It must be her.

'Madame Denis?'

'Speaking.'

'Dupin here.'

'Of course. *Bonjour*, Monsieur le Commissaire. I hope

you're well. I read *Le Figaro*. The case has – how should I put it – become even bigger.'

'True, Madame Denis. Look, I need some information.'

'I'd be happy to help if I can.'

'You spoke about two larger plots of land belonging to Pierre-Louis Pennec, which he himself had inherited, the ones with warehouses. I noted it down: one in Le Pouldu and one in Port Manech. Is that right?'

'Exactly, Port Manech and Le Pouldu. The one in Port Manech is bigger and has a bigger warehouse too. The one in Le Pouldu is apparently more of a shed. But of course I haven't seen either of them myself. He described them to me a little bit. There are other plots of land in the inheritance, but they're smaller.'

'Can you tell me exactly where these two plots of land are? Do you have the addresses?'

'The will just lists the possessions bequeathed. Then it refers you to the land registry entries and quotes the land registry numbers. The land registry entries are in Monsieur Pennec's private papers. Perhaps the Pennecs will know... sorry, I mean, perhaps Madame Pennec might know where exactly the plots are, or maybe Madame Lajoux or Monsieur Delon.'

'I'd rather find out some other way.'

'Hmmm... you could try the mayor's offices.'

'All right then.'

'I'm sorry I can't be more helpful.'

'You've been extremely helpful!'

'Good, it's been a pleasure, Monsieur Dupin. I'm sure you'll solve the case soon.'

Dupin smiled in spite of himself. 'Maybe, Madame Denis. *Au revoir.*'

He had no idea how far he'd walked along the path through the wood. He hadn't been paying much attention to the landscape on the way and he was paying even less now. Port Manech and Le Pouldu. Port Manech was ten minutes away by car, Le Pouldu perhaps three quarters of an hour. He needed the exact addresses.

'Nolwenn?'

'Are you still thinking?'

'I need two pieces of information.'

'That was quick.'

'What?'

'Nothing. And I take it you need both pieces of information right now.'

'Exactly. Pierre-Louis Pennec had two larger plots of land, each around a thousand metres squared, one in Port Manech, one in Le Pouldu, each with a kind of warehouse on it. I need the exact addresses.'

'One is in Port Manech, one in Pouldu.'

'That's right.'

Nolwenn had hung up.

Now Marie Morgane Cassel. He dialled her number. It took her longer to answer this time.

'*Bonjour*, Monsieur Dupin.'

'Yes, it's me.'

'Where should I be headed?'

'Really? I mean, if you could, if your commitments allow... I think you could be extremely helpful to us again. It's possible we're reaching the end of this case.'

'The last act?'

'Possibly. The hotel I think, yes, that would be good. If you could come to the hotel... Inspector Le Ber will be waiting for you there.'

275

'I'm on my way.'

'Thanks. Thank you so much.'

Now Le Ber again. He dialled his number. Le Ber answered immediately.

'Yes, Monsieur le Commissaire?'

'Madame Cassel is on her way from Brest, she'll be with you in an hour. Then I want you to go with her to… I think to Port Manech. I'll let you know the exact address. Is there any news from Labat? From Beauvois?'

'I imagine Labat will only just have arrived in Quimper.'

'Good, it'll just be the two of us then. Which of our colleagues from Pont-Aven are there?'

'Monfort. All hell has broken out here since we last spoke. Everyone has read *Le Figaro*, or at least heard about it. The officers from Pont-Aven, the guests and the whole village, apparently. Of course everyone thinks the painting is still hanging here in the restaurant. A few people have already asked whether they can take a look at it sometime. What should we do?'

'Nothing. Our work. That's got nothing to do with us.'

'And what do we want with Port Manech?'

'You'll see soon enough.'

'Okay. We'll hit the road as soon as Madame Cassel gets here, Monsieur le Commissaire.'

'Hurry. I'm heading there right away, as soon as I get to my car.'

'Where are you now then?'

'I'll see you in Port Manech, Le Ber. Speak soon.'

Dupin thought Port Manech was the most beautiful town on the coast. This was where the Aven and the Belon flowed into a sheltered bay. And from the little beach opposite their estuaries you could either look at both rivers or out to the open Atlantic. A dozen tall fairy-tale palm trees grew in the dazzlingly white, fine sand. The beach sloped gently downwards to the turquoise sea. The coast's landscape was rugged where the Belon met the sea, cliffs towering upwards, twenty or thirty metres high. The cliffs were overgrown with grass in every shade of green, somewhat reminiscent of Ireland. The hills were higher here than in Pont-Aven and it was striking how steeply they fell away to the sea, so that the streets led down to the beach and harbour at a mind-bending incline, dividing the village into three: the Port Manech on the plateau above, the one on the hillside with the magnificent villas and the Port Manech down by the water. Dupin particularly liked its cosy little harbour.

Nolwenn still needed a little time, it was more complicated than it had seemed; she had given him a brief update. Of course, none of the records were digitised yet – everything had to be looked up in bulging files. Dupin urgently needed caffeine. Right on the beach, but set back a little on a raised platform, there was a small, unpretentious café where you could sit and look out on the Belon estuary. There were only a few tables on the terrace but none of them were taken. The waitress, a young girl in a faded blue dress with artfully dishevelled hair, looked very tired. Dupin ordered a coffee and a pain au chocolat. He had just placed his mobile on the table in front of him when it rang. Nolwenn. Dupin answered immediately.

'I have the addresses, both of them. Le Pouldu was easy actually, Port Manech was a bit of a mission. I had to speak to the mayor personally on the phone.'

'Fantastic. Right, let me have it.' He took his notebook and pen out of his pocket.

'Where are you?'

'In Port Manech. Down on the beach.'

'Okay. Listen carefully. Take the road past the beach, it's called the Corniche du Pouldon, and then follow the steep road up the hill to your left, as though you were leaving the village. That really narrow road.'

'Okay.'

'Drive for around three hundred metres and there'll be an unpaved path on your right just before you take a sharp left.'

'Okay.'

'There's a villa on the left hand side. That's where the big pine trees are. Turn onto the path here. Drive for around two hundred metres, in the direction of the Aven in fact. Another path branches off to the left. It's parallel to the Aven and it goes back down the hill a bit. This is the one you take.'

'How do you know all this, Nolwenn?'

'I was faxed a copy of the site map by the mayor's office… and I have Google Maps. Then you keep going straight until you reach the warehouse. It must be about another three hundred metres.'

Dupin had copied down every detail.

'I'm sure I'll find it. Thank you.'

'The big *new* Citroën has an excellent satnav.'

'I know.'

This was one of Nolwenn's favourite topics. And she

was right; he might find a device like that very useful. He must seriously consider it. He drank the coffee in one gulp, stood up, left the money and took the pain au chocolat back to his car with him.

Nolwenn's description had been accurate. Five minutes later he took the last turning onto a path that was little more than a dirt track, and parked the car. He walked slowly down the path. Even this was picturesque. Gentle hills, fields, meadows, little woods. You could see them – the landscapes by Gauguin, Laval, Bernard. You found yourself inside them. Very little had changed here over the last hundred years. Dupin found it astonishing how realistic the paintings seemed once you were here. They were more accurate than any photograph.

To his surprise, the warehouse was not a warehouse at all, but a magnificent kind of barn. Dupin had been expecting something completely different, something smaller. The walls were made of stone, at least fifteen metres high, although not in good condition. And the slate roof sagged dangerously, overgrown with moss.

On the side closest to the Aven there was a hefty wooden door that rounded at the top, but no windows.

Dupin had no trouble with the door; it was surprisingly easy to open. It must have been used recently. An enormous, imposing room appeared in front of him, much bigger than it had seemed from outside. It had a dirt floor. He stepped inside. A thin beam of light fell through a hole in the roof that Dupin hadn't spotted from outside. There was total silence. A musty smell. Dupin flinched. His phone was ringing. He saw Le Ber's number.

'Yes?'

'Madame Cassel has arrived at the hotel. Where do you want us to drive to? And Labat wants to speak to you about Beauvois. I've spoken to Salou on the phone already too, he was outraged not to have been informed of the progress we'd made and then he had to read –'

'I'll call you back.'

Dupin hung up. Not now. He waited until his eyes had grown accustomed to the dark and then walked back and forth across the room. The room was completely empty. Bare. It was odd, but there really was nothing here. Nothing at all. And it seemed as though nothing had been here for many, many years. There were no footprints on the ground.

Dupin had been so sure the painting would be here, but he must have been wrong. Or at least his first guess was wrong. But maybe he'd been wrong about everything.

He went to the door, stepped outside and walked once around the outside of the barn. There was nothing unusual here either. Not in the least. He closed the door and felt for his phone.

'Le Ber, we're going to meet in Le Pouldu, not in Port Manech. At the entrance to the village. You'll probably be there before me.'

'At the sign for Le Pouldu, if you're coming from Pont-Aven?'

'Yes.'

'When?'

Dupin would have to take the small roads towards Pont-Aven, go through the village, over the Aven, through bustling Riec-sur-Belon, around the Belon, westwards slightly, then back down to the sea. Perhaps an hour.

'I'm leaving now. Give me half an hour.'

It was quarter past twelve when Dupin arrived in Le Pouldu, having managed the journey in twenty-seven minutes. He had seen Le Ber's bright red Renault in the distance. It was right next to the sign, so close it looked like Le Ber had crashed into it. It read 'Le Pouldu' and underneath was the Celtic name: 'Poull du', or black sea. And in the same size lettering: 'The Artists' Path'. Dupin still remembered the marketing slogan competition they had held for over a year and a half, the winner of which had been 'The Artists' Path'; Brittany had decided to embrace its artistic inheritance – but as there had been so many painters in Brittany, in so many different towns, the same sign was up everywhere.

Nolwenn had given him just as precise a description for Le Pouldu as she had for Port Manech, he just hadn't been able to write it down while driving. He drove slowly past Le Ber and nodded to him. He could see Madame Cassel in the passenger seat. Le Ber started his car and drove close behind Dupin. It was the first turn off to the right after the entrance to the village, then they had to follow the signposts for the so-called 'Buvette de la Plage' which had recently been turned into a museum. Gauguin lived and painted here for a few months, together with his friends Meyer de Haan, Sérusier and Filiger. The house had belonged to Marie-Jeanne Pennec too but she had sold it while she was still alive after the painters had left the area one by one.

Dupin drove to the 'Buvette' as Nolwenn had called it, then along the little road parallel to the sea and took the first right onto a bumpy track. They drove along at walking pace and followed the path as it veered sharply to the right after some woodland.

Suddenly the building appeared out of nowhere, right in front of them on the path. This one was really a shack, weatherbeaten wood, an ugly corrugated iron roof and not big, just a few metres square. They drove right up to it and turned off their engines.

Dupin got out and went over to Le Ber's car.

'*Bonjour*, Madame Cassel. I'd like to thank you again, once more you are –'

'Here? You think the Gauguin is going to be here? A forty-million-euro painting in this shed?' She was nervous.

'If we find the painting, you might be able to give me an initial, provisional confirmation of its authenticity. That could be crucial. And you –'

'Nobody would keep such a valuable painting here.'

'But perhaps they'd stash it here temporarily. For a little while.'

'How did you come up with your theory that the painting could be here? I mean how did you come up with this place in particular?'

It seemed a little strange now, even to Dupin. It was just a suspicion, and he had set so much in motion. 'It's a long story.'

'Let's search the shed, Monsieur le Commissaire.' Even Le Ber was impatient now.

Oddly enough the door was on the other side of the shed, so they walked around it quickly. It was locked with a heavy padlock which looked neither obviously new nor obviously old. The little windowpane next to the door was blacked out. Before Dupin could even say anything, Le Ber had rummaged in his pocket and pulled out a thin wire. Dupin was always forgetting that Le Ber's practical skills sometimes verged on the magical. Madame Cassel was also looking at Le Ber in awe. It took less than half a minute to pick the lock. Excellent.

'I'm going in. Le Ber, stay here with Madame Cassel.'

The narrow little door wasn't easy to open; it jammed and stuck on the uneven ground. Dupin managed to get it open a crack. It was completely dark inside the shed; the only light came through the small opening in the doorway and it didn't help much.

'I'll get you a torch.'

With Le Ber already on his way back to the car, Madame Cassel and Dupin tried to make out some of the objects closest to the door. The shed looked like it was filled up to the rafters. Right next to the door there was a pile of empty canisters and they could see farming machinery, two big barrels and an old bathtub. A moment later Le Ber was standing next to them with the torch. It was huge.

'An LED Lenser X21.'

Le Ber's eyes lit up for a moment. Dupin shrugged and turned it on. He squeezed nimbly through the narrow opening in the doorway and cleared a path for himself inside the shed. He had to do more climbing than actual walking. It was pitch-black. The torch cast a clear, very bright beam of light on the various objects in the shed. A large, rusty plough with several old wooden chairs balanced precariously on top. The chairs were missing anything and everything: sometimes the backrest, sometimes a leg, sometimes the seat. More canisters of various sizes. The beam of light was dancing around wildly as Dupin moved. He was impressed by the amount of stuff that could fit in a shed of this size; it seemed as though more and more objects had simply been squeezed in over the course of decades, piled up and stuffed down in a manner as chaotic as it was artistic.

Dupin had somehow managed to force his way into the middle of the room, and was now standing still. A sharp, pervasive smell hung in the air. Disgusting. Dupin pivoted slowly around on one leg and moved systematically through the room with the torch.

'Monsieur le Commissaire?' It was just a few metres, but Le Ber's voice sounded far away, muffled. 'All okay over here.'

'Found anything?'

'No.' Dupin cleared a path for himself to the opposite wall, it didn't look as though anything had been changed here recently. The dust lay centimetres deep. 'There's nothing here.' Dupin had to shout so that they could hear him. He moved back to the centre of the room and tried to make his way to each of the corners from there – insofar as this was possible. Anyone who wanted to hide the painting here would have had the same difficulties. This wasn't plausible.

'I'm coming out.' The sense of resignation that washed over him was so great that Dupin couldn't even scream. Nothing. Yet again, nothing.

He clambered back the way he had come. Just before

the door the beam of light fell on the far end of the bathtub, which was effectively divided into sections by a thick pole lying across it. Dupin could make out what looked like a blanket or towel. A white fabric. With some careful manoeuvring, he climbed over the pole jutting out into the room. The fabric looked like a sheet – a pristine one. He was standing next to the tub now. He felt the object carefully. Underneath the sheet was something soft, then something narrow and hard with sharp edges. It was large. With his right hand he felt for the seam in the sheet and tried to pull it away. It wouldn't come off.

'Le Ber?'

'Yes?'

'I need you.'

'Have you found something?' Le Ber tried to open the door a bit wider, but couldn't.

'I'll give you some light, Le Ber. I'm near the door, but you've got to go to the middle of the shed first, and then come towards me.'

Le Ber deftly made his way over to Dupin.

'Hold the torch, I want to pick something up.'

Le Ber did as he was told and Dupin carefully lifted the object. The dimensions were exactly right. This had to be it. Dupin had gone very quiet. 'You go first.'

They made their way towards the door in single file. Marie Morgane Cassel watched the bizarre procession, peering right inside through the crack in the door. They reached the exit.

'You squeeze through, Le Ber, then I'll hand it to you.'

As Dupin stepped outside, he had to keep his eyes closed for a moment. The sun was practically still at its peak and it was blindingly bright. Slowly he opened his eyes. Le Ber had placed the covered object in the field next to the path. Without saying a word, the three of them knelt down in front of it. Dupin pulled back the white sheet, revealing a dark blue blanket. He gently lifted this too.

Even in direct sunlight, the garish orange jumped out at them.

Dupin pulled the blanket off. The painting was in pristine condition. All three of them stared at the Gauguin and were silent. It took their breath away.

Marie Morgane Cassel was the first to snap out of the reverie. 'It can't be kept in the sun like this.'

'Can you comment at this stage, Madame Cassel?' Dupin knew it was a stupid question, they had only just seen it.

'I have to look at it carefully using my tools. I don't know, I think it could be it.' She spoke absent-mindedly.

'Let's put it in my boot very carefully. You can look at it up close there. And Le Ber, walk around the wood and stand where you can watch the path.' He paused for a moment. 'And take your gun with you.'

Le Ber looked irritated for a moment. And Madame Cassel looked taken aback. 'Shall I call for back-up?' There was a touch of anxiety in Le Ber's voice.

'No. Just secure the path. Make sure you're not seen. Come on, Madame Cassel.' Dupin took the painting and carried it slowly to his car. Madame Cassel went on ahead and had the boot open for him when he got there. Dupin placed the painting carefully inside.

'I'll get my things.' Madame Cassel went to Le Ber's car, opened the door on the passenger side and took a big bag from the back seat. She came back over to Dupin. 'I need my stereomicroscope.'

She took out a complicated-looking instrument, turned it on and bent right down into the boot. 'This will take a little while... and I might not be able to give you a definitive answer, just my initial opinion.'

'That's more than enough for me. I'll leave you to work in peace.'

Le Ber had taken his gun, walked up to where the path curved round the little wood and then disappeared behind the trees.

Dupin had to think things through. He walked back to the entrance of the shed and then kept going, towards the sea, which he kept catching glimpses of between the hills and trees. Only now did he realise how dirty he was. The shed had been incredibly dusty. He'd have the smell of it in his nose all day. He tried to brush the dust off his clothes but it was no use. He hadn't gone far when he heard Madame Cassel calling.

'Monsieur le Commissaire? Monsieur Dupin? Hello?'

'I'm coming.'

Half a minute later he was standing next to her, a little out of breath. Dupin looked expectantly at the professor. Her face didn't give anything away and she spoke in a serious, analytical way.

'I've looked at the paint in detail in a few places, the brushstrokes and the signature. I obviously can't say this conclusively, I would need more tools for that, but in my opinion the painting is by Gauguin.' Then Marie Morgane Cassel beamed, 'This is the painting.'

A relieved smile spread across Dupin's face. He had the painting.

That was a start. But there was no time to waste; there wasn't even time to celebrate. Now came the much trickier part. Whoever it was who had hidden the painting here, that person believed the painting to be genuine. It was probably the murderer and they would be coming back here to pick up the painting. Dupin was sure they wouldn't keep it here for long; it was far too makeshift a solution for a painting worth forty million euro.

'I would rather you left the vicinity now.' Dupin sounded more alarmed than he had intended. Marie Morgane Cassel flinched slightly.

'I... I –'

'I'm sorry. I just meant that I don't want to put you in a dangerous situation, or even an unpleasant one – we're dealing with a murderer, perhaps even a double murderer.'

'Oh yes... yes. I keep forgetting that.'

'Inspector Le Ber will bring you back.'

'Great.'

'Thank you very much, Madame Cassel. You've helped us so much; this is the third time in fact. We are forever in your debt, without you –'

'No problem, I've really enjoyed myself. This is where my work comes to an end, I suppose. You should have the Musée d'Orsay do the technical confirmation. You don't have to go to Sauré though; speak to the museum president himself. I'll be keeping up with your progress in the papers.'

'No, I... I'll give you a call.'

'Please do. Let's stay in touch.' Dupin felt somewhat self-conscious for a moment, even he himself didn't know why. But most of all he felt anxious. He went off a short distance, took his mobile out of his trouser pocket and dialled Le Ber's number.

'Le Ber, I want you to drive Madame Cassel back to her car now, it's at the *Central*.'

'Is it the original, Monsieur le Commissaire?'

'Yes.'

'That's insane. There's a real Gauguin in your boot. Forty million euro's worth. That is seriously crazy. What do you think –' Le Ber sounded gobsmacked.

'We don't have time to discuss it now, Le Ber. You've got to put the padlock back and lock it. Nobody can know that we've been here.'

'I'll be right there.' A minute later Le Ber was standing next to them, panting loudly.

'Let's get going.' Dupin shook Madame Cassel's hand, a little clumsily. They smiled at each other.

'*Au revoir*, Monsieur Dupin.'

'*Au revoir*, Madame Cassel.'

Madame Cassel turned on her heel, walked briskly to Le Ber's car and got in. Le Ber came over to the Commissaire and spoke quietly.

'Should I take the painting with me? I think it would be best.'

Dupin thought about it. 'Please do, Le Ber. Take it with you. Best take it to the hotel first, to the restaurant. One of the officers from Pont-Aven can guard the restaurant if you need to get away again. When everything is over, you or Labat can drive the painting to the station.'

'And what are you going to do, Commissaire?'

'Wait.'

'Shall I come back once I've dropped Madame Cassel off? With Labat? We could secure the area.'

'No. I'll stay here by myself.' Dupin knew this was completely and utterly against police regulation. 'For now anyway. We'll see about later. We might need to arrange shifts. Who knows? I want you to be prepared for anything.'

'Okay. We'll be ready.'

'Don't say anything about the painting. And all of this stuff here – not a word to anyone. I'll call Labat.'

'Okay.'

Le Ber went to Dupin's car, covered the painting with the blanket again, carried it very cautiously to his car and placed it carefully in the boot. Le Ber had already dumped everything that had been lying around in the boot onto the back seat: first-aid kit, kitchen roll, a bag of police equipment. He got in and started the car, rolled down the windows, leaned out and nodded to Dupin. Marie Morgane Cassel was in the passenger seat and Dupin smiled at her one more time. Then Le Ber carefully reversed up the path. The car eventually disappeared behind the wood.

Dupin went to his car, turned on the engine and reversed just as carefully up the path. He couldn't let it be obvious at first glance that someone had driven along the path. Back on the road again, he turned in the direction of the beach and parked at the unsupervised car park above the large bay. It was just a few hundred metres to the shed. Nobody would notice his car here; nobody would suspect a thing.

He walked briskly back to the shed across the fields instead of taking the road. He had taken his handgun out of the glove compartment and stuck it into his belt. He would take up his position in the little wood. And wait.

He dialled Labat's number. He could see that Labat had already tried to call him twice. It was half past one; Beauvois' interrogation should be over by now.

'Labat?'

'Yes, Monsieur le Commissaire?'

'What did Beauvois say? Do we know everything?'

'It wasn't easy with that lawyer. He and Beauvois had clearly agreed to say as little as possible. So Beauvois told his story about the copy again, the same one he told you and Le Ber. He confirmed all the details we'd already heard, that he painted it thirty years ago because he was so fascinated that he –'

'Does he have an alibi for both evenings?'

'No firm alibis. He was in the museum on Thursday and stayed late, did tours for some local politicians and was at the art society meeting until ten o'clock that night. Then he went home alone, according to his statement. On Saturday evening he had a convention in Le Pouldu. Some kind of local council thing. Cultural issues. Also until around ten o'clock.'

'Le Pouldu?'

'Yes. The places for these meetings must change. It's on rotation... I've drawn up a list of Beauvois' activities in the last four days, do you want to hear it?'

'Did he leave Pont-Aven in that time?'

'No, just that evening when he went to Le Pouldu.'

'But otherwise he didn't leave Pont-Aven?'

'He says he didn't.'

'Where is Beauvois now?'

'He left the Prefecture a quarter of an hour ago. His lawyer arranged it. But we could call him in again. Should I –'

'I want you and Le Ber to be on standby at the hotel. I might need you.'

'Where are you?'

'Le Pouldu.'

'Le Pouldu?'

'Yes. In a wood near the Buvette.' He was back at the shed by now.

'What is going on?'

'We have the painting, Labat.'

'What?' Labat had yelled into the phone in his excitement.

'We've just seized it.'

'Where?'

'In a shed here.'

'In a shed? The Gauguin?'

'Correct.'

'Is it definitely the real painting?'

'Labat, I need you to get going right away, go and meet Le Ber at the *Central*. He's driving Madame Cassel back to the hotel as we speak. He has the painting with him.'

'Madame Cassel?'

'She has provisionally confirmed the authenticity of the Gauguin.'

'And what are you doing?'

'Waiting. Until someone comes to pick it up.'

There was a long pause.

'Do you know who it is?'

'I think so. Wait with Le Ber at the hotel. And the

most important thing to remember is that nobody can find out that we've seized the painting.'

'But –'

Dupin hung up.

It was already over thirty degrees again and the sun was blazing like it did in the south. In Brittany this was classed as a 'heatwave' and it was going to cause sensational headlines in the local papers tomorrow. The little wood where Dupin stood was not very big; it was perhaps a hundred metres long and very typical of the province. Dupin always used to think of thick, endless woods of birch and oak when he thought of Brittany. In reality, while it had indeed been one almighty, dense wood in days gone by, extensive deforestation since the Middle Ages meant it was now the least densely forested region in France.

This might be a long wait. And there would be all those urgent official calls to make afterwards. He definitely wasn't in the mood for that. He wanted to know if he was right, and he wanted to get it over with. The whole thing needed to come to a head. He wasn't interested in anything else.

It was quarter past five now. Dupin had been waiting for more than four hours. He hated not being able to do anything.

He kept walking back and forth, from one end of the wood to the other. He felt like he knew every single tree, every blackberry bush, every fern. In his boredom he had counted the number of oaks, larches, beeches and horse chestnut trees in the wood. Interestingly there were far more oaks than any other kind of tree.

He had looked for the tallest fern, and for the tree with the most mistletoe. He really liked mistletoe tea. He had spoken to Nolwenn three times and each time he had had an important reason to call her. But he never managed to make the calls last longer than ten minutes. Nolwenn knew how much he hated waiting. He had brought her up to speed quickly. She hadn't asked any questions and she had especially avoided bringing up Guenneugues – or any of the other things that couldn't be put off any longer. She had just reminded him to call his sister. His mobile had rung a good ten more times but he had just looked at the caller ID and let it ring. Only when Salou had called – his fourth attempt since this morning – did he pick up. He actually did feel a little bit guilty about that – maybe there really was some news. Salou was still beside himself with rage and said that Dupin's behaviour amounted to a boycott of his work. Dupin wasn't paying enough attention to get worked up about it. He also didn't feel at all inclined to take Salou into his confidence. In brusque tones, Salou finally reported his findings on the copy in the museum: inconclusive so far. And he announced the 'official result' of the investigation at the cliffs: 'Potential traces of the presence of a second person, but robust traces cannot be documented.' So there hadn't been any news after all.

Dupin was hungry. But more than anything he was thirsty. He hadn't thought of bringing anything to eat or drink. There was a bottle of Volvic in the car, but that was no good as he couldn't leave. He should have had Le Ber come back after all. He had to distract himself. Maybe he actually would call his sister.

He reached for his phone. 'Lou?'

'Is that you?'

'Yes.'

'Have you arrested him yet?'

'What?'

She laughed.

'Nolwenn told me you were trying to get in touch the day before yesterday. So what are you doing?'

'You're waiting for someone somewhere, am I right?'

'I –'

'You always call when you're waiting somewhere.'

It didn't come across mean. And she was right.

'I'm sitting on a roof in Quirbajou. We're almost finished here. It's nearly forty degrees. A crazy house. I'm good though. Lots to do. Good stuff.'

His sister had moved to the Pyrenees with Marc seven years ago, to an absolutely tiny backwater with lots of wine, olives, a real Cathar castle and two magnificent stone quarries not far from Perpignan. She was three years younger than him, an architect and carpenter, and she built crazy houses made entirely out of wood. Low energy ones. Dupin loved his sister, even though they rarely saw each other and seldom spoke.

'Yes, I… I'm on a case. And yes… I'm waiting.'

'Complicated?'

'Yes.'

She obviously hadn't heard anything yet.

'Two dead. And a genuine Gauguin.'

'A genuine Gauguin?'

'A Gauguin that has lain undiscovered until now – probably the most important painting in his oeuvre, according to *Le Figaro*.'

'No way!' She laughed. 'Sounds exciting. Mum will love that.'

Their mother was an antiques dealer and was passionate about fine art. Dupin actually wondered why she hadn't called yet. She would really like this case.

'Wouldn't you like to come to Paris next weekend? And visit her?'

Anna Dupin did not travel out to the sticks. They always had to come to her in Paris. 'I don't think I'll be able to get away. We'll see.'

Dupin didn't really want to go. It was also an aunt's birthday that weekend and he couldn't stand her. One of his mother's three sisters, the worst kind of arrogant, stuck-up Parisienne and he would have to accept everyone's condolences all evening because he now had to eke out a living in the back of beyond.

'Blame the case. You know there's nothing she loves more than a good chance to complain.'

'I'll do my best. How's Marc?'

'Really well. He's in Toulouse. Some engineering convention.'

'Did you build the house?'

'This one? Yes.'

'I'd love to see it.'

'I'll email you some photos... And how are you, apart from this case?'

'Hmmm. I don't know.'

Lou always asked the most complicated questions.

'You never know.'

'Sometimes I do.'

'Still in love? With Adèle?'

'No.'

It had been a while since they'd spoken.

'That's a pity, it sounded so promising. Anyone new?'

'Hmmm.'

'Doesn't sound like it.'

Lou was absolutely convinced that he still loved Claire and she'd told him so many times. And that was why he lost interest in any woman who came after Claire. Lou knew him well.

'Well actually… I just mean I'm not sure.'

'What does that mean?'

'I don't know. I… wait a second, Lou.' Dupin could hear something. The sound of an engine.

'Lou, I think I've got to –'

'Stay in touch!'

'I will.'

He could hear it very clearly now. A car. Coming up the path. He moved a little deeper into the little wood; he must not be seen under any circumstances. The car was approaching now, coming around the bend. It came hurtling up the path at top speed. Then Dupin heard the brakes. A car door opened and slammed shut again. Dupin waited a few moments, then pulled out his gun and moved carefully through the trees towards the shed. Through the leaves and the branches he could see parts of the car glinting in the sun. A dark car. His footsteps quickened. Then he stepped out of the wood.

A large black limousine was parked directly in front of the shed. The fender was practically touching the wall.

'André Pennec,' murmured Dupin in surprise.

An hour and a half later, Inspector Labat was driving to Quimper for the second time that day. André Pennec was sitting in the back of the car and Labat was bringing him to the station. There had been a very unpleasant scene at the shed, but it hadn't lasted long.

Dupin was standing in front of the dark, ugly villa he knew so well by now. Soon Le Ber would come and wait outside the front door in his car.

He gave the doorbell another quick ring. He didn't have to wait long for the door to be opened.

'Good evening, Madame Pennec… I'd like to have a word.' Dupin had spoken very firmly.

Catherine Pennec looked openly hostile for a moment, an unadulterated, scathing gaze which transformed into a look of absolute surrender. She was wearing the high-necked, black dress again. Without showing any emotion or saying a word, she turned around and walked slowly in the direction of the drawing room.

Dupin followed her inside. He had no desire to play mind games. 'We have the painting, Madame Pennec. It has been seized.' Dupin paused for a moment. 'André Pennec told us everything.'

Catherine Pennec gave no sign of even having heard Dupin's words. She just kept walking, inscrutable. She stopped abruptly in the drawing room.

Dupin was right behind.

'André Pennec? Really? He told you everything? No. He did not tell you everything. He didn't tell you anything at all.'

Catherine Pennec sat down on the large, plush sofa. She sat there without moving for a few moments and then suddenly she broke into a short, shrill laugh. Not a particularly loud one. 'What does he know? And what do you know? He knows nothing. Nothing... he told you nothing.'

'You tell me then.' Dupin was standing near the large fireplace, three or four metres away from her. Catherine Pennec was staring glassy-eyed at the floor. She seemed to be collapsing in on herself. Dupin waited for a long time. 'You don't have to say anything, Madame Pennec. You have the right to remain silent.' There was another long pause. 'Inspector Labat will drive you to the station in Quimper. You can speak to your lawyer there.' Dupin turned to go out to the hall. He almost preferred it this way. 'Come with me.'

At first he wasn't sure if he had actually heard anything. Catherine Pennec was speaking so softly, whispering, her voice entirely changed now, deeper, hollow. Mechanical.

'He was a failure. A complete failure. He never achieved anything. His whole life. He was too soft. He had no toughness to him. Or sense of purpose.'

Dupin turned around cautiously and stayed where he was.

'He had courage once, just once. One single time. He hadn't planned it at all, but for a moment he had the courage to stand up to his father. His father destroyed him, he destroyed his own son. He always reminded him of how weak he thought he was. That he was worthless, not a real Pennec, even less so after his mother died. And this constant delaying. But he took a stand once. He had to do it. He mustered the strength for it one time. That one night.'

She stopped. She seemed to be shaking her head slightly.

'Isn't it ironic? The knife was a present from his father when he was young. His Laguiole. It was sacred to him.'

A haunting smile played about her lips for a moment before her face slipped back into its mask.

'We'd been waiting for our lives to begin for such a long time. We waited and waited, for years, decades… he wouldn't die. Always waiting. All of it was ours. The hotel. The painting. The painting would have made anything possible. A different life. My whole life.'

Catherine Pennec had lifted her head and looked Dupin in the eye briefly. She seemed quite cheerful now.

'Did André Pennec tell you that? Did he? That's the truth. That's how it truly was. My father-in-law was infinitely stubborn, an awful old man. What was he getting out of the painting? It was hanging there the whole time, it wasn't benefitting anybody. He may only have had a few more days to live. If only we had known! A few days. We thought he had already changed the will.'

Catherine Pennec spoke as though she wanted to present her argument in a logical, systematic manner, without her emotion getting in the way. Her eyes were fixed on the floor again.

'We knew about the donation. He told my husband that evening. He told him he was planning it and they argued. We only took what belonged to us. The painting belongs to us. Why should the museum get the Gauguin? It has always belonged to the family and my husband had a right to it. Once, he only

300

took action once in his life. And then he got tearful all of a sudden. Pitifully so. And wanted to confess to everything. He was whining that he couldn't bear it. He was so pathetic. I couldn't allow it, for his own sake. I had to do something. He had ruined everything… His father was right to despise him… Oh yes. He despised him his entire life, even if he didn't mean to. Utterly despised him.' She looked Dupin in the eye again, cold and utterly self-assured. 'I did too! I despised him. Anything might have been possible. It was there, everything was right there in front of us. Is that what André Pennec told you? Is it?'

Dupin was silent.

'Did André Pennec come to you? Could he not bear it any more?'

'No. He came to collect the painting. He was planning to take it to Paris as soon as possible. We arrested him in Le Pouldu. He's on his way to the station now.'

Catherine Pennec broke into another of her abrupt, high-pitched laughs. She shook her head for a moment, as though in a trance, and then stopped, motionless. 'How did you know where it was?'

Dupin thought he saw a sudden fear in her eyes. But her voice was perfectly steady. 'I assumed you had to have it. And that you'd need somewhere to hide it at first.'

'Why me?'

'It wasn't anything you said or did – it was what was missing. Everyone was anxious about the painting. You were the only one who wasn't. The only person who had no reason to be anxious was the person who already had it. During our conversation the morning

301

after the break-in, you and your husband didn't even ask what had happened, or whether it might be some kind of smokescreen. And then yesterday, when we were talking openly about the painting, you missed another opportunity to bring up the break-in. If it hadn't already been safely in your hands, you would have, rightly and despite your grief, expressed your worry about the painting. It was your forty million euro. By that point, you already knew that it was legally your possession. Your rightful inheritance. You should have been anxious and you weren't in the least. That was what gave you way, although at first I didn't notice it either. I only worked it out this morning.'

'I –' Catherine Pennec broke off.

'Of course I was meant to think that you were grieving.' Dupin really hadn't wanted to have this conversation, but he felt a deep sense of satisfaction now.

'You played your part very well, Madame, you showed precisely the feelings that were to be expected of you at any given time... but at some point the role became too complex. There was a lot you couldn't control. If Beauvois hadn't tried to steal the painting, you would never have been in a position to make the mistake you did.'

Catherine Pennec was silent. She was sitting there as though she'd turned to stone.

'I didn't know for sure. So, despite my suspicion that you had the painting, in order to prove it I still needed to find the thing. I had to catch you red-handed with it when you came to collect it. I thought you would come and fetch it. The hiding-place was just a guess. Madame Denis had mentioned the plots of land in the inheritance and you had to stash the painting somewhere temporarily – you wouldn't do that here in the house. Nobody else knew about the shed. Only the family.'

Catherine Pennec didn't seem to be listening at all. He didn't care.

'There were a lot of coincidences at work here. If, by pure coincidence, you had found out that Pennec never got around to changing his will, you wouldn't have had to do a thing – the Gauguin would have been yours. You wouldn't have had to switch the paintings that night, you wouldn't have had to involve André Pennec – you wouldn't have had to do anything at all. Not one thing. It would have fallen right into your lap... You...' Dupin stopped. That was enough. He was exhausted. And livid. 'We're going now. That's enough. Come with me.'

Dupin turned abruptly towards the door. Madame Pennec leapt up, as though Dupin had pressed a button. She stood up, her back ramrod straight, and then followed him in silence with her head held high.

The scene had played itself out incredibly quickly. Dupin just wanted to get out of there; he couldn't stand this house a moment longer. Or any of this. He was already at the door, opening it in one swift motion. Madame Pennec was right behind him now. They went outside.

Le Ber had parked his car directly underneath the steps outside and was watching the house. He got out when he saw Dupin and Madame Pennec and went straight to the rear door to hold it open.

He was a man of few words. '*Bonsoir*, Madame. I'll be taking you to the station.'

Madame Pennec got in without a word. She looked utterly undaunted. Le Ber walked calmly around the car. 'You'll definitely call, Monsieur le Commissaire?'

'Yes.'

'And you'll call the Prefect?'

'Yes.'

Le Ber smiled. 'Good.'

He got in, started the engine and drove off. Dupin could see Madame Pennec through the car window. She had lowered her head. He kept watching the car until it reached the bridge and disappeared round the bend. Dupin crossed the street.

He had done it.

A little while later Dupin was standing where he had stood so many times in recent days, by the quay wall at the harbour. The tide had reached its highest point. It was quarter to eight and still very warm. This evening there wasn't even a light breeze; the air was still but not close. A large sailing ship had anchored right in front of him. His eyes drifted slowly over it. It was a wonderful wooden ship, a real Atlantic-going vessel, quite clearly made for rough seas, for the ocean. It must have been at sea for many years. This was not a boat for a river. The tide had come in, the sea was here, you could smell it, taste it, feel it. It was truly beautiful down here at the harbour; and yet he was happy to be leaving Pont-Aven behind him, along with this case, and glad to be going back to Concarneau. The case would keep him busy for the next week anyway with all of the 'follow-up' he'd need to do; interrogations, minutes, forms, dozens of phone calls. The press. 'Communication'. But that was enough for one day.

Dupin drove around the last of Pont-Aven's roundabouts at quarter past eight and soon he was in Névez, then Trégunc, and finally in his own village. He had rolled the windows down and opened the roof as wide as it would go. The traffic was bad. The *Festival des Filets Bleus*, that's where everyone was headed this evening. It didn't bother him. Even the fact that he had to call the station didn't bother him. He would get it over with quickly.

'Monsieur le Préfet, Commissaire Dupin here.'

'Ah, lo and behold! Mon Commissaire.'

'I'm on my way to Concarneau.'

'I've already spoken to Inspector Labat at length – as I've done every day recently; nobody could get hold of you in the last forty-eight hours. I... It...'

He paused. Dupin could practically hear Guenneugues struggling with himself on the other end of the line, deciding whether to get angry. Dupin would have taken it well, but the Prefect decided against it.

'In the end it wasn't such a complicated case after all. We've solved it.'

It was never a complicated case in the end. Dupin was used to hearing this; he heard it every time 'we' closed a case.

'No, Monsieur le Préfet. I mean yes, we've solved it. And no, it wasn't such a complicated case in the end.' Dupin's voice was friendly.

'Everyone will be relieved. The press will welcome it. But I must say, you –' Guenneugues' tone seemed about to change. 'Actually, when I think about it –' He started again. 'It was probably just... I think we can call it a great family tragedy.' Guenneugues seemed to be searching for the right words. 'So many emotions, such strong ones too. Over such a long time. It's terrible really.'

Sometimes he surprised Dupin – even though this was very, very rare.

'Yes, Monsieur le Préfet, that's probably what it was. A family tragedy.'

'Was it murder, the death of Loïc Pennec?'

'I think so.'

'Have you got a statement from Madame Pennec?'

'An initial statement, yes.'

'Reliable?'

'I can't say.'

'I'm going to hold a press conference this evening. I want articles in all the papers tomorrow about the case being solved. That painting made the case a national issue, Dupin.'

It didn't sound like a complaint. There was pride in Guenneugues' voice.

'The papers will be going to print soon. We don't need all the details yet, just the most important ones. My concern is only that our work be adequately conveyed... The police in Finistère have everything under control! I had the painting brought to Quimper straight away.'

'I understand.'

Dupin was used to this. Guenneugues had solved the case. That was the message. That was what it always was.

'Do you think the son planned the murder? Was it premeditated? The press will want to know.'

'I don't think so. That's... It just happened. That evening.'

'Why that evening?'

'Pierre-Louis Pennec had told his son that the painting was going to be handed over to the Musée d'Orsay soon.'

Dupin actually didn't want to say any more. He had remembered the knife. The Laguiole.

'And? What do you think?'

'Nothing.'

'Had Pierre-Louis been planning it for a long time? To make the donation I mean.'

'Not in any detail, but yes. He only started planning the specifics of it after visiting Docteur Pelliet.'

'Yes. I understand. Was it greed? Was it about the forty million euro in the end or not?'

'It was about deep wounds. Humiliation. Over the course of decades. I –' Dupin was irritated, he didn't want to get into a serious discussion with Guenneugues.

'Yes?'

'You're right. It was about the forty million.'

'What do you make of Madame Pennec?'

'Are you asking what her motivations were?'

'Yes.'

'She is a cold-blooded person.' Dupin was irritated with himself again.

'Cold-blooded? That's pretty dramatic, Commissaire.'

Dupin was silent.

'And where did the second copy of the painting come from?'

'I don't know yet. I'd imagine Pierre-Louis Pennec owned it and his son knew about it. That it was in the hotel. We'll find out.'

'About that member of parliament, Monsieur André Pennec. He's entitled to immunity.'

Dupin could feel his temperature rising. He had to be careful. 'That will have to be lifted.'

'I don't know. Does it have to be? He does seem to be a man of integrity. I've been assured of that by many credible sources. And his lawyers –'

'He was attempting to conceal the painting, a stolen painting worth forty million euro. Madame Pennec had offered him a quarter share of the money in the event of it being sold. That would have been ten million euro. Ten million!'

'Madame Pennec gave him the task of selling it. It wasn't his idea. He was due a share of the money of course, but a salesman always gets commission, there's nothing untoward about that. And it is her painting. The Gauguin belongs to her, if I understand everything correctly.'

Guenneugues had been well briefed. That much was abundantly clear.

'Someone has already called you.'

Guenneugues hesitated. 'I've been getting calls. From Paris, from Rennes and Toulon.' He hesitated again, audibly. 'And from his lawyers too.'

Dupin was surprised to hear him admitting that. But he might have guessed. André Pennec had had two hours.

'Madame Pennec didn't know it was her property when she asked André Pennec to sell it. She assumed that Pierre-Louis Pennec had left it to the Musée d'Orsay. She and her husband swapped the paintings the night of the murder because they weren't sure whether the change to the will had been finalised.

And Catherine Pennec called André Pennec that same night, not long after the crime. She told André Pennec what had happened. André Pennec is therefore also guilty of being the accessory to a crime. He did not go to the police. He has systematically lied to me, thereby directly hindering the investigation.'

Dupin was really furious now.

'André Pennec's lawyers are saying that Madame Pennec definitely didn't clearly state that her husband had stabbed Pierre-Louis Pennec that night. She spoke about a 'family crisis'. Madame Pennec was probably extremely hysterical and confused. Understandably.'

This situation was absolutely outrageous. And disgusting. This was what Dupin hated so much about his profession. He hated it with every fibre of his being. His voice rose again. '"Didn't clearly state", "family crisis"? What is that meant to mean?'

'Did he agree to the task of stashing and selling the painting the night Catherine Pennec rang?' Guenneugues' voice was irritatingly matter of fact.

'He... no.'

'You see.'

'But the next day –'

'The next day, Madame Pennec learnt at the reading of the will that there had never been a change in the will. Pierre-Louis Pennec had not managed to write the donation into his will. She knew that the painting belonged to her. André Pennec met Catherine and Loic Pennec because of the reading of the will. He wasn't leaving until the following day.'

'But that's... he knew –' Dupin broke off. He hadn't thought it through. That was his mistake. He really ought to have known better. Yes, this was how it went in cases like this, exactly like this. But in fact this was one of the very reasons he became a policeman; however unreasonably naive and arrogant it might sound, he was absolutely incapable of standing by if someone blithely thought they could get away with something. 'This is a disgrace and you know it.'

Guenneugues ignored Dupin's observation. 'Madame Pennec did not know for sure whether the change had been made to the will. Her husband believed it had already been changed during the fight with his father that evening. But that was obviously an... extremely emotional situation.'

'And what is that meant to mean, Monsieur le Préfet?'

'It means that Catherine Pennec seems to me to be the only person there is to prosecute here... for the murder of her husband, so long as she doesn't retract her confession when she gives her official statement.'

Dupin wanted to argue back. But with a great degree of self-control he managed to stay silent. So this was how the official version would go.

'I think André Pennec wanted to help during, how did you put it again, a great family tragedy? It takes a while to think clearly again after such traumatic events.'

'"Wanted to help"? He "wanted to help"?' Dupin had repeated the words in disbelief.

Again, Guenneugues did not respond.

'And this Beauvois, this art society chairman? That's serious stuff. We should take it seriously. Very seriously indeed.'

Dupin couldn't believe his ears. Now Beauvois was one of the people to be rounded up and charged? He personally thought Beauvois was a creep, a ruthless narcissist. Who would – almost – step over bodies to get what he wanted, but only almost; and Dupin's profession had taught him that this 'almost' was important.

'Beauvois is small fry. Utterly insignificant in this case.'

This wasn't easy for Dupin. He felt angry just saying that. But his anger at what the Prefect had in mind was significantly greater.

'You yourself had him brought to the station. Under questionable conditions. We really, really stuck our necks out there. There was a lot we couldn't control. You knew that. I, of course, supported you.'

Dupin was sick of this. He would find another way. With an enormous amount of effort, he managed to let it go. 'As you say, it wasn't a complicated case in the end, Monsieur le Préfet. And the most important thing is that the case is solved.'

'There now! And I'm very pleased it's solved, Monsieur le Commissaire. That was some good work.' The Prefect broke into a low, conspiratorial laugh. 'Madame Pennec is going to be one of the wealthiest convicts ever to grace a state prison in France, apart from Louis XVI...' Guenneugues seemed to consider this joke a good note to start winding up the conversation on.

'Yes, that's true. *Au revoir* then, Monsieur le Préfet.'

'I would also like to –'

Dupin hung up. It hadn't escalated. He had hung up, but at least he hadn't started shouting.

And something had occurred to him. Dupin's expression brightened all of a sudden. He had become quite friendly with a journalist from *Ouest France* in recent years and had already had 'confidential', off the record conversations with her a few times. Lilou Breval. Perhaps she would learn something extra about the case from an 'unnamed source'. A few details of André Pennec's entanglement in it. Dupin didn't know if it would change things. But still. The press would love something like this. And Pennec would have enemies and they would know what to do with it.

By now Dupin had reached the third of Concarneau's five roundabouts, the one right by the high bridge. He took the road on the left into town, through the deep sea port. The journey had taken an especially long time this evening. Everyone was out and about. It was always like this on festival days. Even from the roundabout you could hear the muffled noises, the bass pounding. It was only just dawning on him that he wouldn't be able to find a parking place as most parts of the centre of town would be closed. And if he wanted to get anywhere near his house he would have to drive all the way round Concarneau and come at it from the other side. But he was not in the mood to go turning around. He decided to leave the car in the industrial harbour, near the big tuna fishing boats and dockyards, and walk along the waterfront. He could always collect the car tomorrow.

The deep-sea port was far from picturesque. But Concarneau did still have an impressive fleet of trawlers that sailed all around the world. They weren't romantic fishing boats like the coastal fishermen's ones, but an ultra-modern, high-tech fleet. However this fleet did not, and this was very important to Bretons, have barbaric drift nets like the large Japanese fleets did. These were powerful boats made for rough seas, with heavy lifting equipment onboard. Laure's father had travelled on a boat like this for three decades and saw the world that way. Dupin had heard the stories. The harbour area, the buildings, the equipment and systems, the machines, everything was in working order here. Dupin liked this port just as much as he liked the much more attractive, historical harbour further downstream where the local fishermen still moored their little wooden boats.

There were in fact some free parking spaces down here, even though lots of the festival-goers had clearly had the same idea. Dupin parked the car near the water. Unlike in Pont-Aven just now, a soft summer evening wind was coming in off the sea. Dupin took a deep breath. There was a strong smell from the sea this evening. Salt, seaweed, iodine. Breathing this air always changed everything.

Dupin strolled along the waterfront. He had almost forgotten the stupid phone call he'd just had. The whole case seemed like some crazy, dark dream from the past; even though he knew that it would be on his mind for a long time to come, long after all the bureaucratic work was finished.

He realised what he still wanted to do. He got out his phone.

'Monsieur Dupin?'

'Good evening, Madame Cassel.'

'Should I get going? Where shall we meet?'

Dupin stopped short, but then he laughed. 'No... no. I –'

'I can't hear you properly. It's so loud at your end, where are you?'

'I'm in Concarneau, at the *Festival des Filets Bleus* – or rather I'm walking down by the harbour and the festival is on today. I've got to walk right through the town; you can't get into the centre by car.' He knew he was babbling.

'I see. So was that the last act in the drama, did you solve the case?'

'Yes. The case is solved. It –'

'Don't worry about it.'

Dupin was glad to hear that.

'That was a crazy case. Do you always get such crazy cases?'

'I don't know.'

'You have a crazy profession.'

'Do you think so?'

'Like in a crime novel.'

'It's not that bad. To be honest your world doesn't seem any less crazy.'

'You're right.'

It was very loud now, Dupin was approaching the main square and a band was playing on the largest of the four stages.

'Well... then, then... I suppose, I'm sure we'll see each other again sometime. It's hard to lose touch with anyone in the back of beyond.'

Dupin laughed. He liked how she put things. 'Hang on... just a moment.' He turned into a side-street where it was a little quieter.

'You live in Brest, right?'

'Yes. Just on the outskirts, right by the sea. When you're coming from the west –'

'Do you like penguins?'

'Penguins?'

'Yes.'

'Do I like penguins?'

'Do you ever go to the Océanopolis?'

'Oh yes, of course.'

'They have amazing penguins. Gentoo penguins, Adelie penguins, King penguins, Emperor Penguins, Blue penguins, Crested penguins, Yellow-eyed penguins, Banded penguins.'

Marie Morgane Cassel laughed out loud. 'Yes, their penguins are amazing.'

'We could go and see the penguins together sometime.'

There was a short pause.

'Let's. You have my number.'

'I do.'

'*Au revoir* then, Monsieur le Commissaire.'

'*Au revoir*, Madame Professeur.'

They both hung up at the same time. A moment later it occurred to Dupin that he had actually wanted to thank Madame Cassel officially for all her help. He wouldn't have got very far without her. He wanted to thank her on behalf of the police but he could do it another time.

Dupin went back to the harbour, and continued on to the main square and Pénéroff Quay and the *Amiral*. The festival seemed livelier than it had in recent years. This was already his third festival. (Which he never

315

admitted to anyone; Nolwenn had explained that he could only mention it on the tenth or fifteenth occasion at the earliest.)

Regardless of how fun it was and how big a part alcohol played (as it tended to do at all Breton festivals) the *Festival des Filets Bleus* was a highly emotional affair for the Concarnese. It was clearly the most important festival in the village, but it was also a shining symbol. The Concarnese were celebrating themselves: their ability not to lose confidence during the worst of times and their ability to overcome hardships together. Every child knew the story... and told it too. Nolwenn told it every year – three or four weeks before the festival she would bring up the topic as if by chance. Up until the late nineteenth century, sardines had been like *gold* in Brittany, there were eight hundred (!) boats in Concarneau's sardine-fishing fleet alone. Nolwenn had a large engraving in the office which showed part of the fleet at sea before coming into harbour. There were so many boats side by side that you could hardly see the water. The fishermen and the whole fishing industry had lived off the erratic, wandering fish that travelled in gigantic shoals. But in 1902, the sardines disappeared overnight; they simply vanished without a trace for seven whole years. It was a catastrophe. Fishermen, factory workers and many other people lost their livelihoods. Poverty, hunger and depression prevailed. There was a stark contrast when the rich Parisian bathers came to stay during the summer. So some of the artists hit upon the idea of organising a charity festival, to which the whole region would be invited. They wanted to help in a very practical sense but more than anything they wanted to create a symbol of hope. The festival was called after the blue nets that hauled the fickle fish out of the sea: as a kind of incantation to call them back. Even the very first festival was a jolly affair. And a great success too, with a considerable amount of money raised. Celtic music, dances and dancing competitions, costumes and costume competitions, tombolas and the crowning of the queen of the festival. There was food – tuna because it was all the Concarnese had left – and above all there was drinking. Concarneau has celebrated its festival ever since, for over a hundred years.

As always there was an exquisite smell in the air, fresh fish grilled over huge wood fires. Dupin was practically fainting with hunger. He considered having one of those delicious tuna fillets; almost raw, very well seared on either side. His mouth was watering but he decided against it. He wanted to be alone for a little while first. Perhaps he'd come back to the festival later. Nolwenn would be there. Along with a few other people he knew.

Lily had already spotted the Commissaire as he walked in. She was standing behind the counter fiddling with the espresso machine.

Dupin smiled. A brief but broad smile.

'Everything worked out all right then!' she called to him, only to busy herself with the machine again straight away. It was hissing beautifully.

Dupin didn't need to say anything to Lily. He sat down. Everyone was outdoors; it was practically empty in the *Amiral*.

The entrecôte would be sitting in front of him in a few minutes, accompanied by Philippe's famous sautéed potatoes (which was the only food Dupin ever allowed to replace his beloved chips). Mustard. A Languedoc. He was sitting in his favourite dinner spot, the restaurant's only round table, tucked away into the furthest corner. You could see everything from here. Through the large window you could see the square and the *ville close*, the harbour with its brightly coloured fishing boats; but above all – even now with the great throngs outside – you could see the sea, always the sea.

Dupin looked out. Far into the distance.

Yes, all was right with the world.